My T^r oyboy is a Twat

PAULA HOUSEMAN

Title: My T(r)oyboy is a Twat
Author: Paula Houseman
ISBNs: 978-0-6482836-4-5 (paperback)
978-0-6482836-5-2 (epub)
978-0-6482836-6-9 (mobi)

Publisher: WildWoman Publishing,
Sydney, Australia

Connect with Paula Houseman
Website: https://paulahouseman.com

Social Networks
https://www.facebook.com/PaulaHousemanAuthor
https://www.goodreads.com/PaulaHouseman
https://www.linkedin.com/in/paulahouseman
https://www.pinterest.com/paulahouseman
https://twitter.com/paulahouseman

For Jeff

CONTENTS

CHAPTER ONE

Shrink-Wrapped

'Walk this way,' the receptionist instructed.

Igor, Doctor Frankenstein's hunchbacked assistant with the shuffling gait, had said the same thing to his master in the comedy–horror movie, *Young Frankenstein*. Where Doc F had misunderstood (or was just a tosser) and imitated the lumbering Igor, we followed the receptionist's directive. She didn't have a hump and she didn't shuffle. But because of a pronounced limp, she waddled like a penguin.

As an adolescent, I'd have thought about mimicking her swaying gait. *Thought* about it. I wouldn't have done it, though, partly because I knew what it was like to be made fun of for being different, and also because I'd be mortified if I were caught out.

Back then, I had no control over my shameful thoughts or the impulse to laugh. Neither the passage of time nor maturity had curbed these. Even so, the urge to laugh wasn't there at the moment. Being here was no laughing matter.

I studied her as we trailed her down the hall. A penguin walk and a penguin build. She was torpedo-shaped, with a thick midsection, narrow shoulders and skinny legs. She was also torpedo-hued: gunmetal-grey hair pulled up tight in a severe bun; dressed in a pale grey, short-sleeved, polyester, O-neck tee, a charcoal pencil skirt and grey stockings; sporting boring, low-heeled pumps in a whale grey colour.

The receptionist's fifty shades of grey reflected my state of mind.

'Doctor shouldn't be too long,' she said as she ushered us into the shrink's office.

I stopped short.

The office was enormous and had a musty, old-house smell. *Ecch.* And with its heavy, murky hues, it must have once been the drawing room of this place that looked like a Georgian mansion.

'Can I get you a tea or a coffee?'

Ralph said, 'No, thanks.'

The receptionist was looking at me, waiting for an answer.

I could do with a cup of confidence. Maybe in a Starbucks insulated paper cup. Not the coffee—fuck no!—just served *in a Starbucks cup to remind me that we're in the twenty-first century.*

'Uh, no. Thank you.' The coffee had probably expired a hundred and sixty-five years ago. Anyway, drinking it when I was uptight gave me wind. And already feeling like I was behind the eight ball, the last thing I needed was to fart during the session.

'Okay. Make yourselves comfy, then.' She pointed to the large black two-seater sofa against the far wall. A Chesterfield—probably the real deal, not a knock-off. I knew the brand name because I'd once worked as an interior decorator. The receptionist toddled out and closed the door behind her.

I remained standing, un-comfy, as I surveyed this room that was in need of a facelift. Gutting it would be a good place to start. Everything in it was pure vintage. Except for the open laptop on the huge antique mahogany pedestal desk in front of the wall opposite the Chesterfield, and the oversized executive swivel chair behind the desk.

A large pocket watch lay on the desk, its chain dangling over the edge. Was this man into hypnosis? *Well, no way am I going to be hypnotised!* It was enough that the retro pattern of the olive flocked wallpaper could send you into a stupor. Was it flocked? Maybe it just looked fuzzy because I wasn't wearing my specs. Either way, it was hard on the eyes.

The Chesterfield faced two armchairs from the same collection. A rectangular mahogany coffee table separated the sofa and chairs. Maybe the table was rosewood; it was almost black. And with its creepy, curved-claw feet, the table could have belonged in Frank N. Furter's house. Rocky Horror furniture. It probably moved when no one was around—a little jump to the left, a little step to the right.

Shit.

Had it just moved? Or did old coffee tables have more than four feet? I rubbed my eyes. Still seeing more than four. Double vision could be a symptom of ... *oh no, a brain tumour*! I felt nauseous—another symptom. Gut clenching and roiling, the possibility of losing control of body functions—yet more symptoms. Throw in sleep problems and bouts of fatigue and *Oh God, why me? Haven't I been through enough these last few months?*

I looked at Ralph. He'd already seated himself at the far end of the couch. I read it as *I don't want to sit close to you.*

Fine. I don't want to sit close to you either. And can't you see how distraught I am!

It was then I noticed the couch was flanked by a pair of matching side tables from the same family as the coffee table. So, not double vision. Or triple vision. Just twelve creepy, curved-claw feet.

On each side table sat a brass lamp with a cream glass shade. The lamps were on. Why? It was midday and a lot of light was streaming in through the tall and wide bay window. Mood lighting, maybe?

Fat lot of good it did. My mood had darkened and I was now like the furniture. Or maybe just still part of it; I'd spent way too much time living in the past. It also didn't help that the room was stuffy and I was a hot, sticky mess. *Helloooo ... yesteryear taste doesn't have to preclude aircon!*

Ralph seemed unruffled—not even the smallest of sweat stains in the armpits of his shirt. Not surprising.

I plonked myself down at the opposite end of the couch and fanned myself.

It occurred to me our seating positions were perfectly configured, much like the room itself with its symmetrical layout. And it might have ponged of antiquity, but it was pathologically neat. It spoke to Ralph's obsessive–compulsive personality disorder.

I slid away from the arm to throw things off balance, and hopefully, fluster him. It annoyed me that he had the edge. Ralph was a psychologist, so he and the shrink would prattle on in their smartypants psychobabble, while I'd be on the outer like an idiot.

I looked at my watch. It was quarter past twelve. The man was running fifteen minutes late. I thought it rude. Or maybe his lateness was a form of psychological manipulation—make 'em wait, make 'em sweat. Loosens tongues.

I snuck a side peek at Ralph. He was still cool. But I was wearing a short dress and my bare thighs were sticking to the leather. There was a squelchy sound as I lifted my left leg up and crossed it over the other, then uncrossed it and did the same with the right. Just as well I was wearing knickers. *Must remember not to cross and uncross during the interrogation.*

Knickers? Interrogation? *Jesus, I watch too much TV.* Even so, if the doc did put the screws on us, my tongue was already loose. *Good luck getting anything out of the iceberg.*

I gave the iceberg a death stare. He didn't notice. I checked the time again. He managed to notice that without even turning his head.

Sighing, he looked at me. 'You need to be patient.'

'Oh, really? The reason we're here is because *you* couldn't be patient.'

He made a wry face. 'You know there's more to it than that.'

I averted my eyes as irritation gave way to sadness. Ralph and I hadn't been married long. We'd overcome many obstacles to even be a couple, but this last one had become bigger than both of us. I feared I'd start crying, but then, a distraction.

A chirping sound issued from the laptop on the ugly-arse desk. The computer might have been at odds with its old-fangled surroundings, but the noise it made—presumably an incoming email notification—was so appropriate for a therapist's office: *cuckoo, cuckoo, cuckoo.*

That missing impulse was back and I feared I'd start laughing. And lose more ground. *Oh God, the endless tragicomedy that is my life! Oh God, I'm turning into my mother.* A sobering thought. A horrible thought.

I shook it off and rummaged around in my tote for my glasses. Best to have my wits about me. I put them on and scanned across the three framed testamurs adorning the wall behind the desk. The first announced a Bachelor of Science degree; the second, a Master in Clinical Psychology; the third was a psychology doctorate. Where was the Bachelor of Medicine?

The specifics on each were in a different font, but the name itself was a constant: Jackson Byron Everett-Lillicrap.

Uh-oh. The urge to laugh ramped up. I thought back to how I'd 'nillicrapped' my Bonds Cottontails laughing when Ralph had texted me the therapist's name a week earlier. But then I'd become angry when I realised why he'd picked someone with a name like that. Now, I was even angrier. He'd deliberately omitted the first part of the double-barrelled surname, which gave undue attention to the second part.

The sound of unoiled hinges interrupted these inflamed thoughts as the doorknob twisted and groaned and the door creaked open a tad. From behind it, a deep, plummy male voice dispensed instructions to the receptionist. I envisaged a tall blue blood about to enter wearing a frock coat, tight pantaloons and a top hat. Probably all in battleship tones. Like the receptionist.

The door swung open. 'Sorry for my tardiness,' he said.

Holy crap!

I gasped.

CHAPTER TWO

Fat Chance!

It wasn't only his surname that was double-barrelled. Filling the doorway, Doctor Jackson Byron Everett-Lillicrap was the shape of a giant wooden beer keg, the likes of which would satisfy the hordes at Oktoberfest. A fat shrink. *Now*, there's *an oxymoron*. A little bit of autosuggestion on himself wouldn't go astray.

But a behavioural specialist with an eating disorder wasn't so much the issue. Cacomorphobia was the issue—a dread of the morbidly obese spawned years earlier by my once-colossal, beastly cousin Zelda.

The gasp hatched little 'uns: '*Ah-ha-ah-ha-ah-ha.*'

'Ooh. Are you okay, dear?' said the keg.

'*Ah-ha-ah-ha-ah-ha.*'

'Might some water help?'

I shook my head and my thoughts hyperventilated. *No. But you ... reducing ... your fluid retention ... shedding about ... a hundred and ... fifty kilos of water, brewski, and fat might ... do it. And ... don't bloody call ... me ... dear.*

Heedless of my body language, Jackson clomped out to fetch a glass of water. Or a pail. Or his oxygen cylinder.

Don't think for a minute ... I'm gonna share ... your mask, buddy!

Meantime, Ralph, who was normally quick to clamp his cupped hand over my mouth and instruct me to breathe slowly, remained jammed against the armrest. From the corner of my eye, I saw him watching me with uncertainty. *Jerk*. His inaction made me angry. And more anxious. But over the last couple of months I'd become proficient at self-soothing.

I slapped my own hand over my mouth and breathed slowly. The anxiety started to abate. I turned to him to say something about his disregard, but noticed the corners of his mouth slightly turned up in an amused smile. What? 'Oh my God! You *knew*?'

The smile vanished. 'Uh, uh, I—'

'I don't think you're in the least bit invested in saving us.' I didn't try to conceal the hurt suffusing the words.

Ralph's face reddened. I got up and stalked out.

It was a big thing for me. In the past, I wouldn't have moved. I'd have sat there drowning in shame rather than leave and risk the therapist thinking ill of me.

I picked up my pace in the hallway, where the torpedo was handing the blimp a glass of water. I nearly bowled him over—a superhuman feat powered by an adrenaline rush—charged through the waiting room, and out into the car park.

I reached my car and wrenched open the driver's door when Ralph called out, 'Wait!'

He caught up with me. 'Look, I didn't know. I was just laughing at the irony.' And he was now trying hard to suppress a smile at the memory. And what irony it was. In the end, I wasn't the one who was strapped for self-control.

I gave him the stink eye. 'Go to hell, Ralph!' I started climbing into the car, but first delivered a parting shot. 'Oh. Happy anniversary.'

His mouth dropped open, a pained expression crossing his face.

Ralph had managed to get us in on a cancellation. When he'd texted me the appointment time last Tuesday, he said it was for Thursday week. With the days blurring into one another lately, I'd lost track of dates. Obviously, so had he. Today was our first wedding anniversary.

Hot tears stung my eyes as I quickly buckled up and drove off.

What had started as a clear blue sky this morning was now overcast. Dark storm clouds were rapidly moving in and it began sprinkling. By the time I reached the exit to the car park, the sky was thunderous, it was bucketing down and I was sobbing.

It brought back memories of another situation three years earlier.

Ralph had been angry with me for keeping our relationship under wraps, and for avoiding him when he became demanding about us going public. I dropped in on him. Cold and distant, he'd told me to go home. The battering rain and my tears of humiliation and distress made for poor visibility. Frightened and unfocused, I had an accident that landed me in hospital with a concussion.

Right now, I steeled myself to remain attentive. The despair of the last months was gaining on me, but much as I felt like I wanted to die, I wasn't prepared to. I wasn't ready to leave my two children, Hannah and Casper. Or my little grandson. My darling, two-year-old Luca. Through no fault of his own, he was the reason Ralph and I had ended up in Shamu's office. Luca's entry into this world had been the catalyst that ultimately turned everyone else's upside down.

CHAPTER THREE

A See Change

I turned right and headed towards Glenelg, where *I* had entered the world.

I'd been tempted to turn left, to go running to my mother-in-law. I had three to choose from: Greta, from my first marriage to Reuben; Auntie Norma, the person I'd known all my life as Ralph's mother (my late mother Sylvia's sister); and Beth, Ralph's biological mother, whose existence he'd only become aware of a few years ago and who had become part of his life a year or so after that, and part of mine a few months before our wedding.

I loved all three of these women and they loved me. But it was Beth I'd go to.

Beth didn't have the Jewish sensibilities of Norma and Greta, who with the very best intentions would attempt to cheer me up. Beth wouldn't. She'd wrap her loving arms around me and let me cry.

For a lot of my adult life, I'd shut down my feelings. But after my first marriage unravelled, I opened up and let the pain express. There was something to be said for letting yourself fall apart; for letting yourself fall. Sylvia had never let me fall. A rescuer, she had tried to 'fix' things for me. But her way of lending a helping hand was more like extending a hand to someone she'd just pushed into the abyss.

I knew Beth would never push me. Still, she'd never discourage me from leaping, and she'd hold a space for me if I dared to. But I decided against going to see her, in part because I didn't want to put her in a precarious position, with Ralph being her son and all, but also because there are times when you just need to sit with your shit. Alone.

By the time I got to Glenelg, the rain had stopped. Dark clouds still hovered, but they'd scattered and allowed the sun to peep through. I loved this seaside suburb that was my birthplace. Sylvia had delivered me at Glenelg Hospital. So she'd said. But I knew better.

I was an unwelcome addition to the family; a 'mistake', they'd said, conceived when my brother Myron was only two months old. And his birth had been premature and harrowing. Endless oceans of labouring. Not a good thing for a grudge-holder like Sylvia, with her low pain tolerance and controlling personality. She would have slammed her legs shut and yelled, 'Stay until you can come out without making me suffer!'

Myron's speech patterns, which didn't include question or exclamation marks were forged before he saw daylight. He'd hung tight for thirty-six hours—his acquiescence spelling a meek, mechanical, *Yes, Mummy*. Then for years after that, he'd kissed Sylvia's arse out of guilt for being disobedient in the end.

My speech patterns were diametrically opposed to

Myron's, as in, *What? Are you kidding? No way! I am out of this shithole!* I'd shot out in ten minutes like a human cannonball.

A good thing, you'd think. Not for Sylvia. Because she hadn't needed to push, she would have construed this as an independent move on my part—a greater cause of suffering for her. With her worth tied to her need to be needed, the circumstances of my gestation and birth were the blueprint for my relationship with her. She made damn sure she was the one to push. I made damn sure I pushed back.

Now, I cruised past Glenelg Community Hospital. I'd dropped in a few years back in the hope of getting a copy of my birth records. These would have been archived on microfiche, they'd said. But, oh dear, all the records leading up to and including the year I was born had been destroyed. Sorry, Ma'am.

So, I had no written proof to refute Sylvia's proud claim that she'd pushed me out in ten minutes. But I didn't need it. I'd intuited that, in this single-storey, sandstone-faced brick building which didn't even look like a hospital, *I gave birth to myself!* End of story.

Addendum: It was a real doctor who'd caught me when I came out. Not a pseudonymbecile like Jackson Byron Everett-Lillicrap, who flaunted the title for window-dressing. Ralph also had a doctorate, but he didn't call himself Doctor Brill, except when he booked an airline ticket because it usually ensured an upgrade. I used to tell him he'd be in deep doo-doo and downgraded to economy if the flight staff called on him to assist someone having a heart attack. After that, he enrolled in a first aid course. After what just happened in the not-doctor's office it looked like Ralph, along with his life-saving skills, would be flying solo. Or maybe it just drove home the point that he already was.

I choked back a sob and made a U-turn, pointing the car north.

Ralph and I regularly came down to Glenelg to get some fresh air, chill out or shoot the breeze. Occasionally we hung out where the crowds gathered, at the beach end of Jetty Road. Or we'd sit on the sand under the jetty. Mostly, though, we lazed on the grassed area at the quieter southern end.

There was a parking spot in one of the small side streets at the northern end. Perfect. I didn't want Ralph to find me, or to deal with the fact that he might not come looking.

I walked down to the main drag and bought myself supplies—my second lunch for the day: a chicken and avocado focaccia, a blueberry muffin, a large bottle of water, and a slice of banana bread in case I was still here at afternoon teatime. Even as I suffered through my darkest hours, my appetite didn't.

Back at the car, I grabbed the tissue box from the passenger seat and the picnic blanket from the boot, walked the short distance to the sand, and found a shady little nook in amongst the rocks. I sat cross-legged on the blanket and stared at the ocean, thinking about Ralph and me. I thought back to when and how the fabric of our relationship had started to unravel.

* * * *

Friday morning, almost one year earlier.

I sat staring at the ocean from the table in the enclosed sunroom at the back of Stella's at Henley Beach. This section of the eatery was usually crowded because of its unobstructed sea view. Today, though, I didn't have to fight for a spot; the whole restaurant was quiet. It was eight-forty in the morning and still school holidays. The gaggle of mums who assembled here for lattes after school drop-off were probably at home in their pyjamas. I didn't miss their stage-whispered Chinese whispers that began the minute they got here, the kind that were prefaced with 'Oh my God, did you hear about ...' or 'I shouldn't tell you this, but ...'

'There you are!' Maxi's voice shook me out of my musings. She and Vette made their way to the table. I stood up and we group-hugged.

Maxine Mayer-Rose and Yvette Klein had been my two closest girlfriends since we'd met as four-year-olds at kindergarten. Maxi was also my boss. Had been for almost five years. She was editor-in-chief of a popular women's magazine, and I was one of its feature writers—its inspirational humour columnist.

I'd sent both girls a confirmation text two days earlier, a couple of hours after Ralph and I got back from our honeymoon. We'd pre-arranged this breakfast get-together: 'You'll need to be debriefed,' Maxi had said just after the wedding.

'So, how many times did he debrief you?' she now asked as she sat down. In our late forties, we three shared our sexual exploits like we were still in the phase of developing sexuality. 'Not much else to do in Fiji other than fuck each other's brains out.'

'Uh-huh. And yeah, often.'

'So, why the long face?' Maxi narrowed her eyes at me. 'Please don't tell me he made you dress up like one of the housekeeping staff.' Ralph'd had an adolescent fetish for women in uniform—from military to French maids.

'No! It's not my thing. And anyway, he's outgrown that.'

'Hmm. Outgrown it or replaced it with another one? He didn't literally get into your pants, did he? You know, dress up in your clothes?'

I laughed at her and shook my head, and became serious again.

Vette put her hand on mine. 'What is it, Ruthie? Is it cystitis? Do you have honeymoon cystitis?'

Quaint. I smiled at my caring friend. 'No, I don't have cystitis.'

'Then what?'

I opened my mouth to say 'Nothing', but nothing came out. It would have been a lie, anyway, and they'd have spotted it.

'Ruthie?' Vette gently prodded.

I blew out. 'Truth? It was a bit of a nightmare.'

Maxi frowned. 'Truth? Can't say I'm surprised. And lemme guess. You had a ménage à trois. Sylvia blew in from hell and raised hell about you marrying your "cousin"?'

'Oh, if only it were that simple.'

Vette gave me a wry smile. 'Well, if nothing else, I'm glad you're singing a very different tune about that, but what—'

'You know I wouldn't have married him if I wasn't.'

'Of course—'

'I mean, there are still times I gotta remind myself we're not *real* cousins.'

'Oh, honey, it'll take years,' Maxi said. 'It took forty-five of them to find out he was adopted.'

'Mmm. I guess. But when it came to sex, it took, like, all of forty-five seconds for him to overlook all those years we thought we were blood-related!'

'Hey, we all know Ralph thinks like a girl, but typical bloke, his dick thinks like a dick.'

Vette and I nodded our heads in agreement, then she prompted again, 'So, what is it?'

I hesitated again. Maxi took another stab at it. 'Buyer's remorse, I'll bet! I did tell you, you should've lived with him first. It's one thing to tolerate his particular brand of crazy when you're not sharing a living space, but Ruthie, you should've insisted on a try-before-you-buy policy.'

It was no secret that Ralph was strange. Both of them knew it long before Ralph and Maxi had become an item for a brief time when we were seventeen. A couple of weeks after they'd devirginised each other, she dumped him, unable to cope with his eccentricities. I was used to them. He and I had spent a lot of time together from the get-go, not only because we were related, but because we were besties. The perfect male–female complementarity. Although, there were times I wasn't sure who held what position. But even after he'd discovered we weren't blood-related, and my minge started thinking like a minge, we rarely spent the night together. I only let him stay over on the weekends the kids were with their dad.

Maxi was still sounding off. 'At least that way—'

'Maxi.'

'—you would've—'

'Maxi!'

'What?'

'It's not that simple.'

She arched an eyebrow inquisitively.

How much should I tell them? Just then, a waiter appeared with a jug of water, three glasses, and a pad and pen.

Vette filled our glasses as the waiter took our orders. It was the usual: scrambled eggs on sourdough with a side serving of avocado for Vette and me, eggs Benedict for Maxi, and three soy milk cappuccinos.

He left, and two pairs of expectant eyes fixed on me.

'Ruthie, you know you can tell us anything.'

Vette was right. And even though I feared I'd be betraying Ralph if I told them, the secret weighed heavily.

Seemed I was no better than one of the *I-shouldn't-tell-you-this-but* school mums who haunted this place, but I took a swig

of water then a deep, courageous breath. 'You were right,' I said
to Maxi. 'We did have a ménage à trois—'

Vette's breath hitched. Maxi's mouth dropped open.

'In a metaphorical sense, I mean.'

Vette's face registered relief. Maxi's registered
disappointment. 'So, who was the metaphorical third party?'

'Alex.'

'*What?* You imagined bonking your *son-in-law*—'

'No. *God, no!* I mean he's gorgeous, but *eww*, no! Please,
just let me tell the story.'

Maxi raised her hands in a conceding gesture.

'Okay. So, you remember I told you how we found out about
Larissa and Alex? About that afternoon?'

It had been an unforgettable one.

Hannah had fallen pregnant with Alex's child when she
was only eighteen; he was twenty-four. They were madly
in love and refused point blank to have the pregnancy
terminated. It made sense then that the families on both
sides should meet. So, Alex's parents, Rhea and Hector,
invited Reuben, Casper, Ralph and me for afternoon tea.

A framed picture of Hector with his arm around a roly-poly
woman—who wasn't Rhea—had caught Ralph's eye. We
found out she was Alex's real mum, Larissa, and that she
died when he was only two and a half. The reason she
looked familiar to Ralph was because he'd dated her years
earlier. When she had a waist.

Larissa had been in love with Ralph, but when she started
making noise about getting married, he dumped her. This
was all news to Hector and it rankled. Never mind that
Larissa had married *him*; seemed he felt like the runner-
up. For the rest of the afternoon, our host behaved like a
Chihuahua pissing on a wall to mark its territory. It was akin
to watching the dumbest dog breed that would drink out of
an unflushed toilet, if it could reach it, taking on a vet who

had a Mensa IQ and who was about to neuter the dog. The 'vet' won, but the runt kept trying to pick a fight with him. From then on, the runt was like a dog with a bone.

Hector was destined to always fall short, though. This small man, in dire need of socialisation and training, was one player short of a solitaire game. He was also one letter short of an alphabet. Literally. He pronounced his r's as w's (a condition called rhotacism). So, it wasn't just that he was punching above his weight with Ralph. Launching his assaults with 'Walph' meant Hector lost every battle before it had a chance to get off the ground—

'Ruthie?' Maxi interrupted my thoughts.

'Huh? What?'

'*Focus*. I said, what about them? What about Larissa and Alex?'

'Oh. Uh. Yeah. Well, here's the thing. Hector wasn't just the runner-up; he was Larissa's sloppy seconds.' I looked from one to the other and waited for a reaction. 'You know, straight after Ralph.'

'*Ugh*—the man is sloppy seconds even if no one's come before him! But what's your point?'

'Think about it.'

'Oh, we are not going to do this, are we, this obscure bullshit?'

This obscure bullshit meant I didn't have to come right out and say it. 'Okay. So. Alex might've been born six weeks early, but he was no preemie.'

'Jesus! Living with Ralph for one week and you're already becoming just like hi ...' Maxi didn't finish the sentence. Her eyes widened.

'Oh my God, no,' Vette said. 'No!'

CHAPTER FOUR

Beached Wail

'Yyyep.'

'Nah.' Maxi waved her hand, dismissing the idea. 'It's probably just wishful thinking on Ralph's part. We all know how much he wanted children.'

'Well, he has one,' I said emphatically. 'Larissa took up with Hector pretty much straight after Ralph dumped her. And—an' I don't think I told you this—when Hannah was in labour and Rhea went off to get a coffee, the schmuck confided to us that Larissa had put out on their first date.'

Shocked, Vette covered her mouth. Maxi's curved down in disgust like she'd just swallowed hagfish slime.

'Arsehole thought it was because he was irresistible, but Larissa would've already known she was pregnant to Ralph and was probably looking for a father for her child. I can't think of any other reason why someone would sleep with Hector on the first date.'

'Only on the first date?' Maxi pretended to dry-retch.

We all gave a little shiver, horrified at the thought of anyone shagging Hector. I knew Rhea no longer was. Maxi, Vette and I had become good friends with her, and from an honest exchange I'd had with her the day after Hannah and Alex's wedding, I found out she and Hector were more like flatmates than husband and wife. Still, she *used* to bonk him!

'Still,' said Maxi, 'this paternity thing, it's all speculative and—'

'Ralph took a test.'

'What? *Jesus.* When?'

'A few weeks ago, when Hannah, Alex and Luca stayed with us.'

'The weekend they were getting their place fumigated, right?' Vette said.

'Uh huh. Alex left his toothbrush behind and we bagged it an—'

'Whoa! Wait a second. Isn't that a little sneaky?'

I peered at Maxi. 'Really? This coming from you, women's magazine editor?'

'That's different. I still have ethics. Situational, maybe—'

'I have ethics too, Max. So does Ralph. Also "situational". But he had the right to know. And realistically, he couldn't very well have gone up to Alex and asked for a cheek swab, could he?'

'Guess not.'

'Anyway, if it turned out negative, well, no harm, no foul.'

'But obviously, it was positive.'

'Yep. And the result's conclusive. It wasn't one of those over-the-counter tests. It was done by a DNA testing company. You either get negative, zero per cent, or positive, ninety-nine point nine nine per cent.'

After a sustained silence, Maxi said, 'Wow. *Wow.*'

'Mmhmm. And the letter came in the mail the morning of our wedding. To my place. Ralph had his mail redirected there a week earlier. And he got ready for the day at his apartment.' I turned to Vette. 'That's why I was distracted before the ceremony. You know, when you came in to get me?'

'Ah ...'

'I'd been in a bit of a quandary. No way was I going to tell Ralph before the wedding that I had the envelope. And I was like, do I wait till after the honeymoon? But it wouldn't've been honest—not the best way to start a marriage, so I gave it to him that night. And the OC behaviour started straight away, and it cranked up in Fiji.'

'Lucky you,' Maxi mumbled.

The three of us sat in silence again, then Maxi said, 'If you've known for a while—'

'I didn't know—'

'Okay. If you've *suspected* for a while, why didn't you say something?' A flicker of hurt crossed her face.

I'd seen a lot of Maxi and Vette after Hannah's wedding, because, along with Rhea and Iris (Reuben's sister, my ex-sister-in-law and dear friend), they helped plan my wedding.

'Honestly, I would've told you both earlier, but until it was confirmed Ralph didn't want anyone to know. And please, you *cannot* let on to him that you know.'

Both swore they wouldn't.

'Anyway, outside of our wedding planning meetings, who could reach you, Maxi?' I backtracked in the hope of appeasing my guilt at having kept her in the dark. 'You've kinda been off the grid for the last five months. When you weren't at work, you were in bed.'

Nice segue. Maxi's face lit up. She was in love for the first time in her life. She'd met Nestor, Rhea's twin brother, at Hannah's wedding. Their slap and tickle had yet to wane.

'Hey, I got up to come have breakfast with you, didn't I?'

'You did, and I'm impressed.'

'It was hard.'

'I can imagine. And I'm grateful.'

'No, really. It was hard.'

Vette and I laughed at her.

She sighed dreamily. 'What can I say? The man's a god.'

Vette splayed her hand over her chest. Caught up in the moment, she said, 'Ahh ... Adonis, the god of desire. Or maybe Eros, the god of love?'

'Noooo. Priapus, the god with the erection that won't quit!'

I could identify. Vette, not so much. Maxi and I giggled. Vette blushed. She was no prude, but where Nestor and Ralph were big feet, big meat, her Henry was more cocktail wiener.

Then there was my bent for ancient mythology. Although neither of my girlfriends shared it, Maxi had allowed me to incorporate some of it into my feature stories.

My affinity with myths had started long, long ago.

Even as a little kid, I thought fairy tales were bollocks. The princess had the brainpower of Barbie and the prince had the charisma of Ken. These two deserved each other. Oh, I wanted a prince, but if that meant being a simpering, doe-eyed fuckwit, then no thanks! So, I fell through the framework of the airy-fairy stories and landed square on my arse in the deep, unedited ones.

Relating to them wasn't a real stretch. With a mum like Sylvia and a dad with a god complex and dodgy moral compass, my home life was imbecilic. Both Sylvia and Joe were from Egypt. She struggled to live the Australian way; he thought he was living it because he could fart the national anthem. It made sense, then, that I was in tune with the crude myths and their schizoid characters. But it took a while for me to discover these freaky, yet strangely soothing stories.

Joe taught me to pray when I was five years old. One of my earliest prayers was 'Dear God, let Sylvia make good on her threat to send me to boarding school, I beg you!' I had my friends—Ralph, Maxi and Vette—but five-year-olds can't save each other. And God took His jolly time.

He hung me out to dry for ten years. *Ten fucking years!* And when He did get around to answering my prayers, He delivered in a cryptic form. He didn't send me to boarding school. Instead, He sent me a mythological character that He'd raised from the crypt.

Mr Zero Kosta was my history teacher. He taught us students about the innate comedy in the tragedy. Mr Kosta *looked* like the comedy in the tragedy. Or the tragedy in the comedy. He was how I imagined Death would appear if it were a person. Cadaverous. Emaciated. Sunken cheeks. Ashen complexion. Greyish teeth. Gnarled hands. But his words helped me appreciate that my ability to discern the humour in everything was why I laughed at inappropriate times, when I should have apparently been mournful. And I laughed from the time I could form sentences.

Sylvia used to slap me and yell, '*Tu es mal élevée!*' It made me laugh harder. Only five years old, but able to see the stupidity in my own mother telling me I was badly brought up. And she used to wash my mouth out with soap when I swore, which was often. Joe was my role model, but Sylvia never soaped *his* filthy mouth. Life seemed unfair.

It got so that I felt bad about my dirty bazoo. But I couldn't help myself.

Through Mr Kosta's teachings, I came to understand that I was destined to live out the whole story of who I am, not some sanitised, morally constipated version. I also understood that I was driven by Baubo, the ancient goddess of obscenity. Yes, my potty mouth was inspired by a divine spark. It wasn't because I was *une fille dégoûtante*, a disgusting girl. So, creepy as he was, I loved

Mr Kosta. He helped nourish my deepest consciousness
—my soul—and made me feel better about myself.

'We're getting off track,' Vette said as she shifted
uncomfortably in her chair. 'So, you're saying Ralph had a
feeling about Alex from the time he saw that picture of Larissa?'

'No, no. It was at Hannah and Alex's wedding, when we
found out Alex has Tourette Synd—'

'What! Alex has Tourette's?' Maxi said.

'Uh-huh. Just after the ceremony during cocktails we saw
his arm shoot up and out. Hector pretended like it was nothing,
but I pressured him into fessing up because Alex kept doing it.'

Vette said, 'Well, that explains his jiggy shoulder.'

'Yep. And his throat-clearing.' Alex *ahemmed* a lot when he
spoke. 'Anyway, something niggled at Ralph, but he couldn't
put his finger on it. Then the day after he and I officially got
engaged and he gave me the ring, he went to visit Beth and
found out—wait for it—his real father's late grandmother was
Aboriginal.'

The two of them stared and squinted as if trying to absorb
the import of this snippet of information. I watched and waited.

Vette slapped her cheeks. 'Oh, my goodness! That explains
Luca's dark skin.'

'Oh, it just gets better and better!' Maxi hooted.

'Yep. And after Beth told Ralph about his great-
grandmother, he was on a mission, and—'

'So, Beth knows? You said nobody else knows?' Vette
interrupted.

'I meant, nobody other than Beth. Ralph told her about the
results last night. She knew there might be a possibility because
he'd confided in her.'

Both girls *mmmed*.

'But like I was saying, the timing of Alex's birth and parallels between Ralph and Alex's disorders planted a seed. But Luca's skin colour didn't mean much until Ralph found out about his biological great-grandmother. Before that, as you know, we'd just assumed it was a throwback from an Ethiopian ancestor way back in my bloodline. I mean, after Alex's initial reaction when Luca was born, you know, when he accused Hannah of cheating on him!'

'Yeah, bad call that one was,' Maxi said.

'Uh huh.'

The girls mulled over everything I'd told them, then Maxi said, 'Huh. Yeah, well, I can see how the honeymoon woulda been fun. Was he touching everything twice and repeating himself and *mmm nom nom nomming* while he ate?'

'Oh, around the clock!'

'*Jesus.* Even without Alex or your mother in the bed —metaphorically speaking—it would've been like having a ménage à trois. Ralph's a double act on his own.'

I laughed. Vette didn't. 'Poor Ralph.'

'Poor Ralph, my arse!' Maxi said.

'Vette. His strange behaviours don't exhaust *him*.'

She gave me a sympathetic look.

'I'm surprised he was able to get it up,' Maxi said.

'Why? Ralph's cure for everything is sex.'

Both nodded. They knew that even though Ralph was way past adolescence, his hormones had yet to come of age. There was no need to harp on it.

'What about Norma?' Vette asked. 'Is he going to tell her?'

I shook my head.

'Don't you think that's wrong? I mean, it might have taken him all these years to find out he was adopted, but she was still his mother during those years.'

'And she still is. Look, I agree with you. I love Norma, and she's well-meaning, but she'd blab. It'd slip out unintentionally. And if Alex found out that way, well, can you imagine?'

'Mmm, true. It's no doubt going to throw him into a tailspin when he does find out, but he needs to hear it from Ralph. And at the right time.'

'Uh huh.'

'Geez, hon. Ralph's weirdness is gonna be revving up until then.'

'Oh, I don't think that's even possible.'

'That bad, huh? All I can say is I wouldn't wanna be in your shoes.'

'Well, that makes me feel so much better!'

Maxi squeezed my hand. 'Sorry.'

'It's okay. Hey, I don't even wanna be in my shoes.'

The food and coffees arrived, breaking up our pensive mood.

We ate our eggs, savoured our drinks and discussed the situation until we tired of it. Then we talked about Maxi's hot relationship with Nestor, and Vette's snug relationship with Henry. Both girls were still happy in their chosen career paths—Vette was a fashion buyer for Myer—and now, both were happy in their personal lives. Apart from the matter at hand, I was also happy in mine, but needed some freshness in my professional life. I told them I loved writing feature stories for the magazine. It wasn't enough, though.

'Hmm ...' Vette puckered her lips and drew her brows together in thought. Then she smiled. 'I know, why don't you write a book?'

'A book? About what?'

'Well, for starters, the last three years! Fictionalised, of course.'

'Fictionalised? Her life's so bloody ridiculous it *reads* like fiction; like an eternal black comedy.' Maxi looked at me. 'No offence.'

I held up my hands in a none-taken gesture.

'But good thinking, Betty Boop.'

Maxi sometimes called Vette that when she pursed her cherry-red-painted lips, which made her look even more like the cartoon character. Both Vette and Boop had short, curly black hair, porcelain skin and wide, innocent green eyes. Both were slim, both had small boobies and ample booties. And like Betty Boop, Vette was all heart and had a pollyanna temperament. But she was no pushover. Nobody could take her 'boop-oop-a-doop' away.

Maxi was drawn differently. She looked like Jessica Rabbit—creamy-skin, slim, big boobs, piercing blue eyes, and long chestnut hair. She also had the disposition to go with the looks: 'I'm not bad, I'm just drawn that way'.

We three were so symbiotic, it was as if it impacted on our respective biologies. We'd stopped growing at the same time— all around five foot three, give or take—and we were often told we looked ten years younger than our current age.

I was closer in appearance to Maxi than to Vette: slim, busty, small bummed, shoulder-length, reddish, mid-brown hair, olive skin and hazel eyes. No cartoon character doppelgänger like the two of them, just those strong ties to Baubo. 'Good thing you don't look like her,' Maxi had said when I'd shown her an illustration of the goddess, often depicted cartoonishly as a headless freak whose facial features were on her belly—nipple eyes, belly button nose, prominent vulva mouth. 'I could still be friends with you if you were ugly,' she'd added, 'but not if your face looked like a pussy.'

Miaow.

'Yep, very good thinking, Boop,' Maxi reiterated. She looked at me again. 'With all the bloody drama you've been through in the last three years—'

'And the synchronicities,' Vette threw in.

'Yeah, that too. Hell, it could end up as a movie. A blockbuster even.'

'Uh-huh. It's been apocalyptic, all right,' I said.

The waiter approached and asked if we'd like more coffees. We said no and asked for the bill. Just as he finished clearing away the plates, Maxi said, 'Ooh, ooh, ooh! How about this for a title? *Apocahotlips*.' She spread her hands apart in the air as if to draw out an imaginary banner with the word on it.

'Perfect!' Vette and I chorused.

We paid the bill, they made me promise to keep them updated and we went our separate ways.

I had semi-fictional places to go, characters to see, things to write.

CHAPTER FIVE

Hell's Bells

I dropped in to the non-fictional supermarket to pick up a few essentials, and got home shortly after ten-thirty.

After changing into stay-at-home duds—shorts and a threadbare T-shirt—I made myself a cup of tea; an organic, herbal blend that Ralph had picked up at the Central Market a couple of weeks before our wedding. Neither of us had yet tried it. It was called 'Inspiration'. *Well, we'll see about that.*

At the dining room table with my cuppa, I booted up the laptop and stared at the winking cursor on the blank Word document. Where to begin?

Yes, a sip of tea. No. Not a sip. I don't know how to sip. Passionate beings quaff and gulp with relish—our food and drink and life! It didn't matter that it was hot. I liked it that way. I took a big swig.

Oh, fuuuuuck!

I spat it back into the cup, shivered convulsively and gagged. I looked down into this brew and shivered again, this time at a memory. Its vile taste and yellowish colour reminded me of the castor oil liquid laxative Sylvia forced me to take when I was backed up. With no chaser.

I bolted into the bathroom and squeezed an inch of toothpaste onto my tongue, filled my mouth with some water, swished and swallowed. Retrieving the teacup, I took it into the kitchen, tipped the offending contents down the drain and was about to toss the box of tea into the garbage, but decided against it.

Ralph might like a cup after dinner. Yes. For inspiration. An inspiring thought, although not quite what I was holding out for.

Sitting down again, I leaned back, interlocked my fingers behind my head, and considered the title.

Maxi's suggestion was a good one. I knew what a personal apocalypse felt like, but had thrown the word itself around loosely and in a general sense. If I was going to write about it, I needed to sound learned. And that entailed wads of research.

I googled 'Apocalypse' and clicked on the first result, an online encyclopedia. It said an apocalypse is a revelation.

Huh? What am I missing?

It went on to say that from within a religious framework, this revelation is a heavenly vision that helps us make sense of our earthly existence.

Huh? What are you *missing?* Details! *The devil is in the details.* No details; no devil.

Jesus, who wrote this crap? It was a romanticised, rose-coloured take that rubbed me up the wrong way with its happily-ever-after tone: 'I have discovered the Holy Grail and everything is now and forever hunky-dory. The End'.

'Get off the grass! "The End" is not the end. It comes first. *First!*' I yelled, then mumbled, 'The end is that rotten, stinking stretch before the revelation, the one where the world as you know it feels like it's coming to an end. And nobody sleeps through that. *Nobody*!' I was yelling again. 'Even if you're pissed as a newt or constantly stoned and macro-nap for a hundred years, you still have to deal with it when you wake up. And there is no Disney Someday-My-Prince-Will-Come to save you from that!'

Still, I had to admit my story would have something of the fairy tale because every budding romance does, the first flush of love and all. Ralph's and mine did. But my book wouldn't be doctored like *Sleeping Beauty*. Ralph was no Disney prince, and even if I wanted to be a Disney princess, I didn't have narcolepsy or stars in my eyes or an impossibly thin waist or a vacuous smile.

Cyclopedia could sod off!

I looked to an online dictionary instead. Dictionaries are written by lexicographers; sober realists who don't have their heads in the clouds or up their arses.

Dictionary said an apocalypse is a serious event that causes fear and loss and destruction, and that results in catastrophic disaster.

Not so woo-woo, this, it was a hard-boiled approach. A grim approach. It was what I wanted to hear but then ... *Ah-ha-ah-ha-ah-ha* ... why was I hyperventilating?

Endings were hard. I hated apocalypses. Was one in the offing? No. Ralph and I had had our share of them in the last few years. A reunion was in the offing. Ralph and Alex, a new beginning. Yes! The disasters had already come; the revelations had already come. Although ... not for Alex. It hadn't yet come for him. He didn't know Ralph was his father. An apocalypse was in the offing for Alex.

With that realisation came a sense of foreboding—a 'whorebringer of doom' as Sylvia would have called it. Why, though? This book I was going to write was supposed to be about my past disasters, not a portent of coming ones for someone else. And Alex's impending apocalypse was none of my business.

Drawing a calming breath, I got up and made myself a cup of chamomile tea, the go-to for relaxation. A tea that didn't taste like castor oil. It tasted like soap, but I was inured to that. I took a gulp, typed the tentative title and studied it. It wasn't quite right. I threw in a couple of square brackets. *Apoca[hot]lips*.

Better.

Now what?

On the drop-down menu, I clicked on 'Insert' and 'Page Numbers', and saved the titled, page-numbered manuscript. It was a start; indicated my intention to write a book. Then I leaned back in the chair again and waited for the words to come ...

Isn't it cool working from home?

Again, not the hoped-for words, but yes, it was cool working from home. Here, sequestered, I could dress like a dag, make myself unavailable, put the answering machine on, and switch my mobile to vibrate or silent. I wrote my magazine articles from the comfort and quietude of my dining room. I didn't have to deal with the distractions of an office space—other people's body odour, the clacking of keyboards, the hum of conversation—the buzz of humanity. I smiled.

I stopped smiling. Shit.

'Nnn zzz nnnn zzz nnnn ...'

'Nnn zzz nnnn zzz ...'

The buzz of insects.

Two filthy blowflies hovered and droned. They sucked my focus away from the blank page. I watched them with irritation, then fetched the swatter. But as I raised my arm, both of them, like a pair of kamikaze pilots, slammed into the wall. At the same time. Huh. Impressive timing, but obviously, poorly trained. They lived. Brain-damaged, maybe. Although, there wasn't much there to begin with.

Still, they were streetwise. They dodged and swerved as I worked up a sweat, thrashing and thwacking—forehand, backhand, and then an overhead smash.

'Nnn zzz nnnn zzz nnnn ...'

'Nnn zzz nnnn zzz ...'

No go.

Sylvia had taken me to tennis lessons when I was ten. I could lob with my mouth but was never quite as dexterous with a racket. I stormed down the hall, grabbed the fly spray from the linen closet, let loose on the little bastards, then stood there watching their frenzied death spirals. It made me feel bad. An apology was in order. 'Sorry. But I'm higher up the food chain. Better luck in your next life, morons!'

As I fished a tissue out of my pocket and bent down to scoop up the little stiffs, something occurred to me: I didn't know anything about arthropods or aerodynamics or how flies flew. I wasn't an entomologist or a pilot or Ralph, so I didn't care. But what were the chances of both flies hitting the wall at the same time? And what were the chances that they'd crash-land within a hair's breadth of each other?

The word Vette had used came to mind. 'Synchronicities!' I said to their enshrouded corpses. And something else came to mind as I tossed them into their final resting place: 'Twin Flames'.

Ralph had introduced me to the theory of Twin Flames. It was Plato's notion of split-aparts. Each of us is supposedly part of one soul—one half of it. The two halves split apart, incarnate into two separate bodies, and then they search for each other. Cosmic forces conspire to bring them together.

Did twin flameship exist in the animal kingdom? Did Noah know this when he filled his ark before Plato gave the concept a name all those years later? No. Noah's two by two was for the purpose of procreating. Did animals have soulmates? Did I give a crap? No. *Jesus*. Maxi was right. I was becoming like Ralph.

Maybe I already was like him because we were Twin Flames, according to him. And even if we hadn't been under each other's noses from the outset as cousins, even if he hadn't been adopted, he reckoned that synchronicity would have brought us together.

The synchronicities in my life had been staggering. Apart from the twist of fate that had my mother's sister adopting Ralph, what were the chances that my daughter would meet and fall in love with Ralph's biological son? And that Alex's Uncle Nestor would look across a crowded garden at Hannah and Alex's wedding and lock eyes with his Twin Flame, Maxi? What were the chances that two filthy airborne pollutants called flies would front up with a message?

The list went on. Call it kismet, call it destiny. Whatever. I was in awe of all these surprise meetings. Divine design was a beautiful thing. If only I could see the perfection in its placement with my stupid family. Maybe writing this book would help me. And maybe synchronicity could be the theme. Or *a* theme.

With a germ of an idea and lots to draw on, I was getting excited! Inspired. All this from one gulp of horrid tea. It had delivered on its promise and the words began to flow. I was really getting into it when the shrill sound of the doorbell startled me.

Bugger.

The doorbell might have been one of Sister Maria's favourite things in *The Sound of Music*, along with creamy ponies and whiskers on bloody kittens, but for me, it had become a bugbear. Too often, Sylvia had unexpectedly been on the other side of the door, letting out a stream of invective the minute I opened it. The doorbell was another disadvantage of working from home. I contemplated not answering it, but the caller rang the bell again. And again.

'I'm *coming*.' Talk about impatient.

I opened the door to a beady-eyed, squat, duck-footed man who smelled like an ashtray. His skin was as ghost-white as a lab rat, but otherwise, he looked unclean. He had dirty, dirty-blond hair and a scraggly, mousy, Amish beard. He wore an ill-fitting black suit, an unironed shirt, cream in colour like Sister Maria's ponies, and a wide tie with a kaleidoscopic pattern—the kind that messes with your brain and makes you feel like you're tripping on acid.

'Hello,' he said. 'I'm Olive Portnoy's son.'

Shit. I am *tripping!* What the *hell* was in that yellow brew?

CHAPTER SIX

What's in a Gnome?

I shook off the feeling, brought myself back down into a grounded state, and laughed. 'Yeah, right!'

The little man was aghast. 'I *beg* your pardon?'

We eyeballed one another. *Sweet mother of Jesus.* He wasn't kidding.

Olive Portnoy lived in the house-cum-dumpster across the road. With her Third World living conditions and a squalid temperament, she was a blight on the streetscape and a blot on my inner landscape. She was an informant who'd leaked porkies to Sylvia, who then 'knew' news about me that was news to me. And for a few years, Portnoy had given me hell with the malicious lies she passed down through the communal grapevine.

Ralph had said she herself was the fruit of the ugly tree. Or more likely, the fruit bat that feeds on the fruit of the ugly tree because she was a nocturnal creature. This was understandable. Portnoy herself was also unsightly, not least because of her one whacking great eye that dwarfed the other (exophthalmia, Ralph had said, an abnormal condition characterised by a marked eyeball protrusion. Cyclops, I had said, a direct link to the mythical, monstrous, savage one-eyed giants). And yet, the words of this little man on my doorstep inferred that someone had known her in a biblical sense.

I couldn't wrap my head around this. The woman was too unprepossessing to fuck. Junior had to have been adopted. Or made with a turkey baster.

He was glaring at me with his beady, turquoise eyes that reminded me of the evil-eye glass beads Sylvia used to hang everywhere to stalk me.

I covered my arse. 'Uh, you don't look like her.'

'No, I don't. I look like my late father.'

'Oh.' *Well, Daddy was obviously no oil painting either.*

'But that's beside the point,' he continued in a haughty tone at odds with his appearance. 'I'm here to tell you my mother passed away a few weeks ago.'

My eyes bugged out, not like Portnoy's—nowhere near like Portnoy's. 'Oh,' again. 'I'm sorry.' It was an automatic reaction. Sylvia had primed me for these situations from an early age, I knew what to say:

Bearer of bad news: 'She's/he's passed away.'

Me: 'I'm sorry.'

I used to think it was my fault he or she died. In a child's mind, it was what sorry implied. But I wasn't in the least bit sorry that Portnoy had died. I would've only been sorry if the fetid smell of her rotting corpse had wafted from her premises; it was bad enough her place looked like shit. Who needed it to smell like it?

'How did she die?' I asked Junior. I didn't care, but I thought it might provide some good raw materials for my book.

'A stroke.'

A stroke of luck!

'I found her on the lounge-room floor when I was dropping off her weekly groceries one night.'

Ha. So, she wasn't hunting-gathering the rats in her backyard. I'd long suspected Portnoy bred them. For a spell, she was depositing dead ones on my front porch as punishment for tattling on her to the authorities. Now, I was envisioning her fall.

It would have had a high terminal velocity—she was a tall, heavy woman with the bulk of fat concentration in her caboose. I imagined her head hitting the ground and her mofo eyeball popping out, bouncing around the lounge room like a rubber polymer Wham-O Super Ball—those nifty balls that *boing-boing* back up two or three times the height of the drop.

And, like a moth to a flame, the eyeball would have made its way back to the distorted diamond shape between the lounge room venetian slats that had been her nosy eye's home for so long: Surveillance headquarters. Did the undertaker have to beat her eye down with a stick? Did he—

'I don't believe it!' Her son's voice rudely interrupted my fact-finding musings. 'I just told you my mother has passed, and you think it's *funny*?'

'Oh, uh, um, I was—'

'Well,' he spat, 'I only came to inform you because she left something for you.'

Huh? I gave him a perplexed look.

'But I'm not sure I want to give it to you now.'

'Why ... what ...?' I was lost for words. But if she'd bequeathed me her frickin' rat colony, I was going to have to decline.

She hadn't. What he said cracked me up, though.

Junior was incensed. He gave me a mouthful, then stormed off.

It looked like Portnoy had had the last laugh. Maybe the old tosspot hadn't been as demented as she'd made out to be.

I rang Ralph. He was between clients. And if he'd been mid-session, I'd have asked the receptionist to put the call through as a matter of urgency.

'Portnoy's gone,' I said.

'What? Did she sell up?'

'Nope. She snuffed it. Flatlined. She's dead.'

'Hm-mmm,' he said in the consoling voice of the therapist. It was shorthand for 'I see'. *Pause*. A pause was shorthand for 'Go on'. But what more could I say? Dead is dead. 'So, she's dead,' he said. *Echoing*. Echoing was shorthand for 'I hear you'. *Pause*. Another bloody pause. *The fucking poetics of therapy. Are we really gonna do this? Change hats, for God's sake, man!*

I waited him out, expecting that at some point he'd break into compassionate jargon. At last, he spoke again. 'What about her eye?'

I lost it. And so did Ralph. The two of us were laughing so hard neither of us could get a word out for a good minute.

He regained control and asked, 'How'd you find out?'

'Her son came ov—'

'Her *what*? She has *offspring*?'

'Uh huh.'

Ralph went silent again. I could almost hear the gears grinding in his mind. I expected him to ask if Junior had an eye like his mother. He didn't. Instead, he said, 'Does he look like a garden gnome?'

I lost it again. Ralph had believed the only penises Portnoy ever had were the ones belonging to her two naked male gnomes.

She'd had a gnome militia guarding her front yard. Little bearded fuckers toting clay guns and short-range rocket launchers. They fell down on the job, though, and the neighbourhood had rejoiced. One neighbour, brave warrior that he or she was, still managed to cross enemy lines, dodge a clay bullet, and slice the knobs off the two nekkid male trolls. Without schlongs, they couldn't go forth and multiply with the two nekkid female trolls. Noah would have thrown the four of them overboard.

My laughter petered out and I answered Ralph. 'Kinda. He's short 'n' ugly. And he's got a big gut and high cheekbones like a pair of peaches, and a long beard—'

'Hmm.'

'But guess what? I'm listed as a beneficiary.'

'Hmm. Gnomes?'

'Uh-huh.'

'Dare I say the two eunuchs and their consorts?'

'Yep. But because I laughed when he told me, he yelled at me and said the only way I was gonna get them is if I contest the will.'

'Well ... I suppose it's time to lawyer up, then.'

'Nah. Forget it. What use are they to me if the boys don't have their joysticks?'

'Hey. You've got me. How much more could you ask for?'

Yes, indeedy! Well-endowed, well-versed in wordplay.

Over the coming months, though, the well-hung silver-tongue would become increasingly testy. And both would be in short supply because I believed, and kept reminding him, it was best to hold out for the right time to say something to Alex.

Still, for the time being, he was happy to take my advice—that he assimilate the knowledge he was a dad. And his feverish, obsessive–compulsive activity settled. But like those who quit smoking, and turn to something else to satisfy their oral fixation—usually eating—Ralph's excessive behaviour took a different form. Pomp.

On the weekend, he decided we needed to throw out my bed sheets and replace them with substantial Egyptian cotton, 1200 thread count.

'But I like these sheets,' I protested.

'The sex'll be better. Not such a rough ride.' He gave me a lewd grin, and we roughed it for the last time on a mere 400 thread count.

He also tossed out all my everyday crockery and assorted mixed cutlery, then he went on a shopping spree. On Sunday morning, I buttered my toast with Royal Doulton and ate it off Wedgwood. And on Sunday night, we had smooth sex.

Ralph had grown up poor. He'd never had new sheets. He'd slept on his brothers' old ones, which were discoloured from all their jerk-offs. And his meagre, cheap meals had been served on old, chipped crockery and were eaten with stained bone cutlery that used to belong to my family. Now, not only was cheap tableware out of the question, so were cheap cuts of meat. No gravy beef, no chuck steak. And mince was okay, but only premium and only for bolognaise or lasagne. Rissoles were *verboten*. I thought it was a bit over the top, but I indulged him. Until mid-week when his poncyness wore thinner than my discarded sheets.

We were having dinner and the food snob tried to educate me on luxury foods. I'd made paella with saffron.

'Mmm. Very nice, but I can taste the saffron. Any great chef will tell you it means you've gone a little overboard with it.' Then he yackety-yakked about other foodie things. Apparently, the fabulously intense white truffle aroma and flavour can be lost if you cook it, unlike, say, foie gras, which should be lightly cooked to give it a greater depth of flavour.

'And you, who used to eat tripe and lamb's fry, know all this because you read it in a library book, what, forty years ago?' (As a child, Ralph had spent hours at the library researching everything.)

He didn't like to be reminded of his el cheapo past, though, and he got uppity. 'No. I know these things because I'm a gastronome.'

I stopped chewing and stared at him. 'Really? What a pity. If you hadn't been so gun-shy, you could've sat in Portnoy's yard and offered some cooking tips to the other dumb-arse gnomes.'

This apparently constituted dirty-talk. A soft moan escaped Ralph's lips and he put down his wooden spoon, which is apparently *the* utensil for eating paella. For the gastronome, refinement went down the crapper where sex was concerned. We did the dirty right next to the fine bone china and expensive silverware on the granite surface of the breakfast bar. Cold and hard maybe, but even smoother than the 1200 thread count of our sheets.

We watched TV later, and at every commercial break—*every single one*—he expounded on the need to share the truth with Alex. My response every single time was unchanging: 'Not yet.'

So was his: 'Fine.' Only, it didn't seem like it was fine.

Post-sex and no longer as cocky, Ralph had become obsessive again. And he remained antsy for the rest of the week. It was worse than living with a pre-schooler, who asks the same question over and over to learn words and build memory. Ralph didn't learn or build. He wore me down. And when the week wound down, my nerves were close to shot.

The Bureau of Meteorology had issued a severe weather warning for Saturday night. But as we got ready to go out, I was more concerned about the potential shitstorm that might take place indoors.

CHAPTER SEVEN

Eat, Prey, Shove

With the Alex thing already a touchy subject, I hadn't shared my fears about tonight with Ralph. And I didn't want to spoil his upbeat mood as we got into the car.

We'd be breaking bread with Hector. We were taking our friends out for dinner as a thank-you for the time and effort the girls had put into organising our wedding. Hector would only be there as Rhea's handbag. I hoped to God he wouldn't be a crocodile or snake skin one (he'd turned up to Luca's ritual circumcision in a croc jumpsuit and python skin boots). And seeing as dinner was on us, I hoped to God he'd be civil enough to resist trying to break Ralph's balls.

Even if Hector did try, as always, Ralph would be a shoo-in. And shooting Hector down was a form of extreme sport for him. But I worried the reptile might goad to the point where Ralph shot from the hip—*Ha, ha, I'm Alex's father and you're not!*

Ralph hummed to himself as he drove, his competitive streak limbering up. He derived perverse pleasure from whipping Hector with words. Usually, I derived voyeuristic pleasure watching Ralph thrash him. Whether or not I would tonight would depend on how Ralph wielded his weapon.

'Try an' be nice to Hector,' I pleaded when he pulled up at a red light.

He turned to look at me. 'Why?'

Don't say it, don't say it—'I mean, just don't let anything slip out about Alex. *Please.*'

He turned away, but I saw his jaw clench.

You had to say something, didn't you, big mouth?

Bugger off. I only hedged.

No, you did more than that. You insulted his intelligence.

I'd also burst his bubble and felt bad about it. I tried making small talk. He grunted in response. We rode the rest of the way in silence.

We were to meet Maxi and Nestor, Vette and Henry, Rhea and the ball sack, Iris and her husband Joel, and Dawn and Harmon (whose place had served as the venue for our wedding) at the swish restaurant at eight o'clock. Ralph and I were the first there.

All was forgiven once I gave the maître d' our names: 'Ruth and Ralph Brill.'

I felt Ralph's eyes on me. He took my hand and squeezed it. 'Ruth and Ralph Brill?' he whispered as D' scanned the reservations list.

Small things. I smiled at him. 'It's easier.' It was also a concession, an appeasement. There had been no concession when I accepted his proposal.

It had taken me a long time to shift my mindset from the idea of cousins to not-really-cousins to lovers to marrieds. And when I'd said yes to Ralph's proposal two weeks after he popped the question, I made it clear I wasn't prepared to take his name. He was fine with it.

Now, gauging his reaction, I wondered if Ralph was more old-fashioned than he thought. Or was there more to it? Was there more to my objection to taking his name than I'd thought? I was happy to compromise, but not be compromised. I was now annoyed at my ingratiating peace offering. Sylvia had treated me like I was her possession. I looked at Ralph with a clear message in mind: *I'm yours, but possession is not nine tenths of the law, buddy—*

'This way,' said D', cutting into my thoughts.

We followed him as he wove around the tables, moving towards the far end of the restaurant. Seeing the female heads turn to look at Ralph shook me out of my pinpricked state. I was used to the leering; Ralph was a hottie.

You haven't seen him starkers, I projected to the attractive blonde stripping him naked with her eyes. And to the smouldering, brunette ogling him, *Yes, he's spectacular in the sack!* I gave her a wan smile when she looked at me. *Your fantasy, my reality.*

Buff-bodied from hitting the gym regularly, and standing at just over six feet, Ralph was an ex-model who could pass for years younger than his age. He wore his medium-length, brown hair in a trendy brush-back that curled up slightly at the end. And aside from fine laughter lines around his brown eyes, his roundish face—with its chiselled jawline, subtle chin dimple and Cupid's-bow lips—showed no signs of sagging.

Five minutes after we'd taken our seats at the end of the large table for twelve, I saw Rhea and the poster child for sag at the greeter's station. Hector of the droopy jowls, Hector of the muffin top with a juddering overhang that cried out for a man girdle. Hector of the carrot-top styled in a floppy Elvis Presley quiff that made him look like a parody of 'The King', and a thin, ginger moustache that made him also look like a parody of *Seinfeld's* Frank Costanza, who already looked like a parody.

Surprisingly, though, with his back to us, Hector appeared conservative, for a change. No animals were harmed in his outfitting tonight, but the rear view was still an eyesore. He wore a black satin shirt that shimmered in the dim light, and tight beige pants.

He leaned forward and reached his arm over the station, presumably pointing to our name on the list the maître d' was surveying. D' looked up at him, feigned a polite smile and held up his hand in a faux-courteous *back-off-mate* gesture.

Rhea's head spun around sharply towards her husband. Even from where we were sitting, I could make out her lips tightening with disapproval.

D' then took a phone call. D' took his time on the phone. It was *a screw-you-mate* gesture.

Hector was getting impatient and made a show of putting his hands on his hips. D' looked away. D' didn't give an eff. Hector then pivoted 180°.

My body contracted and I quickly looked down so as not to be seen. This made no sense; they were joining us. It'd been an involuntary reaction.

I braved the elements and raised my eyes. Hector wasn't looking at us, but it was a full-frontal assault.

'Holy shit!'

'What?' Ralph, who must have been in another world, followed the direction of my gaze. He laughed and shook his head.

Hector's shirt had a Count Dracula ruffled panel. It was fitting. But his trousers were unfitting with an image of two huge, silhouetted cupped hands, fingers pointing downwards printed in black over the crotch area.

'What the hell do you call *that*?'

Ralph snorted. 'A pornographic Rorschach Inkblot test.'

'And your interpretation?'

He looked at me and smirked. 'You tell me.' Typical psychologist. Turning the question back on the questioner.

'What would I know about pornography?'

He gave me an enticing smile. 'You think our sex life is *tame*?'

Ooh. I felt my pupils dilate and my nipples and bean sprout. I looked back at Hector and everything went narrow, soft and shrivelly again.

I said, 'Wishful thinking.'

Still with the amused look, Ralph arched a sly brow. 'Hey, I'm happy to be more adventurous in bed—'

'No! I was answering your first question. The one about my interpretation.'

'Oh. Okay.' His eyes squinched up quizzically. 'Go on.'

'Well. You're always saying he's got no balls, so maybe the image is like an in-your-face attempt to say, "I've got such huge balls, my cup runneth over". You know, like he's overcompensating?'

Ralph smiled, looked back at Hector and slowly nodded. 'Mmm, mmm. That could hold water. But his cup would most certainly not runneth over. And it'd be a demitasse, at best.'

I snickered. 'So then, what's your professional take?'

I braced myself for the mental equivalent of a lettuce sandwich, expecting him to launch into some tedious academic explication. Ralph often did this, but he also reminded me often enough that the brain was woman's largest erogenous zone. He was quite the strategist. I might have been bored shitless by his content, but his superior intellectual capacity was alluring.

'Well, a picture paints a thousand words—'

'Really? You're giving me some boiler plate bullshit?'

'No, no. I was about to say, in this case, it paints one word: handjob.'

I laughed at him, but then I had a disturbing thought. 'What if he gets an erection during dinner? *Eww!*'

'Then so be it. I don't care. He's not sitting next to me. Let Iris take him in hand.'

I laughed again, a little too loudly. It disrupted the restaurant's library-quiet ambience and heads turned in my direction. But I wasn't the centre of attention for long as Hector and Rhea followed a red-faced maître d' to our table.

My fizzling laughter was replaced by the brouhaha-ha-ha-ha of the other diners.

Ralph stood up and gave Rhea a kiss. She pulled out the chair next to me and sat down. I leaned across and we hugged.

'You look lovely,' she said.

'Thank you. So do you.' *How the hell are you with him?* Athletically-built Rhea was tall, dark and handsome—she had an androgynous look—and she was intelligent. She and Hector were mismatched in every way.

He pulled out the chair next to her but took his time to sit down. The show-off had to showcase the garish handiwork between his legs. He greeted us with feigned politeness. 'Hello, Wuth. Hello, Walph.'

We exchanged a few pleasantries, inasmuch as you could with someone as unpleasant as Hector. Then he cleared his throat and said, 'So. Walph? Do you like my hand pwint?'

The corner of Ralph's lips twitched as he understated, 'Interesting.'

'Well, I consider myself a bit of a'—he paused for effect—'handy man! Ha, ha, ha, ha.' Hector was the only one laughing at his naff joke. He folded his arms, resting them in between his moobs and his ample, protruding stomach. He continued. 'I've done quite a bit of pwobing and now have some bwoader knowledge. Symbolically, the hand bwings its owner happiness, luck and health.' He jutted out his chin superciliously. 'I'm cuwious about Walph Bwill's psychological viewpoint.'

Here's mine. Bottom line, you're an idiot and you need to be institutionalised.

'Hmm ...' Ralph rubbed his chin and looked up at the ceiling. He was ralphulating.

Maxi had long ago labelled this whimsy of his. *Ralphulate* was a hybrid of 'ralph' (slang for 'vomit') + speculate, which added up to throwing up an idea he'd chewed over. He was normally quick on the trigger, but when he ralphulated, it meant there was a deluge of possibilities and he was just waiting for da bomb!

Oh, mama! Fear might have dampened my libido on the way here, but now, the anticipation was turning me on.

Ralph draped one arm over the backrest of his chair and rocked back and forth on the chair's hind legs. He narrowed his eyes at Hector. A small, sardonic smile tugged at his lips.

Ooh, you are so gonna get laid tonight.

Ralph delivered. 'Well ... to quote Aristotle, who, by the way, is often regarded as the father of psychology—'

'Yes, I know *that*.'

Bullshit you know that.

'As I was saying, to quote Aristotle, "The hand is the tool of tools".'

Oh God, my cerebral erogenous zone was stimulated off the charts! I wanted to slip my hand under the table and play with Ralph's tool.

Hector raised an eyebrow. Thoughtful. But ...

Oh God. Was *his* cerebral erogenous zone stimulated? *Oh God, please don't let Priapus, that god of the eternal erection, have a hand in Hector's response.*

Hector responded. 'Mmm, mmm.'

Thank you, God. It was not the *mmm, mmm I am turned on, yeah baby, baby!* response. He was trying to sound erudite. *Give it up, schmuck.*

Once again, Ralph had taken the piss out of this tool, who didn't recognise it for what it was. Hector nodded contemplatively. He mirrored Ralph. Leaning back in his chair, he draped one arm over the backrest and rocked back. But there was no forth. His weight was too much for the chair and it tipped over. *Whump!*

Jesus. It was like a slapstick routine. I had the urge to laugh, and I felt bad about that. But in amongst the collective gasp and whispering of the surrounding patrons, I heard Rhea cluck her tongue irritably. Huh? She was inconvenienced?

She heaved an enormous, long-suffering-wife sigh. Her reaction surprised me because she was a warm and compassionate woman. Still, if Hector's own wife was put out, why should I feel bad?

He propped himself up on his elbows as the maître d' fronted up. The man's make-believe concern suggested he saw Hector as a potential litigant. D' helped him up.

Hector hitched up his pants, the handprints adjusted his junk and he sat down again. Strangely, 'Elvis' did not look all shook up.

Ralph would have been, but he never fell off his chair. His chair had never overbalanced, and he often rocked on it. With his tall frame, he was probably heavier than fat Hector, who was about five feet six.

Not so long ago, I'd told Ralph I worried about him falling back, but he was *au courant* with the laws of physics. The reason he would never tip over, he said, was because of Newton's law of blah blah, so because of balance and weight shift blah blah blah, he was safe.

I'd then asked him what law of physics was responsible for his nuts falling out of his shorts when we were fifteen. It was an indelible memory.

A ride on his father's Bantam motorbike in front of the extended family had been like using a vibrator in front of the extended family. Ralph'd braked, but friction and inertia meant his extended man-parts kept going. They came to rest outside his shorts. The image was firmly etched in the beholders' minds.

His answer had been a simple one: 'Newton's law of gravity. Free-falling.'

Mine was simpler: 'Don't you mean "free-balling"?'

He'd been wearing his cousin's hand-me-down Y-fronts. But they were supersized and useless. It was after this humiliating incident that Ralph became obsessed with studying the laws of motion, and he became obsessive–compulsive about pretty much everything else.

As Rhea was now giving Hector a muffled mouthful, Ralph leaned over and whispered in my ear. 'It's probably like climacophilia.'

I turned to him with a puzzled expression. He leaned in again and whispered an explanation.

'That's a kind of sexual paraphilia. You know, a fetish where the person experiences erotic gratification falling down the stairs. In this case, it's falling back on a chair.'

Ewwww! Now I understood Rhea's reaction. It was one thing to be with a man who'd had a women-in-uniform fetish (and who was obsessive–compulsive), but this?

Thankfully, the rest of our party started arriving. Pity they'd missed the spectacle. I doubted that any of them would have seen if for what it was, though. Vette would have poured and handed Hector a glass of water, Maxi and Iris would have made smart-arse comments, and Dawn would have *oh-deared*.

Maxi and Nestor sat next to Ralph. Vette and Henry sat next to them. Dawn and Harmon sat next to them. Nobody was rushing to sit next to Hector.

Iris would be his dining companion this evening. *Hhha!*

Ten minutes later, the flame red-haired firebrand bulldozed into the restaurant with Joel in tow. I waved to them and they made their way to the table. 'Sorry we're late,' she said. No one minded. Iris was always late.

A towering Amazon chick who cut to the chase, she eyed the seating arrangement. Her face contorted as if she'd just thrown back a tequila slammer, and then, as if she'd sucked on a lime wedge, she eased into a satisfied smile. Iris couldn't stand Hector, but she loved giving him a hard time. She would ensure he had a soft-on for the rest of the night. Oh, the handwriting on the wall at its best!

She pulled out the chair next to him; he looked as if someone had thrown him a bone.

'Hello, Iwis,' he said in a sycophantic tone.

'G'day, dick.'

We all tried hard to suppress a smile, Rhea included.

Hector leaned back in his chair. He didn't dare tip back again. Judging by Rhea's hardened expression, Hector must have known he'd be lucky to be left with even a soft-on if he tried that one on again.

Iris didn't notice his crotch, she could barely look at his face. Ralph and I were the focus of everyone's attention. They wanted to know about our honeymoon.

'What does one usually do on a honeymoon?' Ralph said rakishly.

One does not usually say and do things in duplicate.

Everyone gave a knowing laugh, and I swapped knowing looks with Maxi and Vette.

We surveyed the menus and after the waiter took our orders, we discussed the wedding.

Hector became increasingly uncomfortable. Lots of throat-clearing and shifting in his chair. With no one acknowledging his half-baked comments, he lapsed into a bogus coughing fit. That did it. Every one of us stopped talking, only because we couldn't hear each other.

With all eyes on him, he stood up, put his fleshy hands on his back and arched it, as if to open up the air sacs in his lungs. But an arched back = a pelvic thrust.

His coughing stopped as abruptly as it had started, and made way for everyone else's gasps, groans and giggles.

With Hector's groin practically in Iris's face, her eyes went wide. And then she stole his thunder.

'What the *fuck*? Forget to wash your hands first?'

Hector's face crimsoned. Dumb as he was, the implication in those words wasn't lost on him. What did he expect? It wasn't like the picture itself was merely a hint. Ralph's interpretation of the print rang true. Rhea, who'd been put out, was no longer putting out and, obviously, Hector needed to get his jollies somehow. But his falling fetish combined with those tacky trousers, well, it was like a public wank.

I glanced at him with abhorrence. *Go choke the chicken in the shower, you sicko!*

We all resumed our chatter as Hector remained quiet and restrained his impulses, at least until our entrées arrived. Then his jaw 'spoke'.

It clicked and popped. Iris rolled her eyes even though she knew to expect this, having sat next to him at our wedding. And while it grated on her, those opposite Hector were far worse off.

Iris didn't have to see the first stage of his digestive process; they did.

Hector was an open-mouth chewer. *Ecch*. And he was one of that rare breed of men who could multitask. He could chew and slop and spray his food and talk, all at the same time.

'So, bwo-in-law ...'

Nestor looked up as shards of frogs' legs flew out of Hector's mouth and leap-frogged over the floral centrepiece. Nestor quickly looked back down and covered his mouth with his serviette to stifle an almost imperceptible retching sound. Seeing the slime swilling around in Hector's mouth, or ejaculating from it, was something one never got used to. And Nestor wasn't the kind of man to say *shut-your-gob-when-you-eat-motherfucker*. He had the most impeccable manners of anyone I knew. He probably thanked Maxi profusely after every blow job. *Note to self: ask her later.*

Nestor composed himself and looked back up. Hector asked him a stupid question, the only kind in his repertoire. Nestor's serviette went back up to his mouth several times, but he still made it a point to respond. It took a while to get the words out, but they were spoken with the utmost grace.

If only Hector had been as gracious. If only Hector had not tried to bite the hand that was feeding him tonight. Ralph's.

It was as if Nestor's politeness was too boring for Hector. He was looking for excitement, the kind that involved incitement. So, he tried taunting Ralph.

'So, Walph. How's our gwandson? Although, stwictly speaking, he's not weally your gwandson. Pity you never got to expewience the joy of having a child.'

Oh shit, shit, shit! A window of opportunity if ever there was one. I held my breath and grabbed Ralph's thigh, giving it a warning squeeze at the same time as Rhea's sharp, sibilant whisper pierced the lethal silence at the table.

'You fool!'

She glared at the fool, then looked across at her brother, her face a mask of pain, mirroring his. It was then I remembered she'd told me Nestor's wife had been killed in a car accident eight years ago. She'd been eight months pregnant. Their son didn't survive.

Nestor's tragedy provided a diversion, thank God.

But oh, what a monster I am for feeling relieved.

Maxi, who had her arm around Nestor's shoulder, shot daggers at Hector and whispered, 'Bastard!'

This was no longer about Ralph and Alex. Ralph knew this too. He spoke in a controlled but forbidding tone. 'A particularly cruel comment in front of your brother-in-law, don't you think? I'd say an apology's in order.'

Hector shifted uncomfortably in his chair and muttered, 'Sowwy.' It was a paltry attempt, the kind you'd expect from a young child apologising only because Daddy said to.

Nestor's response was an uncharacteristic jaw tightening and unforgiving glare. We all have our limits, all except for sociopaths like Hector. But he must have realised he'd pushed too far. His cheeks flamed a fiery red and he looked down at his obscene lap, shamefaced and taciturn.

Vette was the only other person at the table who knew Nestor's story. She sat there with her hand across her mouth and tears welling in her eyes. The others wore confused expressions. Iris mouthed a curious, '*What was that about?*' I mouthed back, '*Later.*' She nodded.

Like Nestor, Ralph had been pushed to the limit. Unlike Nestor, he didn't leave it there. His thrust and parry with Hector was now turned on its head. Where Hector normally thrust and Ralph parried and disarmed him, for the rest of the evening, Ralph thrust and *harried*. He whooped Hector's 'sowwy' arse.

Elvis would have left the building if he'd been on the receiving end. But with Ralph's barrage of words and his high-voltage delivery, he'd tasered the Elvis-wannabe into a submissive, red-faced silence.

The rest of us resorted to small talk to skirt around the tension. The evening felt interminable, but it ended relatively early for a Saturday night. We girls hugged and Iris gave me the thumb and pinkie I'll-call-you gesture.

Ralph and I were both lost in thought on the way home until we were halfway there. He harrumphed. 'Why didn't I see it earlier? Hector suffers from SPS. Of course!'

'SPS?'

'Small Penis Syndrome.' It would have been funny if his tone hadn't been abrasive. 'I mean, the signs are there. Narcissistic behaviour, anger, unwarranted jealousy, overly dramatic, big-noting and drawing attention to his sexual prowess, drives a big, jacked-up car, wears tight clothes and frilly satin. God, the man wears frilly satin!'

Should I remind you of the silver lamé suit you wore to cousin Zelda's wedding? Maybe not.

Anyway, this was said more to himself than to me. Just as well. I didn't know how to respond. Ralph's behaviour tonight had been unsettling—out of character. His smart mouth had always been his best defence. Tonight, though, he'd been on the offensive. But there was something more that I couldn't yet put my finger on. It hit me when we pulled into the driveway.

Being on the offensive had given Ralph the whip hand. But this wasn't about lording it over Hector.

It was about lording it over me.

CHAPTER EIGHT

Keeping Mum

Ralph knew not to dump on me. When he tried to not long after we got engaged, I told him I didn't want to marry him. I'd had enough of that shit from my family and in my first marriage. I threw the ring at him. It was the drama queen thing to do. Melodramatic, but a dumb move, especially when the rock was a two-carat baby. *Dumb, dumb, dumb*.

Tonight, Hector had been the stand-in, an effigy, the bearer of Ralph's frustrations with me. The man had deserved a good drubbing, but Ralph had been merciless. I didn't like it, but I didn't say anything. Under normal circumstances, I'd have asked him if he'd classify his behaviour as displacement (I didn't know how to ramble in psychobabble like he did, but I knew some bits and bobs). Under normal circumstances, he wouldn't have behaved that way. Still, disturbed by it or not, I was looking after my own interests: I hadn't been the patsy, didn't give a crap that Hector was, and it was best not to poke the bear. Again.

The bear was on a high. Bitch-slapping Hector had aroused him immeasurably, and the bear poked me. Afterwards, I asked him if it was a sign of BPS—Big Penis Syndrome. Typical male, he puffed up with pride.

His higher high lasted a week and a half, and he came home from work on Tuesday with a dozen red roses to mark our one-month anniversary. He was still intoxicated by the idea of being married. Having been there before, I didn't go gaga. But I humoured him, let him take me to the Hyatt Regency for dinner. It was where we'd celebrated our engagement.

We had a sumptuous meal—luxury foods to tantalise the gastronome's palate—and I was his after-dinner cocktail when we got home.

I came, he came, he rolled off and came back down to earth. 'Let's watch a DVD,' he said. Cloud nine had dissipated.

Ralph had swung by the video store the day before and rented a week's worth of movies, amongst them *Losing Isaiah*, *Mixed Blessings*, *Immediate Family*, *Deep in My Heart*. All tear-jerkers, all with adoption themes. Ralph was becoming obsessive again.

He held up *Secrets & Lies*. 'Let's watch this one.'

Hmm. Obsessive or manipulative?

We snuggled up on the couch.

With his laser focus and the patience of Job, Ralph could have been a Tibetan monk. Or a shop-window mannequin. Or a sniper for the 2nd Commando Regiment. Not tonight. When the title flashed across the screen, snuggling turned to jiggling.

As the odd scene triggered something, he'd hit pause, and pause to reflect. He shared his reflections: *Alex should ...; I should ...; I need to ...; my son ...*

Like a couple of weeks earlier, my response was 'Not yet'. After the third 'Not yet' of the night, he exhaled noisily instead of *mmm-ing* again. Tired of being the obedient puppy, he untangled himself, glowered at me and became more communicative.

'Let me remind you what you said to me just before I sent off the samples for testing. Your words, and I quote, "I know if it were me, I wouldn't keep quiet about it"!'

'And I wouldn't. But ...'

'But what?'

'But, but ... synchronicity!' I said it with too much verve, in the same way I'd yelled it at the dead Shrek 'n' Fiona blowflies. I became more solemn and added, 'It comes down to timing.'

'*Whose* timing? Yours?' Spoken like an accusation.

'Everyone's.'

'Everyone's? Not mine!'

We'd been down this road before when I insisted on keeping our romance secret. Now, I was too weary to defend my point of view, so I didn't respond.

His eyes widened. 'Oh, this is about Hannah. Again!'

'Uh ...'

Hannah was feisty. There were times when I wondered who was the mother and who was the child in our relationship. The day she discovered things had changed between Ralph and me, she flipped out, moved out, moved in with Reuben for two months, and didn't speak to me. Or to Ralph. It took another couple of months before her speech patterns evolved into a one-word bark, then into sentences. It was like reliving her toddlerhood but without the cuteness.

The most frustrating part was that what she'd heard about us—that Ralph had pranced around naked in my front yard early one morning—had reached her indirectly via the one-eyed gargoyle across the road. It was a lie. He'd gone out front to collect the paper and he was only *semi*-naked; he'd had a towel around his waist. He'd showered at my place because when he'd come back to apologise for his ill-timed declaration of unchaste love for me, he was unwashed and unshaved. Hannah accused us 'cousins' of having sex.

Something had happened between us, but it wasn't like that. Ralph mightn't have pranced outdoors, but we'd danced around each other indoors:

Burning stares, averted eyes, peacocking, racing hearts, racing breathing, dilated pupils, hardened nipples. Ralph had probably thought about sex with me twelve times in the three hours he'd been at my place—this, based on the average man thinking about it thirty-four times a day. Ralph was an above-average man. He and I were well-matched in this area. And even though I'd also thought about sex twelve times, my line of thinking was how to avoid it.

My protests against Hannah's accusation had fallen on deaf ears, no doubt because there was some truth to it.

I didn't bother to deny Ralph's claim now for the same reason. There was some truth to it.

He pushed himself up off the sofa and said, 'I'm not watching anymore!' What I heard was, 'I'm not playing anymore!'

When we were little and things didn't go Ralph's way, he'd scream those words, throw his toys on the floor and storm off crying. He was more mature now. He stormed off in a sulk. I didn't think it was a good idea to blow a raspberry, like I did back then. Instead, I gave his back the up-yours sign. I was also more mature now.

But I was in a stew. Ralph might have been right about Hannah, to some extent. He'd taken me to task about her 'spoilt brat' attitude when she'd snubbed us back then, and I didn't like his criticism of my parenting. His comment tonight implied the same thing.

Well, guess what, shithead—when your ideas about raising kids come out of a textbook, it doesn't make you an expert, and discovering you've got a son some twenty-six years after his birth doesn't make you a parent!

And yeah, there were times I should have been firmer with Hannah instead of pandering to her, but I knew of people whose children wanted nothing to do with them. Even though Hannah had shunned me, I knew she'd come back. Now, I had more to lose. The thought of being denied access to my grandson scared me. I didn't know if Hannah would do that and I didn't want to find out.

Ralph apologised the next morning. But he was quiet at breakfast; he wasn't at peace. I held mine. Mostly.

'I don't think it's a good idea to watch these sorts of movies.'

He nodded absently.

I returned the DVDs and grabbed a few chick flicks to feed our inner romantic. Ralph loved these movies. He'd always pause them after the sex scenes, jump my bones, then unpause.

That night, we watched *Ghost*. And ooh, that iconic, dead-sexy, pottery scene with 'Unchained Melody' playing in the background floated my boat. But Ralph? No pausing, no commentary. I was tempted to say, 'What's up, honey?' He might have answered a robotic, 'Nothing.' He would have been right. Ralph did not hunger for my touch. He sat impotent, staring at the screen with glazed eyes. It wasn't good. But worse, he might have ranted and raved about what really was up. I didn't want to hear it because it would mean rocking the boat.

Other than Hannah's, I'd rocked too many other boats over the last few years when Ralph and I got it on: Casper hadn't been impressed; Maxi rebuffed me for as long as Hannah had; self-righteous Myron *tsk-tsked*; Joe typically made snide remarks; and Sylvia carped and beat her chest with regularity, claiming I'd be the death of her. It looked like she'd been right. I had to invest a lot of energy in trying to shuck off the guilt of that. And I'd given myself the hardest time of all.

But keeping my mouth shut now would be a decision I'd come to regret. If only I'd encouraged him to talk about it ...

Throwing away a golden opportunity was dumber than throwing away a diamond ring.

CHAPTER NINE

(Nit)Picking Sides

*O*h, *he's just being pensive*, I told myself when subduedness became the norm. But pensive began alternating with thoughtlessness. And little things peeved him. Ralph was often snippy, then apologised. As time passed, he became touchier, but he touched me less. And he stopped apologising.

I wanted to talk to Beth about it. I called her on a Thursday night and arranged to meet her for coffee on Friday, mid-afternoon. Ralph overheard me speaking and said he'd join us. I didn't know he'd be having the afternoon off. It meant the discussion I wanted would have to be shelved.

We hadn't seen Beth or spoken to her for a couple of weeks. She'd gone to Melbourne with three friends. They shopped for the first week and spent the second one camping and bushwalking.

Beth. Camping? Beth, who mooched around the house wearing freshly-pressed slacks and shirt, and shiny, handmade Italian loafers. I knew this because I'd surprised her with a visit some weeks before our wedding. Was she on her way out? 'Oh, no darling. I'm vegging out today,' she'd said as she hugged me warmly. Her short grey hair smelled of citrusy shampoo. She wore no make-up, but she didn't need any. Tall, slim, youthful-looking, Beth was a striking woman.

There'd been no dirty dishes in the sink. The only sign of disorder had been one chair at the family-room table that wasn't lined up with the others, and an open laptop on the table in front of it. 'I was just going through one of my candidate's drafts, but it can wait.' As Emeritus Professor in Philosophy at Adelaide University, Beth chose to work part-time. She was also supervising a couple of PhD candidates.

At two-thirty on Friday, she was all smiles when she strode into Phat Coffee, a café in Hindley Street. 'I've missed you, my darlings!' she said as she embraced each of us.

We placed our orders—coffee for Beth and Ralph, a chocolate milkshake for me, Danishes and friands to share. I asked about her camping experience. 'Did you have to dig a hole to take a dump?'

Beth and I laughed uproariously. Ralph didn't even crack a smile. He waited until our laughter subsided, then dived in, headfirst.

'I have a hypothetical question for you, Beth. If you'd met me, say, twenty years ago and somehow found out I was your son, would you have said something?'

I stiffened. He was recruiting her to help shore up his determination to approach Alex. And if she agreed with him, I expected him to say to me, *'Na-nana-naa-nah, I'm right, you're wrong!'* He often did this when we were children.

'Hmm ...' Beth looked up and rubbed her chin. Like her son, she was a ralphulator. Her response, when it came, was a measured one. 'Honestly? I can't know how I would have reacted.'

'Uh, you can't know how you'd react in the future because you don't know your future self. But I'm not asking you to project into it.' There was a trace of annoyance in his voice. 'I'm asking you to think back twenty years to what you were like. Surely, you'd have some idea as to what you would have done!'

Beth was perceptive. She took his hand as she answered him. 'Darling, I wasn't very impulsive back then. I had been as a teenager, but after the whole situation with David ...' Her voice trailed off.

David Mitchell had been Beth's Twin Flame. She was sixteen, he was eighteen and they were madly in love. After she fell pregnant with Ralph, her parents forbade her from having any further contact with David. They sent her away to have her baby, and then made her give him up for adoption. Beth was disconsolate, but she felt she had no other choice. Her spirit went underground and some years later, she married a well-to-do lawyer. Ideal husband material, according to her parents. She had two other children, Nicholas, thirty-four, and Amelia, thirty-two. Neither had known anything of their mother's previous life and were shocked to learn they had a half-brother. Both were angry at Beth's late disclosure, and although neither had wanted to meet Ralph, Nick had started warming to the idea of a brother.

Beth continued. 'Look. I can't tell you what to do. All I can suggest is that you think very carefully about whatever course of action you decide on.'

It wasn't what Ralph wanted to hear, but I felt relieved. *Na-nana-naa-nah, I'm right, you're wrong!*

He said very little for the rest of the time. Beth and I chatted up a storm. She stole glances at Ralph and tried to draw him into the conversation. He mostly gave her one-word answers.

As we hugged goodbye, I whispered into her ear, 'Where are you at with the David search?' She'd made a decision at our wedding to try and find him. 'Nowhere, so far. His parents have moved or passed on and—'

'Can we go? I've got work to do at home.'

Then you should have bloody stayed there! And I should have taken my own car.

'We'll speak,' Beth mouthed to me.

There was a strained silence between Ralph and me on the drive home and it spilled over into the next week. But the following Sunday, things changed.

Beth called Ralph early in the morning and asked to be put on speakerphone.

'I have some very good news! Nick wants to meet you— both of you!'

It was the first time in a while that I'd seen Ralph smile. His face lit up.

CHAPTER TEN

A Bit on the Side

Ralph called his half-brother. He ended the call feeling uplifted by their brief but friendly chat. We would be having dinner with Nick and his partner, Donna, the following Saturday.

This was a heaven-sent distraction. Ralph relaxed into his old self. He was chatty and he was sexually charged again. Like Patrick Swayze—or the Righteous Brothers—he hungered for my touch. Every night.

Come Saturday afternoon, he was getting nervous.

'What if we don't get on? What if we have nothing to say to each other?'

'You had plenty to say in the five minutes you spoke on the phone.'

'I guess.'

I understood his reservations. Ralph's experience of siblings had not been a good one. He'd grown up with an obnoxious younger sister, Louise (Louwhiney), who squealed like a stuck pig, and his two older brothers, george and simon, were a pair of common numpties unworthy of proper noun status. They were bully boys like their st-t-t-t-tuttering father, Albie.

We got to the restaurant ten minutes early.

Ralph was fidgety, drumming his fingers on the tabletop. Then, like a spectator at a tennis match watching a good, solid rally, his head to-and-froed between the cutlery flanking his plate. He tweaked their placement until he was satisfied they were equidistant from the plate, then he said, 'Can you please, uh, behave tonight?'

I looked up at him. 'Excuse me?'

He didn't answer; didn't need to—I got his drift. With the intoxication of marriage worn off, it now seemed the uninhibitedness he once loved about me had become a source of irritation.

I looked down again, staring with glazed eyes at the plate in front of me, but the rush of air from the restaurant door opening snapped me out of my abashed frame of mind. A couple stood at the entrance and looked around.

We'd seen a picture of Nick, but how much can a snapshot capture? Still, Ralph and the man locked eyes and knew straight away. They both smiled broadly. Like Beth and Ralph, Nick had a killer smile.

Ralph stood up. I wasn't sure about gender-based etiquette. Should I stand? Should I remain seated? Did I care about rules of etiquette? Or rules of anything?

I stood as Nick and Donna approached the table.

The atmosphere was electric as the two men shook hands and gazed at each other. Clearly, it was love at first sight and the beginning of a bromantic infatuation. They glowed, their brains lighting up from the dopamine hit. Having a sibling whose head wasn't untenanted would be a new experience for Ralph.

He introduced me, and Nick introduced Donna, a petite, pretty blondie with a warm handshake. I liked her immediately. If she'd tried to lay a hug on me, it would have been a strike against her. I hated it when people you didn't know went in for cuddle at first sight.

Nick was a male version of Beth with his blue-green eyes and the same shaped mouth. Like his mother and Ralph, he had the roundish face with the chiselled jawline and subtle chin dimple. Good-looking and with close-cropped black hair, he was about the same height as Ralph.

The four of us sat down and chatted easily, the only lull in conversation was when we were scanning the menus. The waiter came over to take our orders.

Donna had decided on the eye fillet in red wine sauce on a bed of creamy polenta and wilted spinach. I chose the Moroccan spice-rubbed rack of lamb on a bed of sweet potato purée with root vegetables, and Ralph ordered osso bucco on a bed of saffron risotto. *Here's hoping the chef doesn't go overboard with the saffron and upset the gastronome.*

'And for you, sir?' the waiter asked Nick.

'I'll also have the eye fillet, but, much as I like beds, I prefer to sleep in them, not to have my steak on one. Can you please ask the chef to arrange things next to each other, you know, rather than on top? Steak, polenta and spinach separate, and can I have the red wine sauce on the side?'

The waiter gave him a strange look.

'I don't like my food groups touching.'

'Of course, sir. And how would you like your steak?'

'Well done, please.' Presumably, he didn't want meat juices leaking into the accompaniments.

The waiter was polite, to his face, at least. He was probably busting to tell the kitchen brigade about the whack job at Table Ten.

And I was busting to tell Nick I had two Dora The Explorer melamine compartment plates for Luca, and would he maybe like one? But the memory of Ralph's warning gagged me. He, on the other hand, spoke freely.

'OCPD?'

Nick nodded and gave Ralph a *what-can-you-do?* shrug. 'No doubt you see clients with this disorder?'

'I *have* this disorder.'

The three of them laughed. *Ha ha ha ha.* I couldn't. If one part's fettered, other parts are too. But why was I allowing him to censor me?

Kiss my arse, Ralph!

I turned to Nick. 'Maxi, a dear friend of ours, once told me about a barista who used to secretly spit in people's coffee if they pissed him off.' I could feel Ralph cringing next to me, but I kept going. 'If the chef gets pissed off at your request and there's a risk he might spit in your food, d'you think it might be an idea to tell the waiter to get the chef to spit *next* to one of the groups—you know, keep that separate as well?'

Eat that, Ralph!

Nick and Donna laughed. 'Mum told me about you. She said you are fabulously irrepressible! She adores you, by the way.'

'It's mutual.' I smiled.

Ralph managed a smile, but it was like I'd stolen his thunder. Was he competing with me? I hoped not.

Either way, it was an enjoyable evening. It was entertaining watching Nick-the-compartmentalist eat, while Ralph—seemingly nursing some nervous energy—*mmm nom nom nommed* next to him.

Ralph and Nick revelled in a scholarly confab, and when Donna confided she was glad these two had found each other because it meant she didn't have to listen Nick's highbrow bullshit, I wanted to hug her.

Unlike that night with Hector, it was over too soon, but we promised to get together again.

And unlike that night with Hector, Ralph hadn't come out on top where I was concerned, so I didn't get laid when we got home.

Once again, he started withdrawing into his own little world. And still, I left him there and kept my mouth shut.

CHAPTER ELEVEN

At Your Indiscretion

My niece's wedding the following Sunday would be a distraction. And a stimulus. Seeing Alex would no doubt stir things up for Ralph, but I wasn't worried he'd say something. He was shrewd enough to know it wasn't the time or place.

Iris and Joel's daughter Leah married Ari in the back yard of her childhood home. Iris knew the ropes; she'd hosted Leah's engagement and Hannah's wedding there. But where Hannah had chosen a rustic theme, Leah chose a rainforest one. With an Amazonian mother, it made sense.

Like Hannah, Leah didn't want anything showy.

Hannah was her only bridesmaid, just like Leah had been Hannah's. Cousins and best friends, they were a plucky pair. Appearance-wise, other than the fact that they both had lovely figures, they couldn't be more different. Where Hannah was tiny, Leah was tall. Where Hannah had olive skin, Leah was fair. Like Iris, Leah dyed her fine hair flame red and kept it short in a well-styled pixie. Hannah's reddish-brown, thick mass of curls fell halfway down her back. She had deep blue eyes, Leah's were brown.

Both girls looked beautiful today. Leah in a cream, full-length, boho wedding dress of tiered lace chiffon, with spaghetti straps that crossed over at the back; Hannah in a dusty pink, off-the-shoulder maxi dress. Shirred to the waist, it had a soft flowing skirt with a front split that showed off a little leg.

Although the wedding was a simple affair, it was still a wild celebration. The only drawback was Hector, who was about as welcome as a squirting skunk, and as usual, just as offensive. I'd have thought he'd be less crass after Ralph blitzed him at dinner a couple of months earlier, but snakes thrive in a jungle setting. Still, although he kept throwing venomous looks at Ralph, he held his forked tongue in front of him.

But Hannah rattled me a little when she sidled up and said in an undertone, 'What's with Ralph? He's acting weird.'

Act normal. 'And that surprises you because ...?'

'Well, it wouldn't normally surprise me, but he's acting even weirder. Like'—she dropped her voice to a whisper—'why is he staring at Alex as if he's just discovered a long-lost son?'

Shhhit. I inhaled a sharp breath. *Keep acting normal. Act nonchalant.* 'Who knows? It's Ralph being Ralph.'

Satisfied with what I said, Hannah went back to her partying and I took Ralph aside. It was my turn to censor him. He wasn't satisfied with what I said.

And he became more and more dissatisfied over the weeks ahead. So did I. At times, it felt like being back in my childhood home, a passive–aggressive reincarnation of it as we silently jockeyed for supremacy. I only conceded in the sack, which wasn't all that often.

On a Saturday morning after months of keeping shtum, Ralph was near bursting point and I took a direct hit.

'Okay, I've had enough. I *need* to say something to Alex!'

'No. You need to be patient.'

'So you keep telling me. But, really? This coming from the queen of impatience?'

I gave him a dirty look.

'Well, I've complied. I've done it your way. I've done it your way for six months! And it's not working for me. If you insist on calling the shots, then give me a Plan B.'

I couldn't, but a Plan B presented itself. It was in my favour, though, not Ralph's. It was heaven-sent—the universe working in mysterious ways.

For the next two months, Ralph needed to exercise sensitivity. Like it or not, he'd become a team player. It was a particularly cold, wet winter and Luca got the squirts, a nasty gastric flu that turned into a hand-me-down. Alex had it, then passed the baton to Hannah. Hannah passed it to Ralph, Ralph passed it to me. We were all well for Hannah's twenty-first, then it was round two. Luca got it again. And so it went, until one fine Sunday spring morning when the temperatures had started to rise and everyone else's had normalised.

Hannah called to say they'd drop over in the afternoon. She was feeling stir-crazy from being housebound for so long, but she didn't want to take Luca to a busy public space and risk exposing him to a germy environment.

Ralph went to my favourite French patisserie and came back with a box of assorted petits fours, as well as Luca's favourite cookies, chocolate-dipped madeleines.

I looked forward to the kids' visit, but also dreaded it. Over the weeks, Ralph had stopped champing at the bit to say something. But I detected a subtle shift in him when they arrived. His OCPD behaviours ramped up—always a dead giveaway.

The night before, he and I had watched *Gotcha!*, an old comedy–action flick. There was a scene in it that inspired me now—a shot in the arse with a tranquilliser gun. I didn't own one, but made a mental note to put it on my shopping list. Maybe a shot of whiskey in his coffee would do. Or not. Loose lips.

I made us alcohol-free coffee while Hannah arranged the petits fours on a plate. Luca zipped around the lounge-room floor making *zoom-zooming* noises with his toy cars, which sparked a discussion between Ralph and Alex about the philosophy of language. It tranquillised me, but invigorated them. Like Ralph (and Beth and Nick), Alex had the nerdlinger gene.

Hannah and I brought the cakes and coffee to the dining-room table. Alex put Luca in his high chair and the two men carried on with their discourse as they sat down.

Luca interrupted them. 'Two! Two! Two!' he screamed. He held a madeleine in one hand and made an open and close motion with the other one. 'Two! Two! Two!' he yelled again.

Hannah sighed and handed him the second one. She looked at Ralph. 'I think he's got OCPD, like you.'

'Mmm.' Ralph looked down at his plate and then shot me an imploring glance.

I shot him daggers.

The tense moment passed and conversation resumed while Luca had a conversation with his cookies. Then, he stopped talking, dropped both on the high chair tray and made frantic, whiny noises as he held up and flapped his chocolate-covered hands.

Hannah wiped them with her serviette. 'Lately, he's been getting upset when he gets his hands dirty.' She looked at Ralph again. 'He really is becoming like you!'

Oh, no. No, no, no!

Ralph's look this time was less importune, more importunate.

I silenced him with a tight-lipped glare. I wish I could have done the same with Hannah.

'Oh, by the way,' she said, 'I ran into Maxi and Nestor at Westfield Marion yesterday.' She sipped her coffee and picked up a vanilla cream puff, bit into it and let out a little moan of pleasure before continuing. 'They're such a cute couple.'

'Mmhmm,' I agreed.

Hannah finished her cake and added, 'You know, if they get married, Maxi'll be my step-aunt. Or my step-aunt-in-law as well as my godmother.' Then she said to Ralph, 'Still, wouldn't be as weird as my relationship with you: second cousin—'

I was about to protest.

Hannah held up her hand. 'I know, I know. He's not my biological cousin.' She turned back to Ralph and said, 'But you're still my cousin. *And* my stepfather, *and* my godfather.'

Oh my God.

Hannah popped another petit four in her mouth as Ralph put his half-eaten one back on the plate. Not a good sign. There was that intransigent look in his eyes as he squared his shoulders. *Don't do it, Ralph. Do NOT do it—*

'And your father-in-law.'

Both Hannah and Alex stopped eating. They stared at Ralph with bewildered expressions.

'Alex is my son.'

CHAPTER TWELVE

Eating One's Jung

Hannah made a scoffing sound, but Ralph didn't recant his words. A deathly silence followed. The point of no return. From that moment, life as we all knew it would never be the same. It would not just be Alex's apocalypse.

Even Luca stopped his renewed efforts to mate madeleine with madeleine, and studied Ralph.

Ralph, who normally thought things through; Ralph who normally weighed Every. Fucking. Word!

Hannah narrowed her eyes. 'What the hell are you talking about?'

Ralph took a deep breath, then blew out.

NOW you weigh your words?

He faced Alex. 'I'm your biological father. I used to date your mother, Larissa. We broke up about nine months before you were born.'

Alex looked askance at Ralph. 'And what? *Ahem.* Based on that, you've decided you're my father?' His shoulder got jumpy. '*Ahem.* It doesn't prove anything.'

'No. But a paternity test does,' Ralph said softly.

'How did you ...' Hannah's words trailed off, then came out in a rush. 'Oh my God! Alex's toothbrush? You used Alex's toothbrush!' She screeched the words.

Ralph nodded. Alex froze. No *ahems*, no twitches, no jerks.

Hannah turned to me. 'How could you do this?'

'What? I, I—'

A now-heated Alex spoke. 'Let's go, Hanny!' The look of anger and anguish on his face was the same one I'd seen when he stormed out of Hannah's birthing suite after Luca's birth.

He pulled a crying Luca out of his high chair and stalked across the lounge towards the front door.

'Fuck you, Ralph!' Hannah said as she grabbed her bag, followed Alex, and slammed the door on her way out.

I sat speechless. Poleaxed. It was the same feeling I'd had when the four-wheel drive had T-boned my car. Ralph sat with elbows on knees and his face buried in his hands. I attacked.

'Are you happy now? You just couldn't wait, could you?'

He sat up and opened his mouth to respond, but nothing came out. Then in a weak and defensive tone he said, 'The timing was right. It was providence.'

'Providence, my arse! You see anything that serves *your* purposes as "providence".'

He looked hurt. 'That's not true and you know it. But the opportunities kept presenting. It was one thing after another. Can't you see that?'

'No. What I *can* see is that you dropped a bombshell without considering the collateral damage!'

I accused him of being selfish and of spoiling everything. He said it was my fault; that it wouldn't have ended up this way if I hadn't kept trying to thwart him. He got up, walked away and locked himself in the study, which was once Hannah's bedroom. I remained at the table, finished off all the petits fours, then went to the en-suite to throw up. So much for comfort food.

* * * *

A sudden, brief gust of wind blew a tumbleweed onto my foot and reminded me I was here on Glenelg beach, in the now, not back there. Yet, reliving the experience made me feel dizzy and weak. It made me cry. Four months on, the shock of that day hadn't dissipated. It was just as acute. Why? Was I suffering from PTSD? I wiped my clammy hands on my dress, hugged my knees to my chest and turned heavenward as if the answer lay in the wild blue yonder.

Plop. A glob of bird shit landed in my hair.

Ecch! Seriously? I wiped it off with my crumpled serviette. That's your answer, God?

I looked up again, seeking out The Almighty's carrier pigeon. A flock of seagulls hovered overhead like a bunch of drones. Did pigeons and seagulls belong to the same family? Ralph would know—

Oh, enough, enough, enough! I was here to give myself time and energy, to focus on *me*. Who the hell cared what Ralph would know?

'I don't appreciate being your toilet!' I yelled up at the birds.

The drones ignored me and started flying in a V formation. It was fascinating to watch. But then, admiration turned to scorn.

'Yeah, follow the leader.'

I'd become that kind of person during my first marriage. Not a leader, a follower. A conformist. And worse, Sylvia's endless browbeating had clipped my wings, so I was more like one of the sheep. A herd mentality doesn't let your spirit soar and it had been a slow psychic death by *blah*. Or *meh*. A painless one because you don't feel anything.

Sylvia.

Why did thoughts of my mother appear out of the blue? What were the chances of being crapped on? Was *she* sending me a message?

Sylvia, the original dumper. 'A psychological projector', Ralph had called her. It was how I best knew her.

Was this synchronicity in action?

Uh-oh. The birds were coming in close. I instinctively covered my head as a useless screen against getting shit-bombed again. But I was safe. Or so it seemed.

They landed on the sand not far from me. Except for the one that perched on a nearby rock: the squadron leader.

The gull gawked at me.

I frowned at it. 'Let me guess, you're Sylvia's go-between? *Hmph.* Looks like you drew the short straw.'

The gull squawked at me.

Jesus. A bird was channelling my late mother. Better than a horse, which had been Sylvia's message-bearer at my wedding a year ago. She, the night-mare. Uninvited, but her plus-one had been Joe, the gelding—he who'd taken a giant dump at the divider fence not one hundred metres from where Ralph and I exchanged vows.

As if it heard my thoughts, the gull shrieked. I flinched and covered my ears. It wasn't so much the terrible noise that hurt, but the piercing words I heard in it. Sylvia's constant refrain from when I was a child: *Nobody will put up with you!*

Indignant, I shrieked back, 'Screw you! Ralph does.'

I remembered the Sunday down at Glenelg just after I'd accepted his proposal; his commitment to put up with me for the rest of our lives. We'd grabbed a quick bite and I made a comment about the hovering seagulls starving if no one fed them. 'Hardly,' he'd said. 'And if they can't get enough insects or rodents, they'll eat young members of their own species.'

I cried again, this time at the thought that Ralph, my love and my protector, was no longer putting up with me. And my mother, who had devoured me when she was alive, was back to scavenge on the carcass.

Sylvia-gull jolted me out of my abjectness as she screeched her demands like a prima donna: *'Gimme bread ... feed me ... or I'll have to feed on—'*

'On *what*? You sucked my soul enough when you were alive!' And dead or not, the psychic vampire had been having a feast over the last two months. I'd had a bellyful.

The freeloading flock on the sand took off. They either got that mommy was about to cannibalise them, or that they'd have to get their munchies elsewhere. Sylvia-gull stayed put, her beady eyes boring into me as she expressed her disapproval. This time, I didn't budge. Her caw was probably a cliché. My mother had so often spoken in clichés, she'd been a walking one. And she'd rarely thrown me a crumb. Now it was my turn to withhold.

I flipped the bird at the bird. She stood there gaping at me. I expelled a resigned breath. There was no getting away from her.

Or from Ralph. Something else he'd said about predators came to mind: they look at their prey when they attack, so a direct eye-gaze could predict imminent danger.

I glared back at the feathered whorebringer of doom, then shooed her away with my hand. She flapped her wings but didn't lift off. We were at a stand-off. Until she dropped a dookie, leaving a thin trail of white running down the rock.

'Nice. Real bloody ladylike. You haven't changed. You might shit white and look white, but a seagull? Oh, I don't think so! You're still a harpy. Sun-bleached maybe, but still a harpy.'

I thought back to when I first learned about the harpies in Mr Kosta's class.

While my fellow students were dying of boredom or cringing, I was engrossed in the story of those bird-bodied, girl-faced fuglies of ancient myth in dire need of deodorant, a makeover and anger management counselling. They were a sorry bunch that stole your food and then pooped on the scraps.

At the time, I hadn't made the connection between Sylvia and the harpies. I joined the dots only a few years ago.

The bird was now preening her feathers with her beak. I gave a harsh, derisive laugh. 'Like that's gonna do it? Newsflash, harpy. You'll never be clean until you start owning your crap instead of dumping it!'

And then it hit me, just like the airborne bird turd had hit me earlier as an answer to my question. Its symbolism now became clear.

The shock of that day when everything changed was still red-raw because of a single event that wasn't a single event. So many of my life's hurts were of the same kind. Everything was my fault, even when it wasn't. I'd always been Sylvia's sitting duck. And Joe's. But when Ralph and Hannah, two people I loved and trusted, blindsided me the same way—apportioning blame to me for this mess of Ralph's making—it felt like all of those times coalesced into a Goliath.

I thought I was done with the role of scapegoat when I'd thrown the ring at Ralph, but one act of rebellion doesn't reverse a default setting. And I sensed there was more to the answer that had just landed in my lap after landing on my head. But I couldn't put my finger on it. Maybe this bird anchored to the rock held the key to the rest of it.

'How 'bout trying to redeem yourself, Sylvia? How 'bout coming clean?'

Nothing.

Typical uncompromising Sylvia. Immovable in life and afterlife.

'Fine. I'll figure it out myself!'

She squawked.

Typical opinionated Sylvia. Always had to have the last word. Well, I would have the last laugh.

Not yet, though.

The gull clucked. She seemed to be crowing over my estrangement from Ralph. Sylvia had never approved of us as a twosome. Hell, Sylvia had never approved of me as a onesome.

'If you've got nothing nice to say, then piss off!'

She held her ground and held her tongue. I didn't.

'I've got a sheepdog and a pet raptor in here,' I said as I patted my bag. It wasn't beyond the realm of possibilities. Sylvia had always scoffed *'What for?'* at my supersized totes filled with just-in-cases. You never knew when you were going to need something. Like a sheepdog or a raptor. *'This* is what for,' I said patting the bag again. I knew gulls feared these breeds of dogs and birds.

It was at times like this I was glad I hadn't completely tuned out Ralph when he'd cornered me in one of his snore-fests, sharing his extensive knowledge about everything under the sun. But it looked like the harpy had upped her little grey cell count. She didn't buy it. So, I made a scary owl face at her. Another one in my bag of tricks; I knew gulls didn't like owl faces. That did it. The harridan scurried back to the flock. And my mind scurried back again to the fall-out from that fateful day.

* * * *

CHAPTER THIRTEEN

Crash and (Slow) Burn

Ralph and I had stalemated. After we'd become an item, we'd have the odd disagreement that always ended in hot make-up sex. (Pretty much everything ended in hot sex. A passionate pair, we were born a week apart—I came first. Ralph continued to make sure that I always did.) Not this time. This time the issue was too big.

I could tell he wasn't confident he'd done the right thing, but he seemed too proud to admit it. It wasn't like him. I took 'tranquilliser gun' off my shopping list—I wouldn't have been able to get a decent shot. When he wasn't at work, he found a reason to go out, and when he was home, we were rarely in the same room. He made sure to come to bed after I'd fallen asleep, and he was out of bed before I woke up. Even if I could get him in the cross hairs, there would've been no point shooting. He was already moving around in a narcotic state, morose and subdued. He had shot himself in the foot.

Hannah wouldn't take or return my calls. I feared my fear was being realised, that I'd miss out on little Luca.

My muse also had attitude. Broody bitch was not putting out. Two weeks on, and I was in a wordless slump. All this fretting over my strained relationship with Ralph and with Hannah's rejection had built a big, unyielding writer's block. I was grateful that I was ahead of myself with the magazine articles—I had a few in reserve.

On a Sunday morning, I sat at the dining room table in front of the laptop. As I felt myself slip into a hypnotic state from watching the cursor blinking, the doorbell and my mobile chimed at the same time. Casper was at the other end of both. I heard the key in the door as I looked at his text.

It's me.

'Hi, Mum.' Six foot of handsome, sunny son burst in and lit up the room, and my world.

'Hi sweetie. You know you don't have to go to those extremes to announce your arrival.'

'Yeah. I do. I really don't want to catch you and Ralph in the act.' He shivered with revulsion at the thought.

I also shuddered at the thought of being caught in a compromising position, but didn't want to say there was no chance of it at the moment.

Casper bent down, kissed my cheek and looked at the blank screen. 'Ah, you've got to the part where you've realised nothing is sacred, huh?'

I smiled. 'Oh, it's nothing new. I've known for a while.' Casper had moved in with Reuben a few weeks before Ralph and I got married. Neither Reuben nor I saw him as often as we'd like. When he wasn't at university, he had quite the social life. 'So. To what do I owe this visit?'

'Do I need a reason to come and see my mother?'

'No. But you usually have one.'

He gave me a boyish grin. 'You know me so well.'

'Of course I do. I pushed you out of my vagina.'

'Oh God, *Mother*! You're seriously gonna play that card?'

It was my trump card, one I'd used a few times. My son the smart-arse always had an answer for everything. From the moment Casper could form sentences, words had been his favourite playthings. He made me laugh. He didn't make his teachers laugh; not in front of him, at any rate. Throughout his primary school years, I'd often felt like his get-out-of-jail-free card.

He covered his ears and walked into the kitchen. I was on his heels.

'So, again, to what do I owe this visit?'

He turned to face me. 'I feel traumatised.'

'About what I said?'

'No. Well, yes. Kind of. It dovetails with my problem.'

'Which is ...?'

'I found a pubic hair in my rice pudding from the uni cafeteria yesterday. I could understand and maybe even forgive it if I'd been eating spotted dick.'

I chuckled.

'They're serving that, by the way. It's popular with the British exchange students. But back to the hair, it was straw-coloured. And'—he dropped his voice to a whisper—'I sensed a conspiracy. Portnoy had blonde hair. This was probably her revenge.'

'Her hair was bleached. And anyway, she's dead.'

'Yeah? So's your mother.'

'*Hmph*. Point taken. But Portnoy's complaint was with me.'

'Hello! I was on her hit list, remember?'

I remembered.

When I'd caught Portnoy in what had become her midnight ritual of planting a dead rat on my doorstep, Casper captured the whole thing on video. We were like a counterespionage task force. I threatened to take the tape to the police if she left any more of her kin on our stoop, or on the neighbours'. It never happened again.

'And you know what they say?' Casper added. 'Revenge is a dish best served cold, and with a short and curly in it.'

'Ewww!'

'Uh-huh, and your experience is only vicarious. Imagine what it was like for me!' He pounded his chest. I theatrically rolled my eyes at his theatrics. I knew he was taking the piss out of his late grandmother. 'Anyways, I figured it's unlikely I'd be ambushed if I ate here.' He opened the fridge and scanned its contents. 'I dropped in on Hannah first for a Luca hug.'

It made me nostalgic, but I was glad Casper had that kind of relationship with his nephew. He'd been in awe of Luca from the minute he was born. The feeling hadn't diminished, and Luca loved his uncle.

'She offered me something to eat, but her fridge is full of sloppy kiddie stuff. As long as I've still got my teeth, I want something I can sink them into.' He took out the leftover quiche. 'Do I need to go through this with a fine-tooth comb?'

'I don't think so. It's from the continental deli and I know the owner. New guy, but I doubt he's a naked chef.'

'Okay, I'll take my chances.' He removed the Glad Wrap and popped the dish in the microwave.

Not wanting him to eat alone, I grabbed two plates. Like I needed an excuse to eat.

I wanted to say something about his thick, wavy black hair, about how wearing it longer was a good look because it brought out the curls. But my wise mama voice intervened.

Sucky timing.

I tucked into my quiche and watched as he sieved through his portion with his fork. 'You do know that you're turning it into something too sloppy to sink your teeth into?'

He glanced up at me. 'Maybe. But I have new trust issues. You know, beyond the long-term ones from my childhood—'

I shook my head.

'—and I don't wanna be flossing my teeth with pubes again, especially someone else's.'

I grimaced and started sifting through the wedge on my own plate.

When we were both satisfied our food was fuzz-free, we indulged in our quiches and some chocolate mud cake, and indulged the kind of banter we often enjoyed. Like being in a sphere of *Seinfeld*, we talked about nothing stuff—about how Casper wished he'd been more specific years ago and should have prayed for a younger brother, not Big Brother in the form of Portnoy's eye, which he believed was still alive, had its own life support system and was a first-rate spy tool operating through rats and—

'Wait up. Through rats? You reckon her dead rats are alive too?'

'No, *rats*. Capital R, capital A, capital T, little s. Get with the program, Mommy! It's an acronym for Remote Access Trojans. You know, that malicious software that lets hackers get remote access and control of your computer.'

'Hmm. So that's why my page is blank.'

'No. Your page is blank because you haven't written anything. And really?' he scoffed. 'You got upset over the-goat-ate-my-homework excuse I used at school, and now *you're* eschewing responsibility?'

My self-parentified son.

I recalled that moment of both pride and shame when Casper's humourless teacher grilled me about why my five-year old was using this excuse, and then warned me that it didn't bode well for the future. Now, trying to act like a semi-responsible parent I said to Casper, 'I mightn't've minded as much if we *had* a goat.'

'Well, even fictional goats eat everything. Everyone knows that. And hey, you would've minded a lot more if I'd said the dog ate my homework, because it would've been too clichéd for your liking.'

My precocious son had been attuned to me even at such a tender age.

I gave him a wry grin and tousled his hair. The two of us continued to shoot more breezes—mostly hot air—when he had a realisation.

'Hey. The man's missing. Where is he?' Casper and Ralph shared a close bond and loved hanging with each other. Casper gave him a good run for his money, managing to checkmate him on many occasions, and Ralph loved the challenge.

'I don't know. He's making himself scarce.'

'Why?'

I sighed. 'We've barely spoken in the last few weeks.'

Casper raised his brow enquiringly. 'You haven't been married long enough for that.'

'I know.' I told him about Ralph and Alex.

'*Wow!* How long have you known?'

'Definitively? Since our wedding day.' I told him about the paternity test results.

'And you never thought to mention it as a by-the-way, like, in passing?'

'I didn't wanna say anything until Hannah knew.' I told him about *the* afternoon.

'Whoa! But, uh, strange that she didn't say anything when I was there this morning. And Ralph. *Man!*' He shook his head.

'I've always admired his forethought, but he's walked into a minefield, hasn't he?'

'Uh, hello! He's created one.'

He nodded thoughtfully then jabbed at the air with his fork. 'You know, I get why Hannah's not speaking to Ralph, but why isn't she speaking to you?'

'I'm an accessory before and after the fact, I guess,' I said as I teared up.

'She'll come around, Mum,' Casper said softly.

I smiled at him and wiped the tears away.

'Dad hasn't said anything to me. Does he know?'

'Uh, I dunno. He hasn't said anything to me either.'

'Then it's a fair bet he doesn't.' Casper was right. Reuben would have rung me, partly because it was a situation involving our daughter, and partly because he wasn't averse to a good bit of gossip.

'Yeah. And I think it's best if you don't bring it up with him. Or with Hannah. Actually, better not to say anything to anyone. You don't wanna be stepping on toes.'

'Or mines.'

'Or mines.'

When Casper left two hours later, Ralph still hadn't come home. He got back at two and collapsed in front of the TV. I was sitting in the dining room with my computer for company.

A hotchpotch of half-sentences reached me from the tube as Ralph channel surfed: 'The beautiful horses had—'; '—was arrested this morning—'; 'What's up, doc?'

Really? Do you not see me here, a stone's throw away from you, trying hard to concentrate on my still-empty work page?

The insensate psychologist who did not hear my unspoken words continued his channel hopping. I got the shits, picked up my laptop and huffed into the study with it.

Monday couldn't come soon enough.

After Ralph left for work, I was back at the dining room table, glad to see the back of him and, again, staring blankly at the blank Word document that I'd filled with trash, and then emptied half a dozen times. Only the low, guttural roar of a Harley interrupted my trance.

It made me think back to Ralph's father's Bantam motorbike's *vroom*. This, though, was like comparing a Krakatoa volcanic eruption to a fart. The flurry petered out into a *potato-potato-potato* sound, then stopped. I refocused on the screen and was about to fill it with more rubbish when I heard the footfalls of heavy boots on the front path. The doorbell rang.

That bloody doorbell.

I trudged across the lounge, thinking it was a good thing I'd got out of my pyjamas and had an early shower today. I didn't expect to see Junior Ugly on my front porch again, but I prayed it wasn't a Jehovah's Witness. I had a response at the ready if it was: 'I'm a Satanist.'

I opened the door.

Oh my. *My, oh, my!*

CHAPTER FOURTEEN

Man of (French) Letters

I stared wide-eyed at the ruggedly handsome man standing on the threshold, a biker's helmet under his left arm.

'Hi,' he said in a silky, baritone voice. 'I'm—'

'Andrew Ellis-Nile,' I said too quickly, like an infatuated groupie.

He raised a questioning eyebrow in feigned surprise. 'Have we met?'

Oh yes. Many, many times. We assumed the missionary position in my bed in my waking dreams as my first marriage was coming to an end.

I shook my head, now unable to utter a sound. From lovestruck to dumbstruck.

He gave me a crooked grin. 'Call me Andy. And you are ...?'

'Uh. Ruth Roth. Uh, uh, Ruth Gold.'

He now raised a mocking eyebrow. 'Still deciding, are we?'

I laughed. It shook me out of my swept-away state. 'No. Roth was my maiden name. I use it as my pen name.'

'Ooh, you're a writer. So am I.'

Duh. No shit. Celebrated forty-two-year-old Aussie king of mystery. First book published at twenty-two. A bestseller, followed by another twenty or so bestsellers. Satyromaniac—the male form of a nymphomaniac. I know this because Ralph had told me. Ralph knows this because he used to be one.

'But looks like you know that?' he added.

Oh boy! Had I said all that out loud? 'Know what?' Embarrassment flooded my cheeks.

'That I'm a writer. We haven't met before, but you knew my name.' Again, that mocking brow hitched up in another display of pretend modesty.

'Uh, yes. Yes! And I've read a lot of your books. Early ones. Page-turners.'

He gave me an aw-shucks grin that didn't fool me, but I went along with it.

'Thank you,' he said and held out his hand. 'And nice to meet you, Ruth-Roth-Ruth-Gold.'

He had a powerful handshake and a powerful, charismatic presence. He was around the same height as Ralph, and like Ralph, he was trim and well built. Clearly, Andy pumped iron. His fawn V-neck jumper, with a bit of white T peeking out above the V, highlighted his well-developed pecs, and his guns were discernible under the aged black leather jacket. It probably had a Hells Angels patch on the back. The man had been a badass in his younger days.

Faded blue jeans half-tucked into a pair of scuffed black Blundstones nicely hugged his muscular thighs and over-used, muscled man bits. I managed to take all this in without lowering my gaze. (Women have mastered the skill.)

He had a light brown, three-day designer stubble and his hair was side-parted, longish and wind-swept. It was a Robert Redford hairstyle, circa *Three Days of the Condor*. In fact, he looked a bit like Robert Redford before the actor's features had become weathered. Blond men had never held much appeal, but if Redford had asked me out years earlier, I would have gone against type and accepted.

Call-me-Andy was just as arresting as Redford. And with his electric blue eyes now X-raying me, I felt self-conscious.

My hair was pulled back in a messy French twist and held in place by a jaw clip. *Thank God I washed it this morning. And good thing I'd epilated my upper lip.* Although, it was nothing like Rhea's. Rhea had a super-hairy upper lip. She also had a mouche—a small tuft of hair under her bottom lip. But she was always made up; I wasn't. No point wearing make-up when you're only hanging around at home. And I saw no point in dressing up like Beth did when I was working from home.

Today, I wore a mismatch of blue warm-up track pants for my writing workout, pink bedsocks and a threadbare green sweatshirt with ... oh shit ... no bra! It wasn't a bad look. My bazookas might be big, but they weren't droopy.

'In la-la land?' Andy's voice sliced through my errant thoughts. He gave me a knowing smile. 'Don't worry. I'm a regular visitor there. It's a writer's thing, isn't it?'

It was a rhetorical question, so I didn't reply. Instead, I asked him one that demanded an answer. 'Um, why are you here?'

'Oh ...' His eyes crinkled in amusement. 'That's not an existential question, is it?' (This was the sort of thing Ralph and I said to each other.)

Andy threw his head back and laughed at his pun, revealing perfectly straight, pearly-white teeth—expensive ones. No Botox in that face, but the king had many crowns.

Ha! I've got all my own teeth. I threw my head back and laughed.

Andy didn't hear my thoughts, but he was pleased with my reaction. He gave me an existential answer: 'Actually, I bought the place across the road.'

'W-what? *You* bought Portnoy's place?'

I'd wondered if the gnome was going to sell or if, Heaven forbid, he'd move in. A couple of months ago, a large skip bin had appeared on the footpath in front of the house, and a month after that, a 'For Sale' sign went up. It was a relief. Even more so when, within a matter of days, a sticker screaming 'SOLD' was slapped across it. The quick sale didn't surprise me. The property screamed 'POTENTIAL'. Only we neighbours knew it also whispered 'Exorcism'.

But it made no sense that Andy would buy it. For a man who was rolling in it, why would he want to live in a middle-class suburb?

He answered my question. 'I did indeed.' Then, he answered the unvoiced one—being a writer, he was probably tuned in to the nuances of thought. 'I'm expanding my property portfolio.'

'Huh. Well, it is a good size piece of land, I guess. So, uh, what are you planning on building after you knock it down?'

'Oh, I'm not demolishing the house. I'll be living in it.'

I eyed him in disbelief.

'Not as it is, of course. I'm going to spruce it up a bit. Repaint it. It's been painted, but it's a slapdash job for selling purposes. I'll put in new carpet; nnnew ... uh, why do you look so shocked?'

'Do you know anything about the previous owner?'

Turned out Andy hadn't heard any of the scuttlebutt about the scuttlebutter, Portnoy. I was the first neighbour he'd introduced himself to. And any realtor worth his or her salt would have done anything to keep a buyer in the dark. Awareness wasn't always a good selling point. Still, Andy didn't strike me as the kind of person to be misled.

I loosely sketched an impression of the deceased beast for him: her mega-arse, her mega-eye, and her mega-mouth. And the monstrous lies she'd spread with it. And I told him about her entertaining alcoholic stupors.

The prolific author was demonstrative. With his eyebrows playing the lead role—mostly the left one—he evinced the whole gamut of emotions as I talked. No wonder he was such a success.

I said, 'That place has to be haunted.'

'Oh, without a doubt. I felt the vibe the minute I walked in. That was the main reason I bought it.'

Huh?

'You've no idea how hard it is to find a haunted house these days,' he said in earnest.

What?

Andy laughed at my stupefied expression. 'You didn't read my last four novels, did you?'

'N-no—'

'Well. My mysteries have evolved into horror fiction. Or maybe that should be devolved.'

I nodded slowly. 'Ah. Got it. Moving in is a bit like method writing, right? Kinda like method acting?'

'Mmhmm. Something like that.'

'Soooo, are you the haunter or the haunted?'

Andy smiled and looked at me with something that resembled admiration. I would have puffed out my chest if I was wearing a bra.

'I'm gonna have to be both if I want to write the roles authentically.'

'Well then, I guess you couldn't have chosen a better place to ... inspirit yourself.'

'Or a better location, by the sound and the look of things.' That inspirited brow lifted suggestively and a small part of me responded the way nature intended. The way Andy intended.

Thank God for the scraping, grinding sound of brakes that caused a distraction. A van had pulled up across the road and a man in coveralls climbed out. He and Andy waved to each other. Andy turned back to me.

'Gotta go. That's Humberto, my painter.' He gave me another one of his disarming smiles. We said our goodbyes and he started to walk off, but then he stopped short and turned back to look at me. 'I'm sure we'll be seeing a lot more of each other.'

Uh-oh. You didn't need to be a writer to pick up the nuance there.

I watched him as he walked back to his place. Andrew Ellis-Nile with his sexy he-man swagger had no Hells Angel patch on the back of his jacket, but he spelled trouble.

CHAPTER FIFTEEN

Hardwiring, Jaw Wiring?

I was dying to tell Maxi and Vette about Andy, but both were overseas. I would've loved to have told Ralph, but the friction between us made even the most mundane communication grating. And for the rest of the week, things became increasingly strained on the home front. My muse remained unforgiving and so did Hannah. She still didn't return my calls. The only high spot was when Andy dropped by again on Friday.

He gave me a lazy smile when I opened the door. 'Morning, Ruth-Roth-Ruth-Gold.' He indicated behind him with his thumb. 'Interesting garden ornaments you've got back there.'

I looked past him. My mouth fell open. *Ugh.*

Maybe there was something to Casper's conspiracy theory. After all this time, Portnoy Junior had reconsidered my inheritance. The executor had made good, and then some. His mother's two garden gnomes were reclining on my lawn, each one sporting a massive strap-on dildo.

It looked like Junior wasn't quite as upstanding as he pretended to be. The sour grape didn't fall far from the grapevine. I shook my head in disgust. *Jesus, what a dick!*

'A pair of them,' Andy quipped.

Crap! 'Did I say that out loud?'

Andy smiled as I pulled up the collar of my roll-neck jumper and covered my face.

I pulled it back down and justified my reaction, giving him a detailed account of my exchange with Junior. He roared with laughter when I described my mental picture of Portnoy's demise.

'What an imagination!' he said. 'Anyway, a gift for you.' He held up four books. 'My last novels—the ones I told you about.'

'Uh, oh, thank you. But ...' I sucked air through my teeth and gave him an apologetic smile. 'I'm not a fan of horror. My son Casper is, though!'

He cast me a dubious look. 'You don't like horror, and yet you named your son after a ghost?'

'A friendly ghost!'

He laughed at me.

'And his real name's Jake. We nicknamed him Casper because my GP at the time told me I wasn't pregnant, and that it was just a phantom pregnancy.'

Andy's gaze raked over my body as if he was imagining what I did to get pregnant with Casper. I felt my face grow hot and, in spite of myself, so did other parts. Again.

I wish you would leave. I'm enjoying my interaction with you far too much.

'Well, I hope your friendly ghost enjoys these.' I thanked him as he handed me the books, but it seemed he was in no hurry to go. 'So, what does Mr Ruth Gold do?'

'Mr Reuben Gold is an accountant, but—'

'He must have a lucrative practice.'

I gave him a bemused look.

'The silver Merc that's parked in your drive every night?'

What? I shifted uncomfortably. 'Uh, I hope your renovations include new window coverings in the lounge room.'

Andy held up his hands in a submissive gesture. 'Sorry. I didn't mean to pry. And I wasn't spying, I promise. It's just that I've been back at the house every night this week moving some of the small stuff in, and I couldn't help notice the car.'

I nodded, embarrassed that I'd misread him. 'Reuben and I are divorced. The car belongs to Ralph, my current husband.'

Current? Oh no. Did I just say current? Hope he didn't notice.

A smile tugged at the corners of Andy's mouth. '"Current"? Odd choice of modifier, that.'

I groaned and felt myself flush under his intense stare. 'You know, living with Ralph, who's a psychologist, well, sometimes I feel like everything I say or do is being analysed. But right now, you've given me insight into what it must be like for someone living with a writer, one who loves wordplay. Maybe not so much for Ralph because he's a wit-meister himself.' *Not lately. Lately, he's a buzzkill.*

'Oh,' Andy said.

With a writer's sensitivity, I read his tone. Seemed the king didn't like to be usurped by another man, much less a commoner.

'Well, better get back to it.' It sounded as if I'd ruined his day. What a narcissist!

As he turned to leave, he added, 'Uh, I can get my tradies to toss the gnomes in the skip bin if you want?'

'That'd be great. Thanks.' *Maybe leave the dildos behind.*

He favoured me with a raised brow and a half-smile. 'Any parts you wanna keep?' The wordsmith had bounced back, but this was way beyond being attuned to nuances. I half expected him to whisper *'I see dead people'*.

'Yes? No?'

Say no, for God's sake! 'No. But, hey, feel free to keep what *you* want.' I favoured him with a raised brow and a half-smile. I'd bounced back.

'Mmm. I just might take you up on that.' No wink followed, no laughter followed. Not even a smile.

What? *What!* Was lady-killer Andrew Ellis-Nile gay? Or kinky? Did this man love to dick around with more than just words?

It was hard to get back into my writing after that. I wasn't sure what disturbed me most: my reaction to his teasing question, the thought that this heart-throb might not be straight, the realisation that I didn't feel like sharing the story of the gnomes on the grass with Ralph, or the fact that he didn't know about Andy.

Another week of in-house cold-shouldering passed, Hannah was still shutting me out and I was feeling weighed down by the greyness. It didn't help that my writing continued going nowhere.

On a Monday morning after pfaffing around doing anything but writing, I looked at the closed laptop and decided to leave it that way. It wasn't a good start to the week, but I needed to immerse myself in someone else's words, not mine. And in a murder mystery, not a romance. I'd just cosied up on the sofa with James Patterson when I heard Andy's Harley. My heart skipped a beat, even knowing what I knew. Or thought I knew.

I ran to the front window and adjusted the angle of the shutters so that I could spy, but couldn't be espied spying.

Dear God. I was becoming like Portnoy. Only, where she'd been as stupidly obvious as Inspector Gadget, I was at least furtive.

I watched Andy as he took off his helmet and dragged his fingers through his hair, like he was in a TV commercial. Humberto came out to greet him. The two chatted, both using a lot of hand gestures. Andy pointed up at the eaves and then at the window. As the painter approached the window frame and rubbed his hand along it, Andy turned and looked in the direction of my place. I ducked back, moved away from the window and checked my colour-coordinated reflection in the mirror above the console table near the front door.

Jesus. What am I doing? Was I so desperate that I was trying to titillate a gay guy?

I raced to the bathroom to wash off the make-up I'd applied just in case there was the remotest possibility that I might on the off-chance maybe decide to go out today. The bra that I'd put on for the same reason stayed on. As I was scooping my hair up into a ponytail, the doorbell sounded.

Andy stood there with three books in his hand.

'Good morning.' He held out the books. 'Not horror this time, just good old thrillers. I assume you haven't read them? You said you'd read the earlier ones. These are more "current" ones.'

I laughed at him. The man was pure mischief. 'Thank you.'

'You're welcome.'

'What do I owe you?'

'Nothing. On the house.'

'Thank you. But, you're bringing me all these books. I'm embarrassed.'

'Wouldn't want that,' he teased. 'So, maybe you can give me one of your books.'

'My books?'

'Yes. Having a pen name implies you're a writer.' Up went the brow. This guy must have done a course on mastering the eyebrow cock.

'Oh, uh. I'm a feature writer for a women's magazine. But I haven't written any ... I'm in the process of writing my first book.' I felt like a fraud.

'Okay. So, maybe a cup of coffee in kind? How's that? Then you can tell me all about this book you're in the process of writing. And I don't wanna be too presumptuous, but I can give you some tips if you like.'

The man had been nothing but presumptuous. And I suspected he didn't hear the word 'no' very often, particularly from women who knew nothing about his tendencies because he wasn't marketed the way he was hardwired.

'Sure.'

He followed me to the kitchen, stopping short at the breakfast bar as he surveyed the place.

'Nice digs.'

'Thank you.'

I put the kettle on. With my gut flip-flopping, tea was safer. I got the dripolator going for his coffee and turned to face him. 'Are you gay?'

Shit. I was hardwired impulsively.

CHAPTER SIXTEEN

Unzipped & Exposed

A ndy stared at me, bug-eyed and gap-mouthed. Then, shaking himself out of his stupor he said, 'Why would you think that?'

Oh boy. Think fast, talk smart. 'Um, what you implied last week, you know, about taking me up on keeping the gnomes', uh, removable parts.'

'Oh, I was only toying with you. I'm not gay,' he sniggered. But then the mirth-filled look in his eyes vanished. 'And yet, you thought I was?'

I should have said something like, 'Oh, silly me', and left it there. But no. I was too proud and didn't like looking stupid. *Think fast, talk smart, act smart.*

Or be a smart-arse.

'Not that there's anything wrong with that if you are,' I said à la Jerry Seinfeld, and chuckled.

His brows were furrowed and there was no humour in his expression. 'I am not gay.'

Let it go, let it go. Keep your mouth shut. 'Hmm. Methinks someone doth protest too much,' I said à la Bridget Jones quoting Shakespeare, an appealing combo of coquettishness and cleverness. I hoped to God Andy wouldn't launch into an exposition of the Bard. Other than knowing he was called the Bard, studying *Twelfth Night* in high school, and knowing the methinks line from *Hamlet* was spoken by a queen—*ha ha ha*—I'd had pretty much bugger-all experience of the Bard's works.

'Like I said, I am not gay.'

I shrunk away from his glare and averted my eyes. I'd overstepped the mark, making myself look more stupid. When Bridget put her foot in her mouth, superstars found it endearing. But Bridget was a fictional character. I wasn't. And maybe Andy wasn't such a superstar. He mightn't have needed to come out of the closet, but it looked like he had skeletons in it.

'I'm sorry. I didn't mean to offend you.'

He waved it away—not a limp-wristed wave. We stood there awkwardly before he inhaled a deep breath, released it slowly and spoke again.

'*Hmph*. Being in the public eye, well, journalistic piranhas write lots of speculative garbage about me. And it's usually about me dating whichever woman I happen to be seen with. But no one's ever suggested I'm dating a man I've been seen with.' He ran his hand around the back of his neck. 'No one's had the balls to.'

Ah. Andrew Ellis-Nile, who didn't like to be outdone by another man and who didn't suffer fools, didn't seem to like his women on top. Had I found his kryptonite? Superpenman, no longer so cocksure, no longer seemed larger than life. I felt like I was on top of things. But then the corner of his mouth quirked up.

'You are one ballsy woman, Ruth-Roth-Ruth-Gold.'

I smiled. Endearing, after all. And bedazzled, again. Yet, I couldn't be ballsy enough to open my mouth with my husband. *God, I am so tragic.*

Andy's steady scrutiny made me uneasy. *Distract him.* 'So, are you gonna put me in your next novel and have your protagonist kill me off?'

'Oh, I'll put you in my next novel, all right. But maybe as his love interest.' He looked at me with bedroom eyes.

Shit. I cleared my throat, turned and took two mugs out of the cupboard and put them on the counter.

'Milk?' I squeaked.

'Mmhmm. Please.'

I opened the fridge door and grabbed the milk.

'Whoa!'

He was loud and I jumped. I spun around, nearly dropping the carton.

'Sorry. I didn't mean to scare you'—he looked down at me, then past me—'but that is one well-stocked fridge.'

I was almost backing into it. Andy was unnervingly close, encroaching on my personal space. It was disquieting, but nowhere near as much as it should've been. The heavenly scent of Giorgio Armani Acqua Di Giò filled my nostrils. I recognised the fragrance because Ralph wore it. It made my nipples stand to attention. Andy noticed; his gaze had dipped. Not good, not good at all.

He made eye contact again. 'How many people live here?'

Tongue-tied, I held up my fingers.

'Man, that is a lot of food for two people.'

Spoken as an observation, not a value judgement, but still, it hit a raw nerve and left me feeling shamefaced. I'd been given a hard time at school because I didn't have a WASP-y (White Anglo-Saxon Protestant-y), bird-like appetite. Shrugging off the shame, I came back at him like an auctioneer.

'We're Jewish. We eat well. Big deal. Ralph came from a deprived background. Before he found his calling as a psychologist, he made good as a catwalk model. Since then, he's always made sure his pantry is full. And his fridge.'

Andy cocked his head. 'A catwalk model, huh?'

Really? That's all you heard in my burble?

He remained within sniffing distance. There was no room for me to move into my well-stocked fridge. Ignoring his comment, I stepped sideways, made our drinks, took a six-pack of blueberry muffins out of the pantry cupboard, emptied them into a wicker basket, and held it up. 'To go with our cuppas. I'm Jewish; I'll eat most of these.'

He laughed heartily, looking like an animated GIF.

I carried our mugs into the dining room. Andy followed with the muffin basket, the plates and serviettes. He placed them on the table and turned to look at the framed pictures on the sideboard.

He leaned forward. 'Who's this little one?'

'That's my grandson.'

He looked back at me, his self-sustaining brows shooting up. 'You're a *grandmother*?'

'Uh-huh. Luca's almost two.'

'Wow. Nannas never looked so young when I was growing up. Or so good,' he said, giving me the once-over, yet again.

He was enjoying himself. I wasn't. And was. Damn!

With his expertise in skirt-chasing, it was clear Andy had the superb tracking skills of the king of the jungle in pursuit of its prey. *Well, I'm old enough to be a cougar, buddy!* But wily feline that I was, I was also wise enough to know that if push came to shove, the lion would come first. Better to treat him like a predator and ward him off.

Ralph had told me blowfish fend off their predators by inflating their bodies into massive, balloon-like shapes. So, with a lot of help from a muffin, I made like a blowfish—shoving enough of the spongy cake into my gob until my cheeks became distended. I knew it wasn't a pretty sight. Maybe like the beefy nannas he'd known from his younger days.

The look on Don Juan's face confirmed I'd burst his balloon. Or not?

He sat down, leaned back in the chair and studied me. The quasi-amused expression on his face said *Man, you are hard work, but I love a challenge!*

With cheeks no longer engorged, I addressed his comment—the part about being a young nanna. 'Hannah, my daughter, had Luca when she was nineteen.'

He nodded slowly. 'Hmm, young.' He kept nodding. 'So, uh, what nationality is the dad?'

'Alex is Greek. His mum was Greek.' *Please don't ask me about his dad.*

'Greek–Cypriot?'

How the fuck would I know? I should *know. He's my son-in-law. Should I pretend to know?* 'Um, I'm not sure.'

Andy looked back at the picture. He scratched his head, seemingly trying to get it around Luca's skin tone. *Jesus, why not just come out and ask?*

'You're wondering about the skin tone, right?'

Andy's skin tone became a smidge rosy. He grinned. 'Sprung.'

Keep it simple. Give him a half-truth. 'We assumed Luca's skin colour's an ancestral throwback. From an Ethiopian ancestor in my lineage.'

'Hmm. If you really wanna know, there is a way to find out. It's relatively new, genealogical DNA testing. It's amazing what they can do these days.'

Yes, it's brought us all so much joy.

Sensing I wasn't interested in hearing more, Andy turned around again and surveyed the rest of the mini-gallery on the sideboard. His eyes came to rest on the wedding photo of Ralph and me. He picked it up and stared at it.

'Wow, you scrub up beautifully.'

'Wow, thanks. I think.' It was like telling a woman she must have been beautiful in her younger days.

'Wow. That didn't come out right. Let me start again. You look gorgeous done up, but you're a very attractive woman without the war paint.'

Oh, you are good. Flattery laid on with a trowel. But it stroked my ego even as it brush-stroked my face pink.

'I assume this is him?'

Him. 'Yes. It's Ralph.'

'Good-lookin' guy.' He peered at me through narrowed eyes. 'It's just an objective observation, nothing more.'

Ugh. 'You're not gonna let me forget that, are you?'

Andy smirked. 'Nope.'

I took a bite out of muffin number two—a smaller one; he put the picture back in its place.

'So, how did you and the catwalk model meet?'

'Long story. The stuff of novels. The stuff of the novel I'm writing, actually.'

'Can't wait to hear it!'

I smiled wryly.

'Or, better still, read it?'

Shit. It was one thing to have a mostly female readership of presumably non-writers following my feature stories, but this man was a novelist of international renown. *What if he insists on reading my draft? I can always say no. Until then, forestall him!* I started loosely sketching out the stuff of novels.

I told him about Ralph and me. How he'd only found out about five years ago that he was adopted. How we'd grown up believing we were cousins, yet from infancy, from the moment we could see a world beyond our own feet and hands, we'd sensed we were much more than that.

Andy sat back and leered at me. 'So, you married your cousin.'

I didn't like his mordant tone. After enduring slurs for three years, I'd had enough. 'He is not my cousin!' *Just like you are not gay!*

Andy was smart enough to back off. His voice softened. 'I hear you.'

He heard what was said and what wasn't said. It used to be like that with Ralph. Ralph always heard what I didn't say. But now?

But now, he wasn't my cousin. What he was to me, though, no longer seemed well-defined. Throughout our lives, even on the odd occasion when he was mad and didn't speak to me, I'd been confident things would blow over. I wasn't so confident straight after I broke off our engagement, but he'd come back less than half an hour later to work things out. Our relationship as it now stood was alien to me. It made me want to cry.

Andy's voice sliced into my thoughts and feelings. 'Please go on.'

I swallowed, took a calming breath and told him how Ralph and I used to crawl around on the floor together and how, when we grew tired, our mothers would find us asleep in a corner with our arms around each other. How, when we were seventeen we both started to notice each other in ways relatives shouldn't, and that we never shared those feelings with each other or anyone, even denying them to ourselves. I told him Ralph's theory about us being Twin Flames.

Andy had heard of the concept, wasn't sure he believed in it, and said, 'So, do *you* think he's your Twin Flame?'

'Well, yeah. I mean, it follows that if I'm his, then he's mine. And Twin Flames are more than just soul mates. Soul mates can come and go, but Ralph says that a Twin Flame relationship is an abiding one, that it stands the test of ... that it stands the test of time.' My voice thinned out with these last words.

'I get that, but he's the one who decided you were Twin Flames, right?'

I didn't know what to say. I'd taken on Ralph's opinion as my own and believed it for almost four years. Andy's question was disconcerting and added to the uncertainty taking shape in my mind. Not wanting to give away too much, I nodded in response.

'Still,' he said, 'whether you're Twin Flames or not, believing for so many years that he was your cousin, well, that had to be weird for you, you know, when the nature of the relationship with him changed?' His eyebrows waggled. Like Portnoy's eye, Andy's bushy-tailed eyebrows would likely outlive him.

His mouth might have said, 'When the nature of the relationship with him changed', but his more forthright eyebrows translated it to *When you first had sex with him*. Oh yes, this man could be as furtive as me. And like me, his mind was mostly in the gutter. But I felt grateful. The gutter was a familiar place, and his innuendo stopped me from going under. It made me want to laugh.

The urge passed as I stared into the distance trying to recall that moment when the nature of my relationship with Ralph changed. I drew a blank because intrusive thoughts got in the way: author Andy, versed in the art of insinuating; author Andy no doubt as versed in the art of foreplay. Smooth. Subtle. Slick—

'Show me the goods.'

'Huh?' My voice inched up an octave: 'What?'

He gave me a wheedling smile. 'Your manuscript.'

I felt the heat rising in my cheeks. 'Oh, uh. No. I haven't gotten very far and it's still rough and all over the place.' *And it's a pile of horseshit.*

'So? Every book starts that way.'

I put my hand protectively on the laptop in front of the seat next to me.

Andy drained the last of his coffee and circled to my side of the table. He sat down and grinned. 'I'm waiting.'

With a reluctant sigh, I removed my hand, flipped open the laptop and booted it up. Better he look at my manuscript than my tits again.

He pushed up his sleeves to reveal strong forearms. They were hairy, but not out-of-control hairy like a gorilla's. That would have been a deal-breaker. I averted my eyes to circumvent the direction my thoughts were headed. I had to get away from this man who looked like a love god and smelled like a love potion.

'Another coffee?'

'Yes please.'

Good. It bought me some distance.

I stood in the kitchen listening to the coffee drip in sync with my heart's *lub-dub-lub-dubbing.* And one of Sylvia's clichés came to mind: 'Watching the pot boil doesn't make it boil any faster'.

Good. I watched the pot intently. It bought me some time. And thinking of my mother was enough to unlight my fire. But what had happened to my resoluteness? I let out a harsh breath. *I am* married*! How does this man keep getting to me? Why do I let him?*

Ah, yes. Of course.

Every woman has an unmarried chick aspect in her psyche. It's been there since birth. You're not born married, you get married. And hopefully, once you do, UC no longer holds the balance of power. But because of the way things were with Ralph and me at the moment, I felt more unmarried than married. Andy's radar had picked up something. Distended nipples were a dead giveaway. They needed to go into hiding, so I ducked into the bathroom and slapped a Band-Aid on each.

Just as I got back into the kitchen, the dripolator stopped dripping and ... oh, dear God.

A memory trickled back.

The moment the nature of our relationship changed was already chronicled in the manuscript in all its glory! I'd described our bedroom antics in such detail, it would probably play out as a blue movie in Andy's head.

Shiiit!

CHAPTER SEVENTEEN

No Cock & Bull Story

One day my words would be out there for hundreds to see. Hopefully, thousands. Maybe, with luck, even millions. And I was fine about sharing it with the masses. Happy to. Yet, there was an uneasiness knowing this particular man was privy to my inner sanctum.

I tiptoed to the edge of the breakfast bar and, craning my neck, peeked at him. And listened. He was reading with rapt attention, but his breathing hadn't turned choppy—no gaspy, chuffy noises. A good sign. Or, maybe not. Maybe he'd got to the juicy bits and found them dry. No, it wasn't possible. Emotion in the writer, emotion in the reader. And I'd been so super turned on when I wrote about that first time, there'd been a need to take a pet-the-kitty interval. Just thinking about it now, the earlier intrusive thoughts drifted away and fragments of documented descriptions drifted back: *He pressed his engorging manhood against me ... he looked at my breasts hungrily, ran his hands over them ... Ralph levered himself above me and guided himself inside ...*

Jesus! Editors of erotica must be in a permanent state of arousal.

I felt squirmy, but at the same time, gave silent thanks for the two uncomfortable, stretching Band-Aids as I came back into the dining room with the steaming mug.

Andy, who'd been smiling to himself, started chuckling and looked up at me.

'You're a very talented writer, you know. I'm a big fan of satire, and you do it so well.'

I gave him a shy smile.

'Such modesty. I mean it. I'm not trying to humour you.'

'Okay. Well then, thank you!'

He took a sip of his coffee and pointed to the screen. 'This here ...' He stared at me.

'What?'

'Be a lot easier if you sat down.' He patted the seat next to him.

I looked down at the seat and snuck a glimpse beyond. No erection. A mixed blessing.

I slid onto the chair, too afraid to look at the 'this here' on the screen.

'Here. This thing. The mythology angle.'

Phew.

'It sounds interesting. What's the deal with it?'

Sitting taller in the chair, I asked, 'How much d'you know about myths?'

'Not much. I mean, I'm familiar with some of the names of the characters, but the stories, well, lots of crazy, twisted, false gods. That's about it.'

'Crazy and twisted, yeah. False, no.'

'Really?' He eyed me with scepticism.

'Really. Worship of false gods is what you see here all around you. You know, glorifying money, status, sex—'

'Sex?' A slow, dirty grin spread across his face.

Shit. I already knew that, like me, Andy would see dirt where it wasn't. *Think quick.* 'Yes, and famous mystery-turned-horror writers!'

Well-played. The slow dirty grin morphed into a vain one. Of course. Andrew Ellis-Nile's most potent aphrodisiac was himself. Pompous ass hadn't even noticed I'd alluded to him as a false god.

His tone became matter-of-fact. 'Look, I'm not religious. But in the face of monotheism, the idea of one supreme God upheld by religion, well, lots of gods in those stories imply false gods.'

'In the minds of the masses, yeah. But that's because people don't understand what the myths and polytheism are about. We're fed fairy tales from when we're little, and then we go on to read adult versions of them. Most people want a happy ending.'

His dirty eyebrow shot up. 'No. Men want a happy ending; women want happily ever after.'

Man, I'm not the only one who's hard work. I sighed impatiently.

He turned side-on in his chair and sat with his legs apart—breathing room for his 'boys'. Resting one forearm on the table and letting the other one hang over the backrest, he said, 'Okay. You've got my attention. Enlighten me.'

He was a little too close for comfort, but I could ignore what that stirred up because I'd be waxing lyrical on an area I was passionate about.

I leaned back in the chair, crossed my legs under the table, folded my arms, turned my head towards him, and spoke. 'The characters in your books, where do they come from?'

'Uh, they're based on people in my life. Inspired by them. People I've had relationships with or interacted with. Often, composites of them.'

'In that case, you've had relationships or interacted with murderers?'

A smile dangled on the corner of his lips and his eyes flickered with interest.

'Well, you do kill a lot of people in your books!'

He laughed at me. 'Yeah, but it's not like I haven't been inspired by movies or other authors' books with murder themes.'

'So, your murders are copy-cat killings, then?'

'No. No! I like to think the methods I come up with to kill off my characters are original.'

'Which means the methods come from within you?'

'Yes. My imagination.'

'I remember reading an article about your "imagination". You know that one after the release of the film adapted from your book, *Covering Tracks*?'

'"Inside the Disturbed Mind of Andrew Ellis-Nile".' We said it at the same time.

He smiled, then shot me a baleful glance. 'And yet, you've still let me inside your home knowing what my mind is capable of?'

I shrugged. 'I'm not worried.'

'Not even a little bit leery because I'm writing those things?'

'No. It's because you *are* writing those things that I'm not worried.'

Both brows shot up. I'd beaten the master of the twist in the tale at his own game. I smiled at him and talked over his dazedness.

'It's the holier-than-thou lot that worry me. Everyone's got a murderous aspect imprinted on their psyche.' I tapped my head to drive the point home. 'You give voice and body to yours; you let it breathe in the form of your bloodthirsty characters. It doesn't mean you're gonna go out and kill someone.'

He narrowed his eyes. 'Yeah ... I get that. But I'm still mystified as to what all this has to do with the gods of myth that you claim aren't false?'

I took a moment to structure my thoughts so I wouldn't trip over the words in my excitement.

'Okay. Here's the thing. You personify that murderous aspect, but those characters are always villains, right?'

'Uh-huh.'

'Well, the ancients didn't see it that way. The blood-lusting perverts in their stories were often heroes or gods. And they revered them! That can be hard to get your head around because what constituted a hero back then goes against everything we know about what makes a hero today. Today, he's more the fairy-tale ideal. And in fairy tales, when the hero killed, it wasn't to satisfy some sick urge. It was to get rid of an evil force. And it was celebrated, but—'

'Well, why wouldn't it be? Maybe he did take matters into his own hands, but as you implied, it was for a good cause. It's that age-old theme of good triumphing over evil.'

'Oh, I don't have a problem with that. What I do have a problem with is, firstly, the message in the fairy tale is the idea that good triumphing over evil means you should kill anything that represents the dark side. Secondly, fairy tales turned the concept of the hero into a one-dimensional, cardboard cut-out figure. They poured all the good traits into Prince Charming, and all the bad ones into the wicked witch. And that's bullshit because nobody's all good or all bad, even if that's how they're perceived.' *Or promoted.* 'It's just a persona.'

Andy looked left and stroked his bristly chin. He was probably considering his suave alpha-male Prince Charming persona.

My neck was getting stiff. I rubbed it, then swivelled on the chair so my whole body was towards him. My knee grazed his and I felt a little spark. He must have felt it too; his eyes zipped back to centre and bore into me. *Oh boy, look away, keep talking.*

'Anyway, back to the gods. Naturally, being gods they're divine beings, but like what you said before about them, they're also twisted and crazy. So, in each one of them you see the *many* sides of human nature represented and personified. Not like in the fairy tales that polarise good and evil. Myths show us that good and evil coexist. In one person. The ancients didn't get all bent out of shape about it because they knew human nature was innately good *and* bad, and that both sides deserved respect— that all sides did.' I paused, then asked, 'Does that make sense?'

'Makes perfect sense.' Andy nodded thoughtfully. 'Hmm. And it turns everything on its head, too. All things considered, I guess when you juxtapose myths and fairy tales, well, the fairy-tale prince is looking more false-god than the gods of myth do.'

'Exactly! And the other thing. Why are books like yours and Stephen King's so popular? Apart from being exceptional writers, I think it's also because you give voice and form to aspects that have been vilified over the centuries. And that satisfies those parts in the reader's psyche that he or she doesn't dare express. You know, all those immoral thoughts or impulses?'

'Thank you!'

Really? 'Well, uh, you are an exceptional writer.' *You egomaniac.*

'No, not that. Well, yes, thank you for that. But to tell you the truth, there are times I scare myself with some of the things

I come up with. But I've never given any thought to the mechanics of it. I don't think I wanted to because I was afraid I'd see something I couldn't handle. Now, looking at it from that perspective actually makes me feel better. So, thank you!'

Oops. Eating crow. Not my favourite dish, but the aftertaste didn't linger. I was chuffed that an acclaimed author had learned something from me. My face lit up like a smiley face emoticon.

'It's a real pity these ancient stories aren't mainstream,' Andy said.

'Oh, but they are!'

'Huh? I spend most of my time writing, but I also read a helluva lot. And, uh ...' He gave a perplexed shrug.

'The classic stories are playing out everywhere today. They're just in obscure forms. Think about it. All the terrible things that go on in developing countries. And then in Western culture, there's the cancer story, stories of terrorism, stories of paedophilia ... And personally, I reckon religion has a lot to answer for. That push to make ourselves in the image of the one supreme God is like saying be spiritual but not human. In other words, purify and purge yourself of your dark side. So, we might work at empowering our spirit, but it's at the expense of our soul. Hardly a surprise, then, that what we try an' get rid of festers and mutates and leaks out. Or leaks in. And hey, isn't that the theme of these monstrous, twisted, modern-day stories?'

Andy frowned. 'My God, you're right.' He nodded slowly. 'So, lemme see if I've got this straight. In a nutshell, ideologies change, the stories then change to suit, and people fall into line, but the original stories are still there?'

'Yep. Permanent. And hidden under layers and layers of changes. And I think there's a deep desire, also hidden, to revert to the original, which is that mythical style of consciousness. An' one way or the other, it's happening. My history teacher in fourth-year high school—the one who introduced mythology to me—used to say that life today is really just ancient myth cloaked in modern attire.'

'Huh. A wise man. I guess if you look at it that way, you'd say the characters from the myths are reduced to just dry things in the modern stories?'

'Mmhmm. De-personified. Little wonder our vitality suffers.'

We both became pensive for a bit. 'You've given me a lot to think about,' he said. Then the corners of his eyes crinkled as he favoured me with a teasing smile. 'Doesn't happen often. D'you know how rare it is to come across ballsy, attractive *and* intriguing women?'

Of course it's rare for you. Mostly, their only requirement would be a pulse.

Now I knew how Casper must have felt when he'd eyed that forkful of quiche and feared what might come up if he dared bite. I didn't bite, just gave Andy a fake smile.

He must have got that there was no point trying to lead me astray. He said, 'But I can see why the fairy tale doesn't do it for you. Still, surely, as a child, you must have been entranced?'

'Not really. Or, not for long. I was never made to feel like a princess.'

He eyed me with pity, like I was Cinderella just tasked with emptying the ugly sisters' pisspots. It was the kind of look that would have warmed the cockles of Sylvia's heart, but it made me want to hurl.

'Besides, I couldn't relate to the damsel. She was too insipid and too ... *nnnice*.' I curled my lip in disgust. 'If anyone needed a firecracker up her bum, it was that goddamn damsel.'

He laughed at me. 'I have to agree. I myself prefer the hot-blooded ones. Firecrackers. Like yourself.'

The heat in my hot-blooded face started to rise. Did this man ever come up for air?

I digressed. Sort of. 'That brings to mind something related to what we were talking about before. We've all got one aspect that's dominant in our psyche. You know, a particular trait that holds sway. Or if you look at it from the perspective of personifying that trait, a mythical figure that holds sway. But I think it's the fairy-tale mindset that makes us define people by that one governing feature, like "She's a victim"; "He's a toad".' *You're a lech.* 'Of course, we're all much more than just one thing, like the ancient stories show us.' The fact that I couldn't take in the whole story where Sylvia was concerned wasn't lost on me. I hoed into another muffin and looked at Andy.

He tilted his head. 'Well then, I can't wait to hear which mythical figure dominates in Ruth-Roth-Ruth-Gold's psyche.'

I swallowed, then gulped. 'Baubo, ancient goddess of obscenity.'

He chuckled, and nodded in the direction of the screen. 'I noticed you don't hold back on the language.'

'No, I don't. And I may not be writing from the murderous aspect like you, but I am writing from an aspect that's so shut down in women because we were taught to make nice. You know, sent to finishing school to learn etiquette and how to arrange flowers and eat fucking spaghetti in public!'

Andy was laughing at me.

'And maybe that's why I had this inexplicable urge back then to knife that damsel!' I made a repeated stabbing motion with my fist.

'You mean your murderous aspect did?'

'Yeah, that. But, like you said, those impulses can be scary when you don't know where they're coming from. And made so much worse if you're stupid enough to share them with your narrow-minded mother.' I groaned at the memory.

'You didn't!'

'Only once. At least she stopped saving for finishing school. She thought I'd have a better chance of ending up in reform school.'

Before he could tell me I was ballsy, attractive, intriguing, *and* funny, I assumed a businesslike tone and said, 'But back to my colourful language. It isn't contrived, it's not just there for shock value.'

'No, no. I get that. You can always tell when someone's writing is unnatural, and—'

'And that's what I love about mythical consciousness. It might be raw, but it's real.'

Andy nodded, and eyed me appreciatively.

Yeah, I know. I'm ballsy, attractive, intriguing, funny, and *real.* But no way was I about to volunteer that the ugly little goddess of obscenity was also the goddess of sacred sexuality. The man didn't need any extra encouragement. And I wasn't going to tell him about my lost years when I'd shut Baubo out and lapsed into a shallow, bloodless, unhappily-ever-after existence. He'd find out soon enough if he kept reading. For now, I'd already divulged more than I'd intended to.

Both of us were silent for a bit. There was one muffin left. He picked it out of the basket. 'May I?'

'Please. It's the only way I won't eat it.'

'And yet, look at you.' Up went that eyebrow. 'You've got a great body.'

Add that to the list. But, great *body* instead of great *figure*? *Body* seemed more carnal.

He took a manly bite out of the muffin and asked, 'So, which god rules the catwalk model's psyche?'

Normally, Pan, famous for his sexual powers. At the moment, Uranus. 'Anteros, maybe. The god of reciprocal love.' The words felt hollow, but I hoped the gist of them might cool Andy's libidinous jets.

It seemed to. He gave me a thumbs-up.

Oh. Had he just buddied up to me? It was what I wanted, wasn't it? Yes. Then why was I disappointed? No. Unmarried Chick was disappointed. Tough! She already had way too much juice, and I couldn't keep stuffing my face as a means of protection. And now knowing Andy considered me a homie made me feel more relaxed around him.

It was what I told myself.

CHAPTER EIGHTEEN

Licked

Andy stayed for two hours. He was interested and interesting, and it looked like I might have misjudged him. He had the vanity thing going, no question, but he didn't pretend to know everything. Without his open-mindedness and depth and humility, he couldn't have been the writer he was.

And it was clear he enjoyed my company because he began dropping in with regularity—three or four times a week. We became like a two-person *kaffeeklatsch*. I always made sure I had cake to go with our hot drinks, and we drank and ate while he reviewed my draft and offered helpful tips. Then we nattered about interesting stuff like celebrity gossip. Andy the A-lister was an insider with lots of wicked stories.

Sometimes he seemed more homegirl than homeboy. Our exchanges were easy, and, homie-whatever aside, every time I saw him walking down the path towards my front door, I felt a rush of excitement. I still hadn't said anything about him to Ralph.

Our exchanges were difficult, and, husband aside, every time he put the key in the door, I got butterflies in my stomach. Or a swarm of moths. Where we once shared the minutiae of our daily existence and enjoyed our repartee, our conversation had become dehydrated. Just factual: 'We've run out of milk.' 'I'll pick some up later today.' He treated my birthday the same way.

'Happy birthday,' he said. My heart sank when he handed me a large grey box with WATERFORD CRYSTAL printed in white. No gift-wrapping, no card. And no ritual dinner at a restaurant. He had to work late.

I felt like crying. And I felt like an ungrateful bitch. Sylvia used to say, 'You're hard to please.'

There was no time to mope after Ralph left for work. Maxi, Vette, Iris and Rhea were taking me out for an early breakfast. We girls made a fuss over each other on our birthdays.

Casper had called just as I was about to leave, so I was running a bit late. All of them were there when I got to Stella's and they started singing 'Happy Birthday' as I walked in, then showered me with lovely gifts. Lovely *personal* gifts.

'What'd Ralph give you?' Iris asked.

'A crystal vase.'

'A vase charm to add to your bracelet?' Vette asked.

'No. A vase to put flowers in.'

They all went silent and looked at me with shocked expressions.

Ralph had always given me jewellery on my birthday. When we were kids, he'd hand-make bracelets from dried macaroni and string. When he started his paper round at thirteen, he gave Norma most of his earnings, kept some for himself, and put the rest aside for my birthday present. It'd be costume jewellery. After he left school and got a job, I got small, nine-carat gold pieces. He graduated to eighteen-carat during his modelling years, then eighteen-carat embellished with diamonds when we became an item.

'It's a Waterford,' I said. It was a lame defence. As if letting them know this would make it okay.

Maxi scowled. Her reaction validated mine. Vette looked at me with sad eyes. Her reaction made me tear up.

Both knew there was tension at home, and why. I'd told Iris and Rhea that Ralph and I were having major issues that I couldn't discuss at the moment. I was tempted to let Iris know the specifics, but telling Rhea would be a conflict of interest. Maybe just as well she was here; I couldn't give in to temptation.

'D'ya want me to come over and kick him in the balls?' Iris asked.

I laughed and wiped my tears. 'No, I might need them again someday.'

'Might?' Vette said as she put a comforting hand on mine. 'Will. You will have them again.'

I cried again, then laughed at the irony of having Ralph by the balls.

I was home by nine-thirty and no sooner had I walked in the door than the phone started ringing. It was back-to-back calls from Reuben, Beth, Norma, Greta, and a good number of satellite friends. A lot of love and best wishes were coming my way, but nothing could fill the void. Even if things had been happy at home and even if Ralph had given me a gem, I didn't like my birthdays. And I didn't like that what I didn't get, or the value of the gifts I got, or who didn't call, overshadowed the good stuff. So I decided to gift myself with a new attitude. Gratitude. Yes. I would be grateful.

Thank you for Ralph's present. It's expensive and it's modern and it's the thought that counts. But if he'd given me an antique, I swear to God I would have ripped him a new one!

No, shh, shh, shh. Gratitude.

Thank you for my great friends and my family and their kindness. I'm lucky to have these people in my life. I have abundance in my life. Many others are worse off than me. Like the starving children in Africa. Oh yes. Those that I had to fucking hear all about when I refused to eat Sylvia's unsavoury vegetables!

Well, thanks a lot. My dead mother had turned up for my birthday. And then she reminded me that Hannah hadn't.

Hannah's had always been the first call of the day and she'd often given me my present in advance because she was too excited to wait.

Just then, my phone pinged. It was a text from Hannah. *Ha, screw you, Sylvia.* I opened the message.

Happy bday

No call, no kisses, no present from my own daughter. Just an abbreviated text that spoke volumes.

Don't be a child. At least she remembered. It is what it is.
I texted back gratitude.

Thank you xxx

And then I fell apart.

I still hadn't pulled myself together a week later when it was Ralph's birthday. I'd bought his present the day before—a personal gift: Armani 'Code' Men's Fragrance. I couldn't very well ask Andy to change aftershaves, so I tried changing Ralph's signature scent. A different perfume maybe, but it was from the same top designer brand.

'It has a spicy oriental fragrance,' the salesman had said as he shoved a card sprayed with Code under my nose. 'It's more masculine than Acqua Di Giò.' Fairly convincing. 'Code is the code of seduction.' Overselling, but it clinched the deal.

I didn't much like Ralph at the moment, but he was my husband. I was still rooting for him to come out on top. And he nodded his approval when I gave it to him before he left for work, thanked me and told me he'd be working late. Again.

Six weeks had passed since the awful afternoon, and we were like a pair of strangers sharing a living space. But Andy and I were growing closer. He still hadn't moved into the ghost house. Even though he wasn't having any major renovations done, there were gremlins in the plumbing and wiring. I told him it looked like Portnoy wasn't so dead.

I told him plenty. Much of it was through the ramblings in my manuscript. He seemed to file away in his memory what suited his purposes. Often speaking his one-track mind, it became clear that Andy did not read about sex objectively. I learned a lot from him and about him. The man wrote with his heart, edited with his head, and thought with his penis.

'So, where's this little French patisserie you've written about, the one with the carnal pastries?' he asked in a velvety tone. From then on, he made it a point to swing by the patisserie to pick up some erotic indulgences before each visit.

Ralph had stopped surprising me with these delicacies since our stand-off. Ralph had stopped surprising me with *in flagrante delicto* since our stand-off. The tension was becoming unsettling. At the same time, Unmarried Chick was enjoying a revival. I looked a little too forward to Andy's visits. The increasing sexual tension was becoming unsettling.

One morning, he turned up on my doorstep with a box of one dozen wanton, mini chocolate éclairs.

I wondered about his intentions as I absently plated the divine little gateaux. I didn't know he was next to me until he took my hand and sensually licked the cream off my fingers.

I let him.

CHAPTER NINETEEN

Hiding the Silly Sausage

A little moan escaped my lips. It was like giving him the green light. Or more like running a red.

Andy turned me towards him, cupped my face in his hands and grazed my lips with his. Then he deepened the kiss, parting my lips and slipping his tongue in. His hands slid down my body, skimming the sides of my breasts. He wrapped his arms around my waist; I wrapped mine around his neck.

Grabbing a handful of my long-sleeved tee, he pulled it up over my head, then unhooked my bra and let it fall to the floor. I groaned with pleasure as his hands kneaded my bare breasts. Then he removed my leggings and knickers and stepped back to survey my body. 'Beautiful,' he whispered. Drawing me closer, he slid his fingers down my belly. And down, down, down ... oh God! He stroked and caressed with such mastery it was as if he'd been there a thousand times before. *Yes, yes, yes, yeeeeees!*

I was left panting as his hands then circled my waist. And with no effort, he lifted me clear off my feet and lowered me onto the kitchen bench. He ripped off his T-shirt and dropped his dacks and jocks.

I gasped at his size as it kangarooed up and down, up and down. He and Ralph were not only an even match in their wordplay prowess—

Shit! Why am I thinking of Ralph? Why now?

Andy slid his hands under my buttocks, gently pulled me towards the edge of the bench and slipped inside me.

Ooh! Well-hung doesn't mean you know how to use it. Ooh! Andrew Ellis-Nile sure did. But then, so did Ralph. *Oh God!* The guilt already inside me exploded.

In an attempt to appease the torturous voices, I imagined Andy was Ralph. Strangely, it helped.

'Ruth?' Andy said. He was clicking his fingers.

Huh?

Andy's voice jarred me out of my dirty daydream. 'Well, someone was way off in never-never land. Looks like I picked the perfect pastries this time. All those little moans,' he said as he favoured me with a wolfish grin. 'Better than sex?'

Ffffuck! Fully clothed, yet caught with my pants down. It had felt so real, my face went bright pink, some of it from the imagined beard burn.

I am one sick puppy. It was bad enough I'd been fantasising about having sex with this man while he was here, but I was mortified that I'd fantasised about having sex with Ralph while I was fantasising about having sex with Andy! *I am so going to hell.*

For the next half hour, I felt like I was already there. Andy sensed it. He picked up on my vulnerable state.

'You seem vulnerable.'

'Why?' Vulnerable and wary.

'You've eaten six éclairs in a row and—'

'So?' Vulnerable, wary and defensive. 'Why would you assume that means I'm vulnerable?'

'Uh, maybe 'cause you say as much in your manuscript. You know, "stuffing down feelings", "comfort food", feeding your "intractable inner bitch".' He raised an inquisitive brow.

'Mm.' I looked away.

Thank God, he left *Mm* alone. If only he'd left well enough alone. If only I hadn't shoved number seven of those little choc-topped phallic symbols into my mouth.

He shook his head and laughed at me. 'Gotta love a woman with that kind of appetite. In my experience, it equates with a healthy appetite for sensual indulgence.' A suggestive brow crept up this time.

Keep cool. 'Hmph.' It was like a bucket of cold water.

Andy looked nonplussed. Here was a woman who didn't want to play with him. 'You okay?'

'Uh, I'm tired.' *Rooted, actually. That was a vigorous bout of sex we didn't just have.*

'*Phoof.* I'm not surprised. Filling up like that can wreak havoc with your liver.'

I didn't respond.

'Okay. I'll leave. Maybe go lie down, hey?'

I will. I have a date with my vibrator.

Pity. It could have been with a pair of dildos. I let Andy out and recalled my strange exchange with him from several weeks earlier—ten days after I'd asked him if he was gay.

He handed me a plastic bag. 'For you.'

My eyes went wide as I pulled out the dildos, held together with a red ribbon tied in a perfect bow.

His mouth curved into a lascivious grin. 'Got rid of the gnomes, but you might be able to put these babies into service. I don't need 'em.'

I felt my cheeks burn up, but then realised something. 'And yet, in spite of your denials that day, you've held onto them for a week and a half?'

We both laughed.

Semi-reluctantly, I threw out the dildos. Andy had had his hands on them, but so had Portnoy Junior. And who the hell knew what *he'd* done with them? *Ecch.*

I banished the sickening thought, went into the bedroom, and romanced myself. Then I called Maxi. I hadn't got around to telling her or Vette about Andy. I kept no secrets from them and I knew they were accepting of pretty much everything, but I also knew they'd disapprove of this. It was a guilty pleasure I'd wanted to keep close to my chest, but now I had to get it off my chest. I told Maxi about the famed author, selectively omitting some things, but I confessed my shameful fantasy.

'Oh, I know him,' she said.

'You know Andrew Ellis-Nile?'

'No, not him personally. I know his type. I've *dated* his type. Charmers. Ruthie, guys like that are dangerous.'

'But I've got to know him. He's a decent person.'

'Really? Does he know you're married?'

'Yes, but—'

'But *nothing*. He knows you're married and he's playing you. End of story.'

I sighed. 'I guess. It's just ... it's just that other than the odd day with Luca, Andy's been pretty much my only source of joy these days. Hannah's still barely speaking to me.' She had started talking to me, but only because she wanted me to babysit. The scope of our conversation when she dropped Luca off didn't exceed beyond what he needed, and then a 'Thanks' when she picked him up. 'My writing's all over the place, and Andy's been a real help. Plus, he's giving me the attention I'm not getting from Ralph.'

'I know, hon. But it's not the kind of attention that's good for you, and that's what you really need. How 'bout we have a girl's night out tonight? You, me and Vette. I'll see if she's free.'

'I'm so tired, Max.'

'I get that. But we're both going away tomorrow and I think it'll do you good to be around people who value you.'

This made me cry. Birthday breakfast aside, I'd been feeling undervalued. Little wonder I was easy prey for Andy.

Five minutes after we hung up, Maxi called back to say Vette was available. I sent Ralph a text saying I was having dinner with the girls. He texted back that he was working late.

We all loved Italian so we met at Chianti in Hutt Street. And Maxi was right. It was what I needed. It was good to get out of the house and be with my dear girlfriends.

After we placed our orders Maxi brought up the subject of Andy. As I told them everything, Vette frowned. Maxi, who'd been irritated during our phone conversation, was now seething.

'Like I said to you, I know his type—bastard's chipping away at your defences so he can get into your pants!'

I wanted to object, to tell her Andy and I were friends, because we were. But there was some truth to what she said. Still, I sensed Maxi's anger was as much at Andy as her past experience of his breed. What Vette said, though, hit home.

'Ruthie, I don't like that he's planting seeds of doubt in your mind about Ralph.'

I didn't like hearing this, but it helped me understand that one of the reasons I was disturbed when Andy had questioned the Twin Flame thing was because he *had* questioned it.

'This man is taking advantage of you and it worries me.'

I shook my head. 'Vette, I wouldn't do anything stupid. The fact that I even had that fantasy worries me.'

'Well then, it's time to cut ties,' Maxi the pragmatist said.

I winced. Her line of attack incited an internal tug of war. Unmarried Chick screamed *Noooo!* Married chick said a forceful *Yes!* But all-or-nothing wasn't a good fit for sensitives; it would send me bouncing off walls. It was why the all-inclusive mythical approach sat so well with me.

Vette tapped into my thoughts. 'Maybe there's another option. Do you think it might be worth you taking the initiative with Ralph? Seems like he's too proud to. And things can't go on like this.'

Maxi was about to protest. I stopped her. 'Vette has a point. And honestly, I don't want to be stuck in this cycle of anger and pride like my mother was.'

Maxi capitulated. They both knew what Sylvia had been like. And maybe I'd retreated from Ralph, in part, because I didn't want to be a suffocating ballbreaker like Sylvia. Maxi and Vette's mothers weren't perfect, but they hadn't emasculated their sons or smothered their daughters. I'd long thought that even though the girls had their share of challenges, they were better able to roll with the punches than I was.

But doing the opposite of what Sylvia did was resorting to black and white thinking. I'd eulogised the many-sidedness of the ancient way to Andy, but I wasn't applying it in my marriage. It made me no different to Sylvia, really. I needed to do things differently, so yes, I would put on my big girl pants! I told them so.

'Good for you!' Vette said.

'Okay. But what about Hannah?' Maxi asked. 'How about we do something?'

'"We"?'

'Yeah, you know, in our capacity as godmothers maybe Vette or I could say something to her.'

'Mmm, I'm not sure that's a good idea. I mean, isn't she likely to dig her heels in even more if we butt in?'

I agreed with Vette. And it suited me to leave it alone. I wasn't ready to put on my big girl pants with my daughter. I feared losing the small concession she'd granted me.

And right now, I wanted to get out of my current headspace of Ralph and Andy and Hannah. So, the three of us talked about other stuff.

Maxi told us about the renovations of the apartment she and Nestor had bought. She gushed about her walk-in closet that was 'big enough to hold a party in'. And we discussed the girls' upcoming trips—Maxi and Nestor were going to the luxurious Hayman Island resort, and Vette was off on another overseas fashion-buying stint. We joked and laughed and reminisced and gossiped. It reminded me what a homespun, organic *kaffeeklatsch* was really like. I went home feeling better than I had in a while.

My good feelings went out the window when Ralph walked in the door half an hour later and I asked how his day was.

'Fine,' he said as he made his way to the bedroom.

He didn't ask how my day was or how dinner went. It hurt that he didn't care enough to.

He came out five minutes later and called out from the kitchen, 'Oh, by the way, I'll be home early tomorrow afternoon.'

It raised my hopes a little. He didn't seem to be in the mood to talk tonight, but another opportunity had just presented itself. I'd broach the subject tomorrow.

'And I'll be bringing my colleague, Anthea. We'll be fine-tuning our presentation.'

It dampened my hopes. I said, 'Anthea?' I knew all his associates. I knew nothing about an Anthea. 'What presentation?'

He told me she'd joined the practice six weeks ago and said the two of them would be flying to Canberra tomorrow night. They were to deliver a keynote presentation at a conference for national psychological society members first thing the following morning, and would be back late that night. Their speech was about the overlap between sex addiction and OCPD. Obsessive–compulsive Ralph was an authority on OCPD; Anthea's area of expertise was sex addiction. It was the longest conversation we'd had in a while. Hope restored. Or not. Why was I only finding out about Canberra the day before? It made me feel like an afterthought.

As Vette had said, it couldn't go on like this. And I didn't think things could get any worse.

I was wrong.

CHAPTER TWENTY

Coy Interruptus

I was standing next to the dining room table at one o'clock the next day with a mouthful of shortbread, when I heard the key in the door. Ralph walked in carrying an unfamiliar, caramel-coloured Louis Vuitton duffle. He placed it on the floor, said, 'Hi,' and held the door open for his colleague.

Sweet merciful crap! I stopped chewing.

Having assumed someone who was sex-savvy would have breasts that hung like flapjacks, bat-wing arms and a worn-out vagina, I expected to see a woman in her sixties, medium-sized, average height, salt-and-pepper hair cut into a neat bob, and black-rimmed multifocals. I'd envisaged her wearing a tailored navy skirt, a loose, off-white, elbow-length, lightweight top in a marled-knit fabric, a single strand of pearls and sensible pumps.

I was not expecting a sex kitten.

Anthea was tall, model thin and well stacked. Probably in her mid-to-late thirties, she had a lustrous brown mane, waist length and side parted. She wore a red scoop neck, painted-on jersey dress that hugged her bod, sheer black hose and black patent stilettos. Anthea probably wore a lacy suspender belt to hold up her stockings. Anthea probably wore no knickers. And Anthea, no doubt, had a well-worn vagina.

Ralph introduced us. 'Anthea meet Ruth; Ruth meet Anthea.'

Ruth. Not, *Ruthie*. Not, *my wife, Ruthie*.

I gawped at this hoochie, my cheeks bulging with cookie as she sashayed towards me, not a single body part of her wobbling, no breast jiggle. She extended her ice-cold hand, with its pristine French manicured nails, and warmly shook mine, with its unfiled, unvarnished nails.

'How lovely to meet you, Ruth,' she said in a smoky voice and with a smile that didn't quite make it to her eyes.

I swallowed most of my biscuit, left the rest stuck to the roof of my mouth, and lied: 'Thame.'

Even without my contact lenses, I'd seen how beautiful she was when she'd stepped through the doorway. Now, close up, I noticed her dark brown, almond-shaped eyes with their long, sooty false eyelashes, her flawless olive skin, her Eva Mendes jawline, Angelina Jolie lips, and straight white teeth. Her face was perfection. It looked sculpted by Michelangelo, or maybe a Dr Michel Angelo, Plastics?

My eyes were drawn down to a Yin Yang pendant.

Suspended on a fine silver snake chain around her neck, it rested a little above her implanted-looking mammaries, which bulged like a pair of orbs spilling out of her décolletage.

Yin and Yang, like a pair of single opening and closing quotation marks mating, were set into a small round silver disc: Yang was mother of pearl inlaid with an onyx dot; Yin was onyx inlaid with a mother of pearl dot. I knew these signified the opposing and complementary forces of female and male. But, the spiritual symbolism seemed to be at odds with Anthea's apparel.

Or, maybe not.

Personally, I thought it was unprofessional and improper to be dressed to the nines when you counselled sex addicts. But in light of the way she was tarted up, this symbol complemented her fuck-me threads. The way I saw it, it said *I am into sixty-nines.*

As Anthea's eyes flicked over me, I became more self-conscious. I wore fuck-off-I'm-writing threads—old black parachute pants, a three-quarter-sleeve black tee, black moccasins.

Shit.

It occurred to me that it resembled the way Sylvia used to dress—always in I'm-a-grieving-widow black (even before Joe died). My relationship with Ralph, being what it was at the moment, might have been the reason I'd chosen this outfit. A far cry from almost ten months earlier, when, filled with life and passion, I dared to don a wicked, sexy red wedding dress. Ralph had loved it so much on me, he couldn't wait to take it off me.

I didn't know Anthea, but I didn't like her. And I didn't like that she was getting on a plane tonight with my husband.

Ralph asked if I minded them working in the dining room; if I minded doing my writing in the study this afternoon.

You bet I mind! This is my *working domain.*

You're a difficult child, said Sylvia's voice.

'No. I don't mind.'

I closed my laptop, gathered up my notepad, relocated, and kicked myself. That need for the approval of the rejecting 'parent' had taken over. It was a pointless struggle that would never bear fruit. And even worse, it felt like I was being punished. Sylvia had often sent me to my room when I was a child because I'd behaved childishly.

I sighed and plopped myself down on the chair, sat staring at the screen, but wrote nothing. My mind was in the adjoining room where Ralph and the tramp were conferring. A lot of muted laughter came from there. Ralph had a resonant laugh. It was the first time I'd heard it in a while.

In my world, even though everything had the potential to be funny, I wasn't happy that Ralph was enjoying himself so much with this woman. I'd never been the jealous type and it irked me that this distasteful side now had me eating out of its hand. It irked me even more that I fed it. I got up and opened the door a crack to eavesdrop. I was about to close it because they weren't saying anything, but then Anthea spoke.

'You know, I find it so easy to relate to you. I feel like I've known you since forever.'

I froze. It was more like adolescent-speak between besties than adult-talk, but it bothered me.

'Mmm. Mmm. Same here. Same here.'

Ah, yes. Repetition. This OCPD symptom was fine in the confines of his home, but in a professional setting, it would be problematic. He was supposed to be a presenter, not a cautionary tale. Show-don't-tell was good for someone in my line of work, not his.

But why had his OCPD kicked in? It usually did when he was nervous. Why was he nervous? Standing up and speaking in front of an audience had never been an issue for Ralph. Was he unnerved by Anthea's sultriness? Was he compulsively obsessed with her? Was she sexually addicted to him?

Their heart-to-heart was the kind that took place between people who were destined to be together. Ralph had never said anything like that to me. *Ah-ha-ah-ha-ah-ha. Breeeathe. Think rationally.*

Yes, of course. He'd never said anything like that to me because he'd known me all his life. But could he have been wrong about us being Twin Flames? What Vette had said last night about Andy planting seeds of doubt was spot on. They were now germinating. Could it be Anthea was Ralph's Twin Flame? Based on physical appearance, a geneticist would say they were a perfect pair. *Ah-ha-ah-ha-ah-ha.*

But wait a second! If Ralph had any doubts about it, why would he bring this woman into our home?

Anxiety gave way to red-hot anger. I needed to cool it.

There were three leftover éclairs in the fridge. I knew Ralph loved these little pastries and would have enjoyed them with a coffee. There was also a head of iceberg lettuce that Anthea probably would have enjoyed with a glass of water. I lumbered into the kitchen, downed the éclairs, and threw out the lettuce. *No treats for either of you—fuck you both!*

Spite now overlaid the guilt I'd felt about my Andy fantasy. I hoped these two would lapse into show-don't-tell during their joint presentation. I hoped Ralph would bore the audience with repetition, and that Anthea would titillate them with her tits. I hoped she had two vaginas (Ralph once dated a woman with two—a condition called didelphys. It was heaven for him. With his deprived childhood, *surplus* was not a word he'd often heard). I hoped Anthea would put out for every member. Except Ralph. *Don't even think about saving the spare vagina for my husband's member, scrubber!* But then, would he be tempted?

Ralph hadn't touched me in months. Was it just pride, as Vette had surmised? Even with all we were going through, with his high sex drive and with sex being an overpowering physical need for a man, why hadn't he at least made a move? Was he suffering from the Madonna-whore complex? No. It wasn't like he viewed me as innocent and pure and motherly, because I wasn't.

I wished Andy would drop around. But then, what if he took to Anthea? She was the kind of gal he couldn't resist. He was the kind of guy she'd want to fix. So much for being the bigger person. *Oh God, my life sucks.*

And then came the lowest blow. I heard Ralph call Anthea 'Anth'. She got a pet name; I didn't.

I went into our bedroom, closed the door, lay on the bed, and silently wailed. *I'm not a Madonna—my daughter doesn't want me. I'm not a whore—my husband doesn't want me. I'm nothing. Nothing, nothing, noooooothing ...*

* * * *

On the beach, I recalled how bad I felt that day. It hurt to think I was nothing. I glared at the bird. 'It's your bloody fault. It's how you made me feel, unworthy of anything good.'

The stupid bird looked at me stupidly. Then it trilled what sounded like a sympathetic coo.

What? It couldn't be the same bird. I studied it. They all looked alike; walking clichés do.

It cooed again.

No. This could not be Sylvia. Sylvia had always been on the offensive. And she never once apologised. Maybe she'd shown a semblance of sympathy on the odd occasion, and I'd had saintly moments of understanding her, but her profusion of nit-picking was stitched together so tightly, it had been hard to glimpse any words of encouragement, hard to keep seeing anything good. Was I like her? It distressed me to think I'd inherited her characteristics. My mind drifted back to the rest of that afternoon and evening.

* * * *

No. Andy wanted me. But was Maxi right? Did he want me for me, or only as his latest conquest? I must be a whore. *I hate my life*.

I lamented my hateful life for another half hour, then stopped when I heard footsteps approaching the bedroom. I sat up, gathered all the used tissues, shoved them in the bedside table drawer, and pretended to look for something in it.

Ralph came in. 'I need to pack a few things.'

Act casual. 'Uh-huh. So, what time will you be back?'

'Late.'

'Do you want a lift to the airport? D'you want me to pick you up tomorrow night?' *She can find her own way. There and back.*

'No. I've booked us a cab.'

Us.

'And I'll cab it back.'

An hour later, they left for the airport.

If I'd owned handkerchiefs, I'd have been wringing one, like female characters did in old movies. If I liked alcohol, I'd have chugged from a bottle of whatever. Instead, I ate. I started on my unmanicured nails, then worked my way through the fridge. Three hours later, I was tempted to call Ralph.

And say what? Even if I had, what if she answered his phone and said he was in the shower? I'd seen a scene like that in a movie once, even though 'he' was not in the shower. The female character was a femme fatale like Anthea. Not the hanky-wringing type like me.

What if I called and he didn't answer and neither did she because they were in the shower ... together?

I imagined them together, naked. *Ah-ha-ah-ha-ah-ha.* Again, I needed to think rationally.

Madonna-whore complex aside, Ralph may have had a lot of women in his past, but he'd been a serial monogamist. He wouldn't cheat on me ... nix that ... he *once* wouldn't have cheated on me.

Ah-ha-ah-ha-ah-ha!

CHAPTER TWENTY-ONE

Synchronishitty

When Ralph returned the next night, he was just as taciturn. Even if his presentation had been a bust, sex would have lifted his spirit. But he wasn't basking in an afterglow. Nor was I. And over the next couple of days, I didn't feel much like following through on my decision to break down barriers between us.

On Friday afternoon, I was at the dining room table sitting opposite Andy.

If I hadn't been lost in glumness, I'd have heard his Harley. And if I'd heard his Harley, I would've pretended I wasn't home when the doorbell rang. He was looking more like a problem than a solution. I'd been cool and distant as I let him in. He'd glanced at me questioningly, but didn't push it.

I was now bent over the computer, gnawing at a cuticle and groaning. He stood up, came around to my side of the table and sat next to me. I tensed up.

'What's up?'

'I'm not going anywhere.' *And I wish you'd go anywhere but here.*

'Your problem is you're tense.'

I made a wry face. 'Past, present or future?'

Andy smiled. 'Present.'

You don't know the half of it. My present writing has become clichéd and shallow. Just like my present life.

Andy pushed my hair aside and started kneading my neck. I tensed even more, but then surrendered to his touch, which was gentle but firm. I needed to find a way to be gentle but firm with him.

We both started at the sound of the front door slamming, and wheeled around to see Ralph standing there stock-still and staring at us.

'Who are you?' he asked Andy. His voice was frosty.

'Andy. You know, your neighbour.' He stood and pushed his chair back, walked over to Ralph and extended his hand. Ralph didn't take it.

'Neighbour?' Ralph scrunched up his face.

'Yes. I own the house across the road.'

Both men looked at me with bemused expressions. I hadn't told Andy that I hadn't told Ralph about him. I gulped.

Andy cleared his throat and said, 'Okay. I guess I'll leave you two to it.'

Ralph opened the front door for him, closed it behind him, then turned to me. He spoke in an imperious tone. 'Well? Do you have something you want to tell me?'

Shit.

'He's Andy Ellis-Nile.'

Ralph gave me a blank stare.

'The famous author?' I said, as if speaking to Ralph's affectedness would make things okay. I told him Andy had introduced himself to me several weeks ago.

'And you didn't think to inform me?'

'Well, we haven't exactly been speaking, have we?'

He didn't respond.

I told him Andy had very generously offered to help me with my writing and that he dropped in every now and then.

'How often is "every now and then"?'

'Once or twice a week.' *Four times a week.*

Ralph sneered.

Feeling backed into a corner, I continued defensively. 'He's been like a tutor, a mentor.'

'Yes. I can see he has a real hands-on approach.' His voice was tempered steel.

Mine became strident. 'Oh, as opposed to your hands-*off* approach the last couple of months?'

He glared at me.

'Anyway, how is this different from you spending so much time with Anthea?'

'Anthea's about work—'

'Andy's about work, too!' It annoyed me that he dismissed my writing as a hobby. Only a soft knocking at the door sliced through the heavy silence.

Ralph opened it to a blubbering Anthea.

She struggled to get the words out. 'I've just c-c-come from the h-hospital. My f-f-father had a h-h-heart attack. He didn't m-m-make it!' She threw herself into Ralph's arms and let out a howl of anguish.

I felt sorry for her. It brought back memories of my devastation when I learned of Joe's fatal heart attack. But why couldn't she find comfort in a relative's arms? Why Ralph's? I felt like a bitch.

Ralph helped a shaky Anthea into the lounge and onto the sofa. He sat side-on next to her, holding her hand.

Looks like I'm not the only one with a hands-on approach.
Again, I felt like a bitch.

He asked me to get Anthea a glass of water.

I'm not your bloody flunkey.

Like the dutiful wife that I wasn't, I filled a glass and brought it over to her. It didn't score me any brownie points with Ralph, but she thanked me with a pitiful look on her tear-streaked face. I stared at her. Her hair was all mussed like she'd just had sex and rolled out of bed. Her mascara was intact, though. *Must be waterproof.* The 'Maybe it's Maybelline' jingle started playing in my head.

Don't start humming, for God's sake!

Ralph gave me a *Get lost, I'll take it from here* look. I extended my condolences and left them to talk. I took my laptop into the study, but left the door half-open. I still didn't trust this woman. Or maybe I doubted Ralph the same way he doubted me.

Between bouts of crying, Anthea spoke about her father.

'For twenty years, I believed my mother's pregnancy with me had been the result of a one-night stand.' Sob, sob. 'It wasn't until she was on her deathbed ten years ago that I found out the truth about my father.' Resentful sob, sob. 'Daddy didn't even know I existed!'

A grown woman who refers to her father as Daddy? Isn't that kind of puerile?

'When I tracked him down—he was living in Sydney—he was devastated about having missed out on my life. He said if he'd known Mummy was pregnant, wild horses wouldn't have kept him away—'

A grown woman who refers to her mother as Mummy? Yeesh!

'—And they weren't going to anymore. Knowing he had a daughter, he moved back to Adelaide. But it brought back painful memories for him of earlier years. Daddy had been madly in love and he got the girl pregnant. Her parents made her have an abortion and wouldn't let her see him again. It was why he left Adelaide. He'd been desolate and wanted to get away from it all; you know, start afresh. It was why he moved to Sydney.'

Anthea told Ralph that Daddy started at university there. After he graduated, he became a lecturer and met Mummy several years later. The two initially bonded as ex-Adelaideans, but then towards the end of her degree, it turned into a sexual relationship. 'She was one of his students,' Anthea whispered, like it was the dirty secret that it was. Well, apparently, Daddy grew a conscience and decided he wanted to adhere to a code of conduct. 'He dumped Mummy just before she graduated and she discovered she was pregnant not long after graduation. She didn't try to contact him. Just moved back to Adelaide to have me.'

Well, dear dead Daddy, clearly you had a problem keeping your pecker in your pants, you prick! And you have a daughter with questionable morals, but who, strangely, counsels people just like you. Gotta be something Freudian in that one.

Maybe the glue that held Anthea and Ralph together was the parallels in their lives. He loosely sketched out his story for her, but he sounded like he was at a psychology symposium talking about himself as one of his case studies—no names. He didn't mention that this particular case study also used to have a problem keeping his pecker in his pants, and had become an unwitting father *and* a grandfather.

But if they both felt like they'd known each other 'since forever', why did they not already know each other's story? Odd, that.

Maybe, as he'd said, she really was about work.

The next few days suggested otherwise. Anthea took to dropping in each night at around seven to cry on Ralph's shoulder.

On the morning of day four, I approached Ralph at breakfast just as he'd scooped a spoonful out of his rockmelon half. 'Why is Anthea coming here all the time?'

He narrowed his eyes at me. 'She's just lost her father. She needs to talk.'

'Well, can't she talk to you at work?' Spoken like a petulant child.

'She's grieving. She's not *at* work.'

I shuffled my feet and muttered, 'Doesn't she have any friends to talk to? Or family?'

His scathing look shamed me to the core. 'Of course she has family and friends! But maybe they want to gag her.' A barely veiled dig at me and I didn't like it. I bit back.

'Or, just maybe she's gagging herself around them, you know, not prepared to share her feelings with those closest to her!'

He got my drift.

Out-psychologising the psychologist didn't go over well. Ralph became flustered, and with a melodramatic flourish, he dropped his rockmelon-laden spoon back into the fleshy shell. It was like, *I'm going to punish you, I'm not going to eat any more.* Where was the bloody logic in that?

He scraped his chair back and rose abruptly to his feet, binned his half-eaten breakfast, carefully placed his Royal Doulton and Wedgwood in the dishwasher, and loped off in a snit.

The next five days were Anthea-free. And Andy-free. No visits, no calls, no mentions. Neither name came up. There had to be some sort of dialogue for that to happen, and there was even less than before.

On Monday morning, I asked him why he was wearing a suit to work.

'Anthea's father's funeral is this afternoon,' he grunted.

I spent the rest of the day trying to get the creative juices flowing. A fruitless attempt. My impasse with Baubo was no closer to being resolved when Ralph walked in at five-thirty. He closed the front door and leaned against it. He was white as a sheet.

'You okay? What's wrong?'

He looked up at me, his face a mask of shock and consternation. 'Anthea's father was David Mitchell.'

'David Mitchell?

'My father,' he said impatiently as he pushed himself off the door. 'My biological father!'

CHAPTER TWENTY-TWO

Dead End

'W-what?!'

Ralph trudged past me without responding.

'How do you know?' I called after him.

He stopped, turned and stared at me like I was stupid. 'His picture was up there. In the cemetery chapel. And it was an open casket.'

Like I'm supposed to know this? They don't put pictures up at Jewish funerals, and they don't have open caskets.

Ralph stomped the rest of the way towards the bedroom. I heard the door to the en-suite slam shut.

I wanted to scream at him, 'IT'S NOT MY FAULT THEY HAVE PICTURES AND OPEN CASKETS AT NON-JEWISH FUNERALS! IT'S NOT MY FAULT YOUR FATHER DIED BEFORE YOU EVEN MET HIM!'

Be sympathetic, Ruthie. He's feeling very bruised. Play nice.

Yeah, well, what about ME?

Shh. Shh. It was no time to make things about me. I got up and went into the bedroom. It pained me to hear his soft weeping coming from the bathroom. I knocked on the door. 'Ralph?' I tried to open it, but it was locked.

'I need to be alone right now,' he said in the tone of a tormented teenager.

I sat on the bed waiting for him to surface. Hearing him vomit made me gag. I'd never been good with other people's vomit. He came out about five minutes later and headed for the kitchen. I followed him, watched him poke around in the pantry cupboard as he muttered about how untidy it was. Untidy for Ralph meant there wasn't a grid-like, alphabetised arrangement of all the elements.

He grumbled as he extracted the box of aspirin from the middle of the jumble: 'These are meant to be at the front. A for aspirin!'

Up yours, A for arsehole!

I bit my tongue. If it wasn't such a terrible time for him, I'd have said it. Still, I felt bad for even thinking it. I didn't want to be insensitive.

'Ralph, I'm really sorry about your—'

His right hand shot up like a cop stopping traffic. 'I can't talk about this at the moment.'

Terse. I stiffened; bit my tongue again. *God, give me patience.*

God gave me guidance instead. 'Fake it till you make it,' came the whisper.

Are you kidding? The Omnipotent was throwing bumper sticker slogans at me? What next, God? 'KEEP ON TRUCKIN'? 'I ♥ WHINE'?

I took a few slow, deep breaths and convinced myself that faking occasionally might have value (as long as I didn't apply this to orgasms). So, I faked altruism.

I waited for Ralph to fill a glass with water and pop his two tablets, then asked in my most cordial fake tone, 'Do you want some dinner? I've made spaghetti bolognaise.'

'I'm not hungry.'

Brusque. *Well, fuck that.*

He chugged the rest of the water.

Another couple of slow, deep breaths. Another try. 'Are you going to tell Beth?'

Like before, he looked at me as if I were stupid. 'What do you think? Of course I'm going to tell her!'

'Jesus! Why are you mad at me?'

He didn't answer, but gave me a where-do-you-want-me-to-begin? look. He washed his glass, stood it up in the dish drainer, put the aspirin box away—at the front of the pantry where it apparently 'should' be—made sure it sat parallel with the edge of the shelf, then went into the study and closed the door.

I gritted my teeth, violently shadowboxed until I was puffed out, then collapsed on the sofa in a torpid state.

I heard him talking to someone, presumably to Beth. Or maybe, himself. Or maybe, Anthea. Or ...

Oh, my Lord! The hard-hitting truth: Anthea, the siren, like those beautiful but dangerous mythical creatures that lured sailors to their doom with their mellifluous voices. Anthea, his ... sister!

No wonder he was so pissed. Ralph had been bewitched by his witchy sister! Half-sister. Whatever. They shared the same sperm donor.

I started to laugh. Silently, though. I doubled up and shook with laughter and, at the same time, prayed that he wouldn't come out of that room and see me.

By the time he emerged half an hour later, the hilarity had passed. In an aloof tone, he announced he was going to bed, he was tired.

Sweet dreams, wackadoodle.

I got up, filled a bowl with a large portion of the spag bol, nuked it, and sat at the kitchen bench eating. I wondered if Anthea knew. Had Ralph told her? *I hope so.* I laughed at the thought of what that would have been like, then the humour started to ebb.

Eating alone had never fazed me, but loneliness came out of left field and washed over me. Tears stung my eyes as a more sombre realisation crossed my mind. I'd have thought this turn of events would lessen the tension between us, bring us closer together. Instead, it was looking like it might drive us further apart.

I put my bowl in the dishwasher, moved back to the lounge and lay spread-eagled on the sofa.

Should I ring Beth to see how she was after hearing the news about David? No. I couldn't be sure Ralph had called her yet. And if he had, calling her now would be more about my needs than hers. Better to wait a day or two and hope that reaching out to her would be a goodwill gesture rather than a self-serving move.

I stared at the ceiling for an hour. It wasn't much of a conversationalist, so I called it a night.

I slipped into my jim-jams, slipped under the covers and turned onto my side to face Ralph. He lay on his back, breathing evenly. Should I reach out and touch him? Wake him by initiating post-funeral sex as a means of affirming life? Maybe not. It would probably negate mine if he knocked back my advances, and I feared I'd feel used if he succumbed to them.

Flipping over to face the window, I indulged in some useless rationalising:

a. Ralph's discovery was one of epic proportions.

b. His reaction to me isn't about me. It isn't personal.

c. Everyone has his or her own way of dealing with grief.

I'd made no overtures, and so I hadn't given him the opportunity to rebuff me and negate my life. I did that all on my own when I addressed the ABCs of my rationales:

a. All the more reason he should share it with me.

b. Seriously? His rudeness towards me isn't *about me?*

c. I've always been his go-to girl when he's experienced grief in the past. Always.

Panic set in and I felt oxygen deprived—*Ah-ha-ah-ha-ah-ha*. It was probably how Sisyphus had felt. This king in Greek mythology would roll a huge round rock to the top of a mountain, only to have it roll back down. The schlub kept at it again and again, each time with the same result. In his defence, the gods had condemned him to this in perpetuity. He didn't have a choice. I did.

Or, maybe not.

I stopped rationalising, but then my mind rapid-fired through the proverbial five stages of my own grief: denial, anger, bargaining, depression and acceptance. I recycled them. After the fifth circuit, and tired from the rock and rolling, I fell asleep.

I slept through the night—a rarity—and woke with a start. Ralph's side of the bed was empty. The clock showed **7:35**. Almost eleven hours' sleep, yet I was dog-tired.

The room felt like a cesspit. I groaned, dragged myself out of bed, waded through the swampy energy towards the bathroom, and splashed cold water on my face. It didn't help. I donned my bathrobe and shuffled into the kitchen. A showered, shaved and dressed Ralph was loading his breakfast crockery and cutlery into the dishwasher.

'Morning.'

'Morning,' he said without even looking at me.

'Ralph—'

His traffic-cop hand went up like it had the day before.

'Can we please talk?'

'Not now, I'm going to work.'

Not now was repeated so often by the end of the week, it had taken on an air of banality. Ralph remained incommunicado. The crusader for Anthea's free expression was not allowing me mine.

He was leaving for work early, coming home late, and eating dinner by himself in front of the television or in the kitchen. Wherever I was, he made sure he wasn't.

Things were getting out of hand. Something had to give.

It was about to.

CHAPTER TWENTY-THREE

Fanning Old (Twin) Flames

I hadn't seen Andy or heard from him since Ralph had walked in and caught us doing nothing. Was Andy scared of Ralph or just being respectful of me? Whatever the reason, his unexplained absence hurt. I knew it was for the best, but it felt like another loss.

Loss seemed to be the prevailing state of affairs.

I'd spoken to Beth a couple of days after David Mitchell's funeral. I didn't have to fake it till I made it with her. She had an open heart and was willing to talk about her pain. Even though I knew the story of her and David's star-crossed love, I also knew that retelling helped the grieving process, so I let her talk.

Somehow, it didn't feel right to mention my increasing sense of despondency. But, I needed a shoulder to cry on. My husband the psychologist had always been it. Now, he was the reason I needed one. Anthea had his shoulder; I didn't. Maxi and Vette were both still away (and still knew nothing about

Anthea), I couldn't talk to Rhea without revealing the root of it all, I didn't want to burden Casper, Hannah still kept me at arm's length, and much as I loved Iris, who, like Maxi had a take-no-prisoners 'tude, it wasn't what I needed right now.

I felt very alone.

I wondered who Ralph was unburdening himself to. He'd told Beth about David that evening after the funeral, but she hadn't spoken to him since. She'd left him messages; he hadn't responded. Had he been talking to Anthea? Surely he'd told her the truth. Or had he? I was dying to ask him, but didn't dare. By Saturday late afternoon, I'd have my answer.

'Hello, Ruth,' Anthea said when I opened the door to her.

Jesus, I'm going to get a doormat. A personalised unwelcome one emblazoned with, SHIT, NOT YOU AGAIN, ANTH.

Reluctantly, I let her in, called out to Ralph, and gave her a quick once-over.

She wore a pair of red and black paisley leggings with red, rhinestone-studded sandals. Her white, gossamer-thin, off-the-shoulder gypsy shirt with three-quarter length sleeves was a loose fit, but it still accentuated her curves and nipples. And it enhanced her deeply bronzed skin, which suggested she'd been sunning herself daily for a month in the tropics.

Really? This is your mourning look?

Ralph emerged from the bedroom. The wide-eyed expression on his flushed face when he saw her said it all. The vamp didn't yet know.

Showtime! It was the most excited I'd been all week. I hated that about myself.

Ralph didn't have to ask me if he could claim the living space. He gave me a look that said *On yer bike.* I retrieved my laptop from the dining room table, took it into the study and stood by the door, listening.

'How are you? How are you?' said the parrot to the vampire.

'Oh, you know ... I've been spending a lot of time sitting by the beach.'

Explains the tan. But then, we also need to factor in that Daddy's nanna was Aboriginal. Did Daddy tell you that?

'I've missed our chats,' she said in a sultry tone. 'You haven't returned my calls. Is everything okay with you?'

A silence followed. I strained to hear.

'Ralph?'

'Anthea. There's something you need to know.'

Huzzah! But hold the phone ...

There was something Ralph needed to know, like, I didn't appreciate it that each time this Playboy Bunny came over, I was relegated to what felt like the servants' quarters. In my own home, the one I'd bought with the proceeds of my divorce—my own money!

'Her name's Beth,' Ralph said.

'What? Whose name is Beth?' Anthea said as I came out of the room, reclaiming my rights. Sort of reclaiming them. I stole into the kitchen and pretended to forage for food. Ralph wouldn't have questioned this even though I'd had a huge afternoon tea. Domesticated ruminants graze all day.

I moved to the breakfast bar where I had a clear view of Anthea's face.

'The woman who was the love of your father's life. Her name's Beth.'

'Uh, yeah, I know. But,' Anthea squinted at him, puzzled, 'I don't recall telling you that.'

He shook his head. 'You didn't tell me. And Beth didn't terminate the pregnancy, as David was led to believe.'

'Wha—how—'

'Beth had me.' Ever the cryptographer, Ralph would have been an asset to the Allies during wartime.

Anthea stared at him, a confused expression crossing her face as she tried to digest the implications of what he'd said.

Come on! It's not that hard. Then again, when digestion wasn't required often, it didn't work too efficiently.

I projected telepathically: *David was HIS father too.*

She must have heard it. Her breath caught and she slapped both hands over her mouth.

Yeeeeeah. He's your half-brother. So, any designs you had on him—

I knocked over a glass in my exuberance. Ralph turned around and shot me daggers. I quickly moved back to the servants' quarters with the sounds of Anthea's wheezy chant playing in the background: 'Oh my God, oh my God, oh my God!' No more the alluring siren song. Instead, the sound of Echo, the tragic wood nymph in Greek mythology who couldn't tell Narcissus she was in love with him.

The nympho started wailing.

Did this mean she *had* slept with Ralph? *Oh my God, oh my God, oh my God!*

The thought of it was disgusting. It was wrong on so many levels, but that one thought that he might have cheated on me left me feeling like I'd been steamrolled.

Not wanting to hear anymore, I closed the door, sat down, doubled over, and rocked. It had a calming effect. The fear and uncertainty lingered, but I was thinking more rationally. Maybe Anthea was also rocking, because her keening abated. Muffled conversation replaced it. And as much as I didn't want to know, I needed to face the possibility that something had gone on between them. So, I cracked open the door. Ralph was speaking.

He was spilling his guts, telling Anthea about Alex and Luca. And like a backing vocalist, she was making *hm-mmm-I-see* noises. Clearly, she wasn't focused because it was the wrong chorus. *Whoa-aah-no way!* would have been more appropriate.

But how could you be focused when you've just found out the man you had the hots for and, God help me, probably slept wi—

'As for you and me, it explains the kinship we've both felt.'

Kinship? Did Ralph say kinship? Oh God, he said kinship. He didn't say attraction. He didn't say he was attracted to her. And he hadn't said anything about them being Twin Flames or showering together in his hotel room in Canberra and him pinning her against the tiles as they had wild sex and both came at the same time as the water cascaded over their spent, naked bodies! Oh God, had I read it all wrong? I must have.

Relief flooded my fully-clothed body, but then I was awash with shame. I closed the door again.

Rocking didn't do diddly-squat this time. It wasn't going to fix my impaired imagination. I'd been unfair to Ralph. I needed to make amends, was determined to.

For the next ten minutes until I heard the front door close, I rehearsed what I would say. Ralph knocked on the study door and opened it a little.

'Ralph, I—'

'I'm moving out.'

CHAPTER TWENTY-FOUR

A Cold Day in Hell

'Wha-what?' I stammered. I hadn't rehearsed for this.

'The tenant's lease on my apartment is up and he's not renewing. I'm going to move back in there for a while. I think it's best.'

'I-I, best for whom?' I felt sick. 'Best for *you*? What about me?' It didn't seem that long ago he'd asked me the same question when I told him not to say anything to Alex. I could tell by the look on his face he was also remembering it.

He opened his mouth to respond, to throw it back in my face, but then just shook his head. 'I'm too tired to keep doing this.'

Before I could challenge him, he disappeared into the garage and came back wheeling a suitcase. I moved into the lounge and collapsed onto the sofa, feeling nothing and staring at nothing as I listened to him sliding open the wardrobe doors and drawers.

Twenty minutes later, he walked out without a word.

I moved to the bedroom, got under the doona and turned on the electric blanket. It was a sunny, warm 28°C outside. Inside me, it was sunless and sub-zero.

* * * *

Thinking about it now made me shiver.

Sylvia-gull shivered. It was hardly an empathetic response. My mother's suffocating and interfering ways had always meant *what's yours is mine and what's mine is yours,* especially where feelings were concerned. No boundaries.

I cried and thought back to how pitifully I'd howled when the thaw came on and reality hit.

* * * *

When I was all cried out, I lay there immobilised. The ringing phone startled me.

'H-hello.'

'Hi, darling.' It was Beth. 'I'm sorry I didn't call you back yesterday. It was a rough one.'

I couldn't respond, save for a small whimper that escaped my lips.

'Ruthie? What's wrong?'

The dam burst. I started crying. 'H-he doesn't w-want me, Beth. Ralph doesn't want me. He's moved out.'

'What?!'

'He l-l-left me.'

'Oh, sweetheart. I'm coming over now.'

'No. It's—I'm a mess.'

'I'm coming; it's not negotiable!'

Twenty-five minutes later, I fell into Beth's loving arms. She held me as I cried, then we moved to the lounge and sat next to each other. I told her everything and I didn't hold back when it came to Anthea.

Beth gasped, and like Anthea had, she slapped both hands over her mouth. 'Good God! He told me she was just a colleague.'

'I don't think he did anything, but she was definitely hitting on him.'

'Oh Lord, can you imagine ...?'

I didn't tell her that I already had. In the shower with her legs wrapped around his waist, on the bed, on the hotel dresser, in the—

'Ruthie, Ralph will come around.' Beth's tone was kind but firm as she cut into my thoughts. 'I think he's angry with women at the moment. And if he was attracted to this woman before he knew, it would certainly add insult to injury.' She became pensive, her brows furrowing as she considered this. 'And look, I knew the day would come when he got angry with me. He still hasn't returned any of my calls. I expected the honeymoon phase to pass. You know, that joy of discovering his long-lost mum, then the bitterness over my abandoning him, even though it was out of my hands. It seems like David's passing has dredged everything up. The whole damn lot,' she muttered. 'He's angry with Larissa for depriving him of his son, understandably. And like a child, he's angry with you for not letting him get his own way.' She took my hands in hers. 'And darling, trust me, all his training in human behaviour won't make a scrap of difference.'

I nodded as I took this in, then said, 'He's not angry at Anthea.'

'No. Anthea's not part of the "conspiracy".'

I understood what she meant. She continued: 'There's a lot there for him to work through, but he's a smart man. He'll figure it out. He will.'

'But Norma left him alone to work through his stuff with her and it took him almost three years to even begin to make peace with her! What if it's the same with me?'

Beth shook her head. 'It won't be. And I'll give him a boot up the backside if he drags his heels!'

'Thank you. That makes me feel better.'

'For now.' Beth gave me a knowing smile.

I smiled back at my wise mother-in-law and said, 'I love you.'

'I love you too, sweetie. You're like a daughter. And I'm always here for you.'

Beth wanting me was framed against Ralph not wanting me. It brought fresh tears to the surface.

After she left, I demolished a packet of Tim Tams in the hope of lapsing into a food coma. It didn't work, so I crawled back into bed. I lay there, wretched, thinking about Mr Kosta and how his teachings had sustained me in the past; how they'd shown me not to take life too literally, too personally or too seriously. Yes. The tragicomedy of life. But right now, none of this helped.

'He literally left me. It's personal. And seriously, fuck you, Mr Kosta and God! All I can see is tragedy.'

I cried myself into a deep sleep that was haunted by a series of disturbing dreams. And there was no reprieve. Yet, I slept through the night without having to answer the call of nature. I woke at six and went to the loo, splashed cold water on my face and groaned as I took in the puffy eyes reflected in the mirror. I went back to bed and cried until I fell asleep again.

Bed became my habitat for the next couple of days. I was wracked with grief, made even more acute because there was no word from Ralph. It was like I ceased to exist.

On day three, I contemplated ending it all. The intensity of the impulse scared me enough to reach out to someone, but it didn't feel right to call Beth. Maxi and Vette were back from their respective trips. I called them. Both wanted to come over. I told each I wanted to be alone, but that just telling them had defused the death-wish and some of the pain. I didn't have the energy to talk, much less gossip, so I didn't say anything about Anthea. I didn't have the wherewithal to crow over anything. Besides, that sense of schadenfreude had boomeranged—who was now laughing at whom?

Both girls said to call if I needed them, and they'd drop everything. I knew they would. We three had always been there for each other, except for that one time when Ralph and I had changed the status of our relationship, and Maxi shunned us both. Our union had brought up painful, deep-seated feelings of insecurity for her that she didn't know how to cope with. Was it the same for Ralph now? *Who knows, who cares?*

On day five, late afternoon, I suspended my yo-yo of anguish and animosity. Worry had overtaken me.

Maybe he's dead. Would I have heard? Am I listed as his next of kin?

I called the practice. The receptionist Sonia knew my voice, so I disguised it—increased it in pitch and put on a Scottish accent. Sleuth Ruth.

'Wad Dawkter Rrralph Brrrill be thar t'dey?'

No, he wasn't in.

I felt a lurch in my stomach. *Oh God, something has happened to him, I know it.* I called his apartment. He answered; I hung up.

Real mature. It was the sort of thing Maxi, Vette and I used to do as teenagers: 'Hello, are you on the line? You better get off, a train's coming!'

This was different. I needed to know he hadn't been hit by a train. Anyway, he didn't have Caller ID. Or did he? *What if he's added it? Shit. Still, if he has, shouldn't he have returned my call to see why I was calling him?*

By nightfall, back to hating him again, back in my unmade bed and curled up in a foetal position, I stared at the electronic number display on the bedside clock and watched the time change. Digital, red, light-emitting diodes; little limbs on a black background. What it must be like—must have been like—in utero, advanced pregnancy. Imprisoned. Restricted movement in a confined space.

It was the colour of hell and it was hypnotic.

CHAPTER TWENTY-FIVE

Funny Farm

Ding dong. Ding dong. Ding dong.

The doorbell jolted me out of my trance. Or a deep sleep. The red stick segments showed it was just past midnight.

With my heart racing, I bolted out of bed and made for the front door, flicked the porch light on and ripped the door open.

Ralph stood on the other side with a 9mm Beretta pointed at my head.

Bang, bang!

I woke with a start, my mouth dry, my breathing ragged. *Ah-ha-ah-ha-ah-ha.*

Shh, shh. It was just a bad dream. *Shh, shh.*

I took some slow, deep breaths until I calmed. Better. But how the hell would I have known what type of gun it was? *Man, I watch way too many cop shows.*

I dragged myself up to a semi-sitting position, slumped back against the bedhead and massaged my throbbing temples. Even my hair hurt.

What day is it?

Oh, yes. Day six. Or was it seven? Or eight? Who knew? I cried again and fell back asleep.

Ding dong. Ding dong. Ding dong.

The sound of the doorbell was like cymbals striking against the sides of my head. No dream this time. I looked at the clock: **7:05** am.

What? It was too early to have visitors. *I'm closed. Go away.*

The bell rang again; the caller was insistent.

Oh God. What if my dream had been a premonition and Ralph really was there with a gun?

Who cares? At least it'll put me out of my misery.

Ding dong. Again!

It couldn't be Ralph. Hit men are supposed to be calm and patient, and it was clear the person at the door wasn't. Ralph was generally calm and patient. Maybe that was a pretence. Could it be his early modelling career had been a cover and he *had* been a sniper for the 2nd Commando Regiment? Maybe he was preying on my fear. He knew I wouldn't ignore the doorbell now because I had a thing about early-morning and late-night phone calls or visits—these potential whorebringers of doom.

Another *ding dong* was followed by a loud rapping.

It was the sort of thing the police did, rang the bell then rapped if there was no answer. In TV shows, at least. What if something had happened to Ralph? I must be listed as his next of kin and this would be the police!

Too terrified to move, but then, needing to know, I slipped into my bathrobe and yelled, 'I'm coming!' as I held my head and stumbled to the door.

I partially opened it, peeked out and rubbed my eyes. It was not a pair of men in blue. But what fresh hell was this?

A pair of hillbillies stood on the other side.

'Yes?' I grunted.

'Hi. We're your new nixt door neighbours,' the man said.

Phoebe and Zac, who'd owned the adjoining duplex, had moved out a week ago. We'd hugged our goodbyes and promised to stay in touch. 'Oh, and say bye to Ralph,' Phoebe had called out as she got into her car. Who knew her words would be prophetic?

I'd heard the comings and goings of another set of removalists on Tuesday, but I'd been too disconsolate to even go watch the action through the lounge-room window.

I rubbed my eyes again and stared at the new owners. A corn-fed Ma and Pa Kettle, they looked to be in their mid-forties. They stood there grinning like manic monkeys as I sized them up.

Wide-mouthed Ma had pasty skin; a flat, turned-up nose; and jellyfish-blue eyes with saggy bags under them and an un-tweezed, mono-brow pelmet above them. She had a large head that sprouted black, woolly, Maggi Noodle hair, and she wore a khaki midi-skirt and a clinging beige tee with a plaid peplum. Her big tits, along with the three tiered rolls of fat under them, resembled a dog's four sets of post-partum teats.

Pa had a thatch of red hair, his freckled face was shaped like a butternut pumpkin, and his ears stuck out like a pair of ailerons—a desirable feature for a winged being, but it would have got him beaten up in the schoolyard. His duds complemented hers—khaki tee under tight, beige overalls. The straps needed some serious lowering to overcome the unsightly moose knuckle and cut his balls some slack.

He and she were the perfect combo, and not just because they were mix and match. He was the shape of a triangle, she, the shape of an inverted triangle. Their sex life was probably interesting.

He cleared his throat and formally introduced himself and his pardner. 'I'm Bin en' thus us Bitty.'

Huh? 'Bin an' Bitty?'

'No. Bin en' Bitty.' He emphasised the names.

'Uh ...' I scratched my fragile head. 'Isn't that what I said?'

'No. You sid Bin en' Bitty.'

Huh? 'Oh.' They were Kiwis. 'Ben and Betty!'

'Yip. End you are ...?'

Too goddamn tired to hobnob. 'Ruth.'

'Hi, Ruth.' He lunged forward, grabbed my hand, which I didn't offer, and started pumping it. It was like he was shaking a bottle of bubbly. What was inside my head started to fizz and was threatening to explode if the pressure jacked up. Thankfully, he stopped, but he didn't shut up.

'Jes' wanting to warn you, you'll prob'ly cop the smill of pissed aside wafting today. Bitty here hess bun bedlee butt'n.'

I once worked with a New Zealander. It hadn't taken me long to grasp the vernacular. I was good enough with languages that I didn't need storytelling with props. I wished I'd said so now.

Bitty lifted her skirt to show me a whole lot of nasty red welts on her inner thighs. It was too much information for this early in the morning. Hell, it was too much information at any time of the day. Or night. I had to look away.

'End litting you know too, I'll be benging away working un the beckyard. Not tilling you on what, though. Et's a surprise.' Bin clicked his tongue and winked at me.

Like I give a rat's arse. I responded with a wan smile.

It took a few moments of awkward silence for it to become clear to Bin and Bitty that I wasn't going to invite them in.

Bin said, 'Right. Need to git working. En' Bitty's stull got lots of unpecking to do. The early bird cetches the worm, eh?'

Maybe in the country, but there are no fucking roosters in suburbia. I hoped to God this man, who was used to waking up to *cock-a-doodle-doo*, didn't start his 'benging' so early in the coming mornings.

I closed the door and leaned against it. 'Jesus. From Portnoy to this? Not funny, God. Why me? Why me?!'

An answer came from above—from the land of the long white cloud: *'You wanted comedy. Be careful what you wush for.'*

I laughed, then I cried. I had a shower, cried, made myself some breakfast—toast and tea—cried, and went back to bed. I stayed there for most of the day, only leaving it for sustenance: packets of chips, bags of lollies, biscuits, Panadol.

It was a long day. Come eight-thirty, I was exhausted from my tormented emotional state. And the on-and-off headache was now a mother of a headache, made worse by Bin's benging and the strong chemical stench of 'pissed aside'. I upgraded to two Panadeine caplets, returned the box to the *front* of the pantry, and opened the bedroom window. But the air outside still stunk. I closed it again, got under the doona and turned the light out. I was unable to sleep, and again, was unable to stop the tears. I finally dozed off after about an hour, but was then woken by a faint noise.

The red diodes said **11:13**. I strained my ears to try and discern what I was hearing. It sounded like the mewling of an injured animal. I got out of bed, moved to the window and cracked it open.

'Uh oh ah oh uh uh uh. Oh Bin ...'

Oh.

Howdy Doody, who had benged in his beckyard all afternoon, was now benging in his bidroom! Lucky bitch Bitty was gitting laid. I stayed at the window and tuned in to the live broadcast. It was the closest I'd come to having sex in a while. Real sex, not imagined.

The volume went up a notch; the homespun, high-frequency rhapsodies went on and on.

'Oh OH UH OH AH UH ...'

And on and on.

Their stamina was impressive, but it was becoming wearisome. I rested my forehead against the cool pane.

'Oh OH UH OH AH UH ...'

Jesus, would ya come already so we can all get some sleep.

'AAAAAAAH YES YES AAAAH OH GOD!'

Thank Christ.

A minute of silence passed. Then ...

'Uh uh uh UH ...'

Huh. Dowdy, but hot stuff in the sack. Bitty, who had barely said boo, was having multiple orgasms. It made me nostalgic, but it was hardly a turn-on. Again, I heard the words, *'Be careful what you wush for.'*

'Hello—I didn't "wush" for this! All I'd said was their sex life was probably interesting.' But it wasn't like I'd imagined it.

Now, the image of these two bumping uglies was enough to make me consider celibacy. Consider? I was already celibate.

I thought of what Ralph might say in this situation. His sharp wit and his comebacks were priceless. I sniggered. And then I was in stitches, roaring with laughter.

The *uh uh oh-ing* stopped. A window slammed shut.

Oops. I felt guilty, so I closed my window. But I laughed even harder. Until the laughs turned to tears and heaving sobs.

The next couple of days were a blur. Bin benged by day and by night. I laughed and cried by night after making futile attempts to beng away at my keyboard by day. Like Ralph, Baubo had also jilted me. There was no word from either. And I remembered there had been no word from Casper.

That one didn't trouble me. I assumed it meant he was having a good time. He was on uni break and holidaying in Bali. He'd left the day before Ralph moved out, and we exchanged texts the day after, but I didn't mention this in the text. I didn't want to spoil my son's vacation, and I didn't have the energy to explain anything. But I had to when he got back and called me.

Casper was upset. Did I want him to read Ralph the riot act? No. Did I want him to chew Hannah's arse? No. Could he, though, for all the grief she'd given him as a child? 'Knock yourself out,' I told him. Did I want him to bring over some comfort food like maybe some rice pudding from the uni cafeteria? My boy! Words of comfort and a small ray of light in the dark.

One morning, I flopped out of bed at eight, feeling punch-drunk from another angst-ridden night. I was tucking into a bowl of industrial-strength chocolate ice cream for breakfast when the phone rang. It was Hannah.

She'd just spent a fortnight on the Gold Coast with Alex and Luca. She didn't know about Ralph. I'd called the day before they left to wish them a safe trip, but she didn't take the call. I'd left a message. Then I'd called yesterday, a couple of hours after their scheduled return, to welcome them home. She'd taken the call.

Did they have a good time? 'Yes.' Silence.

How was Luca? 'Good.' Silence.

Hannah's responses yesterday had been monosyllabic, her tone clipped. Now, her tone was offhand.

'Can you babysit Luca tomorrow morning?'

There was no *Hi*. No *How are you?* No *Please*.

I didn't answer.

'Are you there?'

I sighed. 'Yes, I'm here.'

'I said, can you—'

'I heard what you said. And I can. But no, I won't. Frankly, I'm getting tired of your coldness and your rudeness. I'm sick of you taking out your anger at Ralph on me. And until you're ready to show me some respect as a human being—not just as a mother, but as a human being—then don't ask me to do things for you. In fact, don't call me.' I put the phone down.

It was a tough call, but one I needed to make. I adored my grandson and I was more than happy to babysit him whenever, but I didn't much adore feeling used and abused. Especially not by my own child.

After the horrid past few days, the uneasy past few weeks and months, I felt a bit stronger. And inspired. I sat in front of the computer and the words that had been backed up for too long came out in fits and starts. I wrote for two hours without a break. Only the jarring sound of the doorbell stopped me.

Now what!

Could it be Andy? I'd lost track of time but it had to be a good month since we'd had any contact. I hoped it wasn't him. I was still in my nightie. Not that I cared about how I looked this time, I just wasn't in the mood. I entertained the idea of ignoring it, but thought better of it, darted into the bedroom, grabbed my bathrobe, and threw it on.

I opened the front door and immediately regretted it. It was the hick.

'Morning, Ruth. Would you like to unwind wuth me en' Bitty on my brend-new dick.'

What the fuck?

Apart from the fact that only a sea slug was capable of regrowing a brand-new dick, it seemed that Bin and Bitty were into some very kinky sexual practices.

Bin stared at me. I stared back with a look that said *You sick, dirty bastard.*

He shuffled uncomfortably and cleared his throat. 'Et's what I've bun working on. Iricting a dick.'

I still couldn't find words.

He cleared his throat. 'New tumber dicking in the beckyard.'

Oh. My language interpretation skills had momentarily gone AWOL, but they were back. New Zealand-speak for new timber decking.

'The old dick was worn out.'

No surprise there, try taking a night off. 'Uh, um. Look, thank you. But'— I turned and pointed to the computer—'I have so much work to do today. Haven't even had time for a shower yet.'

His gaze roamed over me. It made me want to throw up in my mouth.

'Will, the offer stends. Pop by inny time.'

Right. Just like you do. UNANNOUNCED. 'Thanks.' *Now piss off!*

I closed the door, made a dash for the bathroom and ran the shower hot to wash away the scuzzy sensations. Twenty minutes later, I was back in front of the computer with a cup of coffee and a piece of toast. Another hour of clacking away at the keyboard sped by when the doorbell rang again.

Jeeeeesus! WHAT? Who the hell is it this time?!

Bin asking me again to sit on his dick? Peter Pandy from across the road wanting to hang with me again because I'd hung on his every word—every noun, verb, adjective and the other five fucking parts of speech? Jehovah's Witnesses wanting to quote biblical verse to me and share the word of God? *Go next door, arseholes.* She *shares the word 'God' every fucking night!*

With a clenched fist, I marched over to the door and ripped it open, ready to deck (or dick, as Bin would say) the trespasser.

It was Hannah.

CHAPTER TWENTY-SIX

My Sorry Lot

She looked miserable. 'I'm sorry, Mum.' She started crying. I pulled her into a hug and cried with her.

Hannah had a couple of hours to herself. She'd left Luca in Norma's care and he was having his daily nap. We moved to the kitchen and I made us tea while she scanned the contents of the fridge. Finding nothing worthwhile there, she raided the pantry and pulled out the biscuit barrel. Hannah was like me. Her appetite never waned, no matter what.

'It's been so hard,' she said as we sat opposite each other at the breakfast bar. 'Alex has been moody and snappy and, for a while there, he was barely speaking to me. Like, as if this is *my* fault!' Her cheeks flushed as realisation dawned. 'Oh. It's not yours either. I really am sorry, Mummy.'

It warmed my heart on the odd occasion that Hannah called me Mummy. But unlike Anthea, she wouldn't be caught dead referring to me as Mummy when she spoke *about* me to someone!

Still, a warm heart, not a bleeding heart. 'Okay,' I said. 'But you freezing me out like that, it's not the first time, Hannah. I hope it'll be the last, though, because I don't deserve it and I don't appreciate it. It hurts.'

'I know. It won't happen again, Mum. Promise, cross my heart.' She made the sign with her finger.

We both relaxed and took a sip of tea. Then Hannah blew out a ragged breath and said, 'To make things worse, I've had Rhea in my ear about Alex. Wanting to know why he's being cold and distant with her.'

I laughed. Hannah looked at me in horror.

'Oh, I shouldn't laugh; it's not funny. But it kind of is. Like father, like son. Ralph's not speaking to Beth and ... he's moved out.'

Her jaw dropped. *'What?'*

I brought her up to speed on what had happened between Ralph and me after the big reveal.

'What is the *matter* with him?'

I gave her a helpless shrug. 'I wish I knew.'

She brought me up to speed on what had happened between Alex and her and about their holiday up north. I told her what Beth had said. I told her about Andy—a censored account—and about Portnoy's gnomes. She giggled. And when I told her about Anthea—also a censored account—she shook her head in disbelief. 'Oh, wow, this is the sort of stuff you only expect to see in movies!'

Then I gave her a blow-by-blow description of Bin and Bitty. Hannah whooped with laughter but cringed at the thought of 'old peeps doing it'. I cringed at the thought of being in her 'old peeps' category.

We were on our second cups when we got down to the nitty gritty. Hannah was ready to talk about the issue itself.

I told her what had raised Ralph's suspicions and how finding out about his indigenous great-grandmother had more or less confirmed them. I watched as the cogs in her head cartwheeled for a few seconds before they came to an abrupt halt. 'OhmyGod! It explains Luca's skin tone ...'

'Mmhmm.'

I defended Ralph's right to know, but not the way he went about letting Alex know. She agreed with me.

It was good to reconnect with my daughter again. We talked and ate non-stop for two hours and could have kept going, but Hannah needed to get home to Luca, who'd be waking soon. I asked if she'd said anything to Norma.

'No way! I haven't told anyone. Alex needs to be okay with it all first.'

Oh boy, please don't ask me if I've told anyone. I doubted she'd mind that Maxi and Vette knew, but I didn't feel resilient enough at the moment to wear her anger if she did mind. She didn't ask.

'And to be honest,' she continued, 'pissed as I am at Ralph, I'm also kinda relieved Alex's idiot father isn't his real father. Or, God, Luca's real grandfather!'

'Ooh, can I please, *please* be the one to tell Hector when the time comes?'

'Nuh-uh. When the time comes, he's all mine!'

I told her I hadn't heard from Norma, so I assumed she didn't know about Ralph moving out. 'Please don't say anything to her. It'll upset her, and I'm in no space to try an' placate her.'

'I won't. Ralph can do his own dirty work, anyways.'

Hannah invited me to her place for dinner that night. It was an opportunity to mend fences with Alex. And even though the thought of going out touched off some anxiety, I knew if I didn't leave my hidey-hole, it would become a prison.

I hyperventilated on the drive there, but Luca's greeting and cuddles were a panacea. Hannah gave me a belated birthday present—Pandora charms—and apologised for not calling on the day. And then, the three of us laid everything bare. It helped tear down walls and repair our relationships all around.

The creative blocks also completely dissolved. For the rest of the week I cried profusely and typed away in equal measure. I was hurting. Productive, but hurting. Andy still kept his distance, adding to the hurt. Bin and Bitty stayed away too, which didn't hurt. Not even a teensy bit. But the thought of going to Maxi and Nestor's party the following Saturday night was agonising.

They'd moved into their penthouse apartment on Monday. A couple of weeks before that, Maxi sent out official, jazzy, snail-mail invitations to their housewarming. It seemed a bit over the top, but Maxi never did anything by half measure.

Some weeks earlier, she'd told Vette, Iris, Rhea, and me to save the date. Because Ralph and I were barely speaking, I hadn't said anything to him about it. The invitation arrived after he'd moved out and it was addressed to Ruth. Not Ruth and Ralph. This had upset me. Was I already considered a single entity? Unyoked? Did Maxi really see me this way? Or, maybe not inviting Ralph was her way of being protective of me. I thought back to our conversation.

'I did invite him.'

'Oh.'

'I thought it might be easier on you if I sent out separate invitations.'

'Mm. He hasn't accepted, has he?'

Maxi hesitated. 'He texted and yes, he accepted.'

It felt like a kick in the gut. Newly separated and he was ready to party!

'Well, I'm sorry. I'll have to warm your house another time. Preferably when he's not there!'

Maxi sighed. 'Look, Ruthie. My loyalties lie with you first and foremost. And you know that. But he's been a big part of my life too.'

'I know he has, but it's not like it's a gala, it's just a housewarming.'

I heard the sharp inhale over the radio waves, then she spoke in a small voice that was so unlike her. 'It's important to me.'

Shit. Maxi, who'd put herself on standby for me. Me, who'd been so self-involved. 'Oh, Max, I'm sorry. That was insensitive. And unfair.' And I didn't want to be that person who asked my friends to choose between Ralph and me.

The tension vanished. 'Honey, I know you're going through a really shitty time, but you *have* to come. Please.'

Maxi didn't ask much of me. 'Okay. I'll be there, I promise.' I needed to suck it up and do the right thing by my friend.

I woke on Saturday morning with the terrifying realisation that I'd be seeing Ralph that night, followed by the grisly realisation that I'd also be seeing Hector. *I'd rather plug my twat with a jalapeño suppository.*

CHAPTER TWENTY-SEVEN

Not So Black & White

At eight-twenty, I buzzed the intercom. Thirty seconds later, the private elevator's doors opened.

Wow! State-of-the-art. The lift's interior matched my exterior. Black and white. It had a shiny, black-tiled floor, sidewalls in horizontal panels of white back-painted glass, and an ebony veneer ceiling. I was wearing a man-eating, Dalmatian-print jumpsuit that I'd bought a month ago. Sleeveless, it had a plunging neckline, a fitted waist with a tie belt, and relaxed legs elasticised at the ankles. I'd teamed it with black, strappy kitten-heel sandals and a black shoulder bag with a white appliqué trim.

Synchronicity? Or system integration? Whatever. *I am so meant to be here tonight.*

As the lift ascended, I took in my image in the full-length, mirrored back wall. The ceiling's recessed downlights cast a soft glow that made me look hot. The mirror: my erstwhile nemesis was being merciful.

Eat your heart out, Ralph!

Or not. *Crap.*

The price tag was still attached. I pulled it off and shoved it in my bag.

I rested the bag on the sleek satin, stainless steel handrail and tightened the tie belt. Despite eating garbage for the last few weeks, the waistline of the jumpsuit was looser than when I'd first tried it on in the shop. Anxiety has a way of whittling away flesh, and the closer the lift got to the top, the more weight I was shedding!

The doors slid open and the silence gave way to a hubbub of chatter and laughter.

Ah-ha-ah-ha-ah-ha. I am so NOT meant to be here tonight.

I wanted to remain the chameleon in the lift and was tempted to hit the G-button. *Ralph knows where my G-button is—*

No, no! I had to stay present; I didn't want to leave *me*. But I couldn't leave the party either. Wouldn't. I needed to stay as much for myself as for Maxi. So, I took several tentative steps across the marble foyer.

I stopped and stood in the imposing entryway; felt dwarfed by it as I looked into a massive lounge. The apartment itself seemed stately. With floor-to-ceiling window walls, it'd be a bright area by day. But now, the city skyline was putting on a spectacular light show without even trying. Pity it didn't lighten my mood.

I took a calming breath and scanned the sea of faces, left to right. My bad. I clapped eyes on him. My husband. My *estranged* husband. Standing about seven metres away with his left shoulder casually propped against the wall, he was talking to Henry and Joel. The two women in front of him moved away at that very moment, affording me a more or less full-frontal view of him. He looked devastatingly handsome in a slim-fit white shirt with black buttons, a black collar, black cuffs, and a two-tone chest pocket. He wore it tails untucked over black chinos.

Awesome. We're in sync. But I feel more at one with the black-and-white lift than I do with you. And, what? You went out and bought yourself new clothes rather than come home to pick up something to wear tonight, and risk seeing me? Wimp.

A small group of people on the wimp's right moved away, exposing a variety of boxy shapes piled high on the floor, like a small Christmas tree. Presents. Shit. I'd come empty-handed.

I looked back at Ralph. *I suppose yours is in that pile; I suppose you bought something at the same time as you shopped for your new get-up; I suppose you gave them a Waterford Crystal vase!*

As if he heard me, he swivelled his head in my direction. I should have swivelled mine, but I didn't. We locked eyes. Did I see a flicker of longing and regret in his? I was wearing my contact lenses, and Ralph was obviously wearing his, but with a good distance between us in the dimly lit room, I'd probably imagined it. Either way, I wanted to cry. Not the time or place, so I quickly averted my gaze.

I saw Vette, Rhea and Iris on the other side and zigzagged through the gathering towards them.

On the way, I met Casper, Hannah and Alex. They were huddled together with Leah and Ari, and Alex's brother, Paris. My two kids hugged me warmly and asked if I was doing okay. Again, the tears welled; again, I held them in check.

Moving on and pushing through the crowd, I said hello to Rhea and Nestor's older brother, Otus, and stopped briefly to greet Maxi's brothers, Ronnie and River. I was then accosted by their mother.

Daisy Mayer-Rose used to be Roma Mayer-Rose. Until she blossomed into a flower child. I loved her. She was loopy, but a kind and (free-)loving spirit. She hugged me warmly, then drew back, clasping my hands in hers as we took each other's measure.

A petite woman in her mid-seventies, she made an impression. Always had, with her off-the-wall values and off-the-wall appearance. I rarely saw Daisy, but when I did, I never knew what to expect; what era or movement she'd be embracing. Tonight, it was a pastiche.

Her hair was 1960s. Short, geometric, angular bob. Platinum blonde with a pink tinge. Her make-up, 1970s. Pearlescent maroon eyeshadow. False eyelashes. Enough berry shade on the apples of her cheeks to rival a pair of juicy Pink Ladies. Opalescent foundation—the shine made it look like she was sweating after a vigorous bout of sex. Knowing Daisy and her husband, Wren, the artist formerly known as Jules, it was possible that that was the case. And most likely in their daughter's walk-in closet.

Daisy's attire mapped the decades. A 1920s black beaded and fringed flapper dress, 1930s black elbow-length gloves, 1950s cat-eye specs. And harking back to her 1960s hippie days, a hammered silver peace symbol suspended on a long chain. It was in a teardrop shape that might have started off as round, but then sagged like ageing breasts. Her black fishnet stockings and black patent leather Mary Jane platforms screamed 1970. And a silver jacket with gridiron shoulder pads represented the 80s. I couldn't account for the 40s or 90s, though. Probably, her undies. Her ample knockers looked pointy, so a 40s bra, and maybe a 90s thong with either 'Fresh as a Daisy' or 'Fuck Me' printed on it. Only Daisy's presence here tonight indicated she was in the twenty-first century.

She spoke. 'Darling, you look gas!' 1970s parlance. It was a compliment. I thanked her and told her she looked cool. It was the only term I could scare up that cut across all the decades.

'Thank you, my love. And how are you? I hear you married Ralph.' She leaned in, her voice dropping to a conspiratorial whisper: 'I don't care what anyone says. There's nothing wrong with marrying your cousin.'

Jesus. I didn't know whether to laugh or cry. I didn't have to do either. A pair of hands clasped my shoulders. 'You're here!' Thank God for Maxi. Saved by the belle.

I turned to face her. My eyebrows shot up.

She was full-on Jessica Rabbit tonight. A long, sequin-covered, strapless red sheath dress with a thigh-high slit on the right; JR purple satin, above-elbow gloves; red stilettos and cherry-red lipstick.

I laughed at her. 'You didn't tell me it was fancy dress.'

She gasped. 'What!' She turned towards Daisy, then looked back at me. 'My mother normally dresses like that.'

'Oh, I, I ...' I felt my cheeks becoming a shade of Maxi's dress.

She and Daisy laughed at me.

The three of us chit-chatted for a bit, then Maxi dragged me away. 'Did she say something stupid?'

I repeated Daisy's words, then asked, 'Didn't you tell her Ralph and I aren't biologically related?'

'I told 'er. And I'd blame her forgetfulness on old age, but we both know crazy Daisy smoked too much weed in her heyday and has never really come into full bloom.'

Lucky Daisy. I envied her spacey state.

'Ruthie!' A booming voice jolted us out of our tête-à-tête. Wren wrapped me up in a bear hug. A handsome man, he was trim and fit, had a relatively unlined, tanned face with a chiselled jawline, and piercing, sapphire-blue eyes that hadn't dulled with cataracts or age. Unlike his wife, Wren was pure 60s: a fringed, tawny suede vest, black leather pants, loose white buttonless shirt with flared sleeves, and a bronze Ankh on a black leather necklace. His shock of dyed brown hair was pulled high into a coiled bun that, in the ambient glow, looked like a steaming dog turd on top of his head.

Wren told me I looked 'neato', that this was an 'outta sight' party, and that he'd love to stay for some more 'lip flappin'', but he needed to 'take a whiz'.

Like I needed to know this?

I turned to Maxi after he left. 'How'd you turn out so normal?'

She was aghast. 'You think I'm *normal*?'

I made a wry face. 'Sorry. Sane. Sane's probably more apt.' The only one in the family of sound mind.

'Better.'

I told her about Hannah's visit and that our relationship was back on track.

'Yay! So glad to hear it. One down!' she said, then looked in Ralph's direction. She turned back to me. 'I know it's hard, honey, but having you here tonight is so important to me.'

Her words made me as happy to be here as I was unhappy to be here. I nodded and sighed. 'I gotta be honest with you, Max, I don't know how long I'm gonna last.'

She took my hand and squeezed it. 'I understand. But please, just hang in there for the next hour.'

Again, it wasn't a big ask. Again, I relented. 'Okay.'

'There's some great entertainment planned.' Maxi was well connected. She'd done stuff like this before—managed to secure the services of well-known personalities to perform at some of her office parties.

'I don't doubt it!' I said, then screwed up my face. 'And I'm really sorry I don't have a housewarming present for you yet.'

She waved away my apology and the two of us made our way arm-in-arm over to the girls. I told her that what I could see of her new home looked 'gas'. She laughed at me, then offered a guided tour, but everyone she passed seemed to want a piece of her. It'd have to keep, just like the present.

As soon as Vette, Iris and Rhea saw me, all three pounced and we group-hugged. I couldn't control the tears this time.

I'd let Iris and Rhea know a week ago about Ralph moving out, and like Maxi and Vette, they'd been in touch regularly since then. I was still circumspect with Rhea but had told Iris about Ralph and Alex and Hannah. I hadn't said anything about Anthea. I was no longer busting to tell anyone about her.

It took a lot to throw Iris off balance. Excessive hairiness on women did it—she suffered from chaetophobia—and my predicament did it. Ralph's rashness and Hannah's brush-off had angered her.

While Rhea was now saying something to Maxi about the apartment, I whispered to Vette and Iris that all was good with Hannah. Both were pleased, but Iris was still annoyed with Ralph. She said, 'Honeybun, I reined myself in over his rubbish birthday present, but this? Lemme go over there and kick him in the nuts.'

I shrugged. The hope I'd held onto the last time I'd seen them—both the girls, and Ralph's nuts—was dashed. As Iris made a move, Vette put a restraining hand on her arm and shook her head. 'It's probably better if we don't say anything to him. Or do anything.'

It was what I needed even if a part of me wanted my friends to step in, like the adolescent who sends her girlfriends on a fishing expedition to find out if her crush likes her.

Maxi had caught this exchange. She kept quiet but I sensed her discomfort. I said, 'I think Vette's right. And anyway, we don't want to spoil Maxi's party.'

She nodded her gratitude.

The five of us schmoozed for a bit and then Maxi left to go mingle with her other guests.

I was tuning in and out of the natter and beginning to wilt. By the time Maxi came back half an hour later, I wanted to bolt and told her so.

'Please don't. The show starts in ten minutes. Promise me you won't leave? Please, Ruthie. *Please, please, please!*' It reminded me of how we used to speak as children. I couldn't bear to disappoint my childhood friend.

'I promise.'

'Good girl.' She turned to the others and said, 'I'll be back. Stay here. And don't let Ruthie go!'

About twenty long minutes later, an amplified, effeminate male voice spoke: 'Helloooo. Could I puleeeease have everyone's attention?'

We all turned in the direction of the talking head that had silenced and parted the crowd.

'Fuck a duck!' Iris said. 'I think we've just found Nemo.'

A clownfish impersonation stood in the centre of the lounge. Fifty-something, he wore an iridescent suit with a blue wave pattern and large orange fish dotted here and there. Nobody could ever lose Nemo again. Ever.

Iris said, 'Rhea, sorry, girlfriend, but this clown's just bumped Hector from the top of the Worst Dressed list.'

We all laughed, Rhea included. Where was Hector, anyway?

Too unwell to go out, apparently. That one could top the list of Forty Little Things in Daily Life That Bring Us True Happiness.

Nemo issued instructions to those of us on his left. 'Sssso. Could youse on this side take a few steps back?'

'Did he just say "youse"?' I whispered to Iris.

'Yep. Nemo lives Down Under, so it makes sense he'd know how to speak Ocker.'

Nemo now faced those on his right. Ralph's crowd. 'And could youse on this side also take a few steps back?'

As the youses opposite us shuffled backwards, Vette nudged me. 'That woman standing next to Nestor, isn't that ...' Her voice trailed off and she gasped.

I turned to look. *I* gasped.

CHAPTER TWENTY-EIGHT

My Achy Breaky Heart

S he was at the other end of the lounge and the lights had been further dimmed, but there was no mistaking it. It was the marriage celebrant who'd officiated at my wedding.

Before I could say anything, the room filled with the strains of Whitney Houston and Jermaine Jackson's ballad, 'Nobody Loves Me Like You Do'.

There was breath-catching all around as heads turned in the direction of the hallway.

Maxi emerged looking like an ethereal sex bomb. She wore a lacy white knee-length, figure-skimming dress with a plunging neckline. She carried a bouquet of white roses. With her eyes glistening, she focused on Nestor as she walked towards him. He was crying unashamedly.

'Far out, man!' her father yelled.

Everyone laughed when Maxi replied in Wren-speak, 'Don't wig out, Daddy-O.' Still drawn like Jessica Rabbit even as she looked like a pseudo-virginal incarnation of her.

She briefly paused as she passed Rhea, Vette, Iris and me, and whispered, 'Not a single word about me being in white!' She sent us an air-kiss, then continued the march towards her beau.

Maxi and Nestor gazed into each other's eyes and then kissed. The four of us were dumbfounded, our faces beginning to streak black mascara as we linked arms and witnessed their unreserved love.

My tears also burned for my unrequited love. Like that line in the song, without Ralph I felt like a poem without a rhyme. Sappy. I caught him staring at me, wearing a look of profound pain. The whole thing would have touched him in a very deep place and, as with me, brought back memories of our wedding ceremony less than a year ago.

I was in too much of a black hole to hear the celebrant's words, but it was a quick service. The burst of applause brought me back up into the room, which fell silent again when Nemo *shh shh shh'd* into the microphone and handed it to Nestor.

He and Maxi, standing side by side with their arms around each other, were both beaming.

'How gorgeous is my wife?' the usually soft-spoken Nestor called out. The two of them kissed again, passionately this time. Everyone clapped, many whooped, some wolf-whistled. And when the noise died down, Nestor said, 'I was so thrilled Maxi said yes when I proposed to her up in Hayman. But then she told me she didn't want to take my name. And I was fine with that, but I was curious. I asked if it was because she's an independent woman, or because she's a feminist and doesn't think the traditional reasons that women once changed their names are legal or social realities today. Or was it because she's built a career in her name? Or maybe just because she's had her own for so long. She told me all these things were true and she loved that I knew her so well. But the main reason, she said, was that being Mrs Poulos would make her feel like a chicken.'

We all laughed.

'And that's one of the many reasons I adore this beautiful woman.' He turned towards her and spoke as if they were the only two in the room. 'My darling Maxi, for a very long time I never thought I'd experience laughter and joy again. And then you came along and brought them back into my life. You are the love of it.' Staring into his new bride's eyes, Nestor said something that sounded like *'Eesay cardia moo.'*

'It means "you are my heart",' Rhea told us, her hand over her own heart and her voice shaking with emotion.

Vette and Iris wiped their eyes, but Rhea and I couldn't stop the tears. Hers were ones of elation for her brother, who'd suffered such tragedy but had now found happiness. Mine were tears of elation for my dear friend, who'd waited a long time for this kind of love. But they were also anguished ones for myself.

Nestor's 'heart' then made her speech. It was short and sweet and typically Maxi. 'Please eat, drink, dance, and then bugger off so I can jump my hot new husband!'

We laughed and clapped, and, as one, we joined the well-wishers closing in on the newlyweds. But Nestor politely cut through the crowd to embrace his sister and brother. Maxi also cut through and embraced us, her 'sisters'. We then *oohed* and *aahed* over her wedding ring—a wide, white-gold band encrusted with channel-set baguette diamonds and two rows, top and bottom, of small, brilliant-cut diamonds. She whispered in my ear, 'I was dying to tell you and Vette, but he swore me to secrecy.'

'That must've nearly killed you?'

'Oh, you have no idea. But I was kinda glad. It meant I didn't have to tell Daisy and Wren.'

Rhea broke away from her brothers and pulled Maxi into a warm sister-in-law embrace. Other guests swarmed to congratulate her, and Vette, Iris, Rhea and I stepped back to the outer limits.

The soft music did an about-turn and we had to shout above loud, back-to-back love songs throughout the decades: swing, rock and roll, doo-wop, pop, bubblegum, disco, hard-rock, soft-rock, hip-hop, rap. Daisy was no doubt delirious.

After an hour of hearing about baby love, everlasting love, burning love, sweet love, secret love, muskrat love, and fast love, I was all out of love and didn't think my heart would go on. This music and the talking and laughter swirling around me threatened to swallow me up. I felt myself disassociating. It had sometimes happened to me when I was a child, and it was not a nice place to be. A sense of being no place. Here, yet not here, disconnected from a world that seemed unreal, I was struggling for air.

I looked over at Ralph. He was chatting to a woman and ... and ... what? *What!* He was *laughing*?

Like the Wham-O Super Ball, I recoiled, bouncing back from my split-off wretchedness. How dare he laugh, how dare he be happy! I now couldn't bear to be in the same room as him.

I said goodbye to my friends, gave my apologies to Maxi and tried to curb the tears as we hugged. 'I'll speak to you tomorrow,' she said.

I hate you, Ralph, I thought as I made a hasty exit.

There was no solace to be found this time in the lift's black-and-white space in my black-and-white get-up with my detested, crazy-making, black-and-white thinking. The lift descended and so did I.

Breaking down as soon as I got into the car, I wept uncontrollably on the drive home.

By the time I turned off the ignition in the garage, though, I felt a blessed nothing.

Inside, I went through the motions—dropped my bag on the floor next to the bed, undressed, dropped my clothes next to the bag, donned my nightie, lumbered into the bathroom, removed my make-up, and brushed my teeth.

The brief respite from the heartbreak ended when I slipped under the covers. I was overcome, half-suffocated by sorrow. And then, there was rage.

I pounded my fists into my pillow, screaming. Silently, though. Spontaneity with conditions attached. It wasn't perfect, but it was better than all-out restraint. And the wrath came in waves, like labour. After the third one, I felt more focused. I grabbed *his* pillow and pummelled that instead.

Exhausted, I collapsed onto my back and lay there, inert and staring glassy-eyed. A few minutes passed when my mobile pinged from inside the bag and cut through my benumbed senses. I turned over, reached down and fished the phone out.

A text from Ralph.

CHAPTER TWENTY-NINE

SMS (Suck My Soul)

I fumbled with the phone in my hurry to access the message.

> I need to know you got home okay.

What? You've got to be kidding me!

I assumed this need related to the night of my accident three years earlier, and that maybe he feared I'd had another one, given my obviously tortured state at the party. Let him sweat! That would fulfil *my* need and put me back in the driver's seat. Wouldn't it?

Maybe not. There was never anything to be gained from the dog-eat-doggedness of my relationship with Sylvia. So I texted back.

> What do you care!

It should have ended with an interrobang—‽—that neat little WTF mark. But my smartphone was an idiot. It didn't have one. At the very least, I should've typed ?!, but his text had knocked the stuffing out of me. He texted back:

> ?

Was he actually correcting me? He followed this with another text:

> Do you honestly believe I don't
> care?

Okay. So maybe he wasn't correcting me. I answered:

> Yes!

And then cried as I wrote another on the back of it:

> You left me!!

No. I deleted that, retyped and sent:

> YOU LEFT ME!!!!

It took him five minutes to respond.

> I did not leave you. Just needing
> to be alone to get my head
> straight. Don't think for a minute
> this whole situation doesn't make
> me sad.

It took me no time to respond to that one.

> Oh yeah. You looked REAL sad
> when you were talking to that
> woman tonight!

If he was so sad, he could go cry on Anthea's shoulder! To think I'd feared he'd slept with her. I was now hoping he had, and that he was languishing in guilt and revulsion.

What woman?

What? There was more than one?

Blonde, green dress.

That was Gemma from our disco days. She stopped to talk to me. What was I supposed to do, ignore her?

Really? *Really?*

Ooh no. Mustn't ignore Gemma. Or anyone else. Just reserve that for ME!

I fired that one off and my thumb went hell for leather on the next:

WHAT DID I DO SO TERRIBLE THAT WOULD MAKE

Strike that one. Instead:

WHAT UR DOING IS MEAN!

I deleted this one too.

There was a reason I couldn't come up with more. If those words I'd text-shouted, then nixed, had produced a sound, it would've had the quality of a high-pitched nasally whine. The poor-me posturing that had shaped Sylvia's life and left its (interrobang) mark on my psyche. I needed to let it atrophy, not keep developing muscle. And what Beth had said came to mind, about leaving Ralph alone to figure it out. Fine. This text match had agitated me. I wanted to go back to the earlier state of flatness. My thumb was poised over the on–off power key when the phone pinged again.

> It's not you, it's me.

AARGH! Breathe, let it go. Let it go. And I did. Brave me. I breathed in for four, *ooooohm*, and out for four, *wheeeeeew*. In, *ooooohm*, and out, *wheeeeeew*. I took the high road; wasn't going to get on my high horse. Nope. I was the bigger person—

Well, fuck that and fuck Ralph. My thumb furiously hip-hopped over the touch pad.

> Really? You're insulting my
> intelligence with a cliche! YOU
> SOUND LIKE MY MOTHER!

This text of mine annoyed me. No need for an interrobang, but where was the accent over the 'e' in cliché? Did I have to select 'French' in the phone's language settings? Why didn't this stupid smartphone automatically know there should be an accent? The word 'cliché' was so fucking clichéd!

GRRRR! ???

Still, notwithstanding the missing acute accent, content-wise the text would be the ultimate insult to Ralph's intelligence.

Cliché queen Sylvia had not been the sharpest tool in the shed, not the brightest crayon in the box, the elevator didn't go all the way to the top floor. I remembered one of her many daft rationales. It was when Ralph and I became an item. She declared our relationship 'voodoo' (instead of taboo), and as my liaison with him evolved romantically, she didn't let up:

> '*C'est dégoûtant!*' It's disgusting! 'It's not the natural order
> of things.'

I knew about the concept of natural order. Ralph had once explained it as the physical universe being an orderly system subject to natural laws, not human or supernatural ones. So, when Sylvia said 'natural order', my ears pricked up. Had she started reading something other than Mills & Boon?

She continued. 'At least he's taller than you. The man is supposed to be taller than the woman. But the man is supposed to be *older* than the woman too, not the other way round. You're older than him It is not the natural order!'

Defending myself was part of the natural order for me. '*What!* I'm only one week older than him!'

'*Oeuf!* It doesn't matter, *pest!*' She was bordering on hysteria. 'You are still older. He's your ... he's your troyboy!'

Oeuf, French for egg, had been Sylvia's euphemism for *fuck*. A mild alternative. Not ever having asked her why she picked egg was one of my regrets after she died. *Pest*, English for pest, had been her dysphemism for *Ruth*. A disparaging alternative. And *troyboy*? It might've been clever if the premise wasn't so stupid. Her tendency to flub her words had always diminished her firepower.

My phone pinging again brought me back to the present.

> You're projecting. So, more to the
> point, you are like her.

The supreme counter-insult, being psychologised with that accusation! And he hadn't even cared enough to yell it. Or at least exclaim it. It was that cold detachment again that made me see even redder. *You wanna be left alone to figure it out, to figure out why it's YOU and not me, then so be it.*

> Fuck you, you wanna be alone?
> Fine!

Go interrobang yourself!

When he didn't respond after ten minutes, I turned off the phone. I turned off the lamp and lay in the dark trying to calm myself with slow, measured inhales and exhales. I didn't want to think about Ralph anymore.

Let's think of Maxi's wedding. God, she looked beautiful. And oh, Nestor's words to her and that choice of song for their wedding march ...

It made me think of Ralph's vows and speech, and our wedding march: 'Endless Love'. The tears came. The short-lived anger that had emboldened me a couple of minutes earlier gave way to endless pain. I wept bitterly, feeling as though I would die of despair. Hoping and praying I would.

'God, please let me die.'

The pain increased, then abated, then gave way to deadness. My prayer was answered. Doctored, but answered. And yeah, I'd leave Ralph alone. But I'd never felt so alone.

I heard a whisper come from within: *'You're not alone.'* Then I heard a whisper come from without:

'Ooh ah oh eeee uh uh uh UH. Oh Bin, Binny ...'

I started to laugh. In that moment, I realised something bigger, although not yet available to my senses, was working undercover. I silently urged on the something—big or small, didn't wanna know—that was available to my senses and working under the covers.

Go Bitty go! Come Bitty come!

'AAAAAAAH YES YES AAAAH OH GOD!'

Yes! Yes! I felt the release and calmed. With Bin and Bitty fucking like rabbits, Bitty getting her rocks off was like being rocked to sleep. It had become a kind of lullaby.

For the first time since Ralph moved out, I didn't go to sleep overwrought. And for the first time in months, I didn't feel unhappy. Not happy, but not unhappy.

After a sound sleep, I woke the next morning, unhappy and with a muzzy head and runny nose. I had a cold.

I switched on my mobile and dropped it on the bed next to me. A minute later, the tritone sounded. I checked the screen. Disappointment, yet at the same time, a bit of excitement. It was a hopeful message.

> Thought it best to give you some space. But I'm worried about you. How are you doing?

CHAPTER THIRTY

Apoca [Read My Cold] Lips!

A man who cared, even if it was only Andy. I pardoned his weeks-long evasion and texted back.

> Lousy. Have a head cold.

He wrote back:

> Not much fun. Take it easy.

He followed this with another text:

> Haven't seen the Merc in the drive lately?

Shit.

> He's away.

It wasn't a lie, but I hoped Andy wouldn't ask where and why.

Okay. Stay in bed.

Phew. But what if he keeps noticing the car's not there? Maybe I can park mine in the drive and say that Ralph's is in the garage? Another text came through disrupting this insane line of thought.

Let me know if you want some company.

If I want some company, like, in bed? I pressed the phone lock to protect myself. I didn't want to text stupid things in my foggy state. Instead, I dragged myself into the kitchen, made some toast with a thick layer of strawberry jam, booted up my laptop, and wrote stupid things.

* * * *

'Fark. Fark.'

Another disapproving squawk from the annoying gull. But at least this foul fowl incarnate of my puritanical mother was now speaking my language.

I answered her. 'Right on, harpy!'

The storm had moved out to sea. Or maybe it was a new storm. A jagged lightning bolt in the distance was followed by a faint thunderclap. Nature's fury. And mine. It brought me back to that day, clearly remembering it because of the sting in my written words. Troyboy, who was once my Trojan warrior and all that that entailed—not least, courageous determination—had lost his warrior status. He'd now become just a Trojan, like a virus that invades computers and misleads users of its true intent.

I'd reworked and reworded my manuscript that morning, divulging intimate details about Ralph that exposed him as a total prick, without the protection of a Trojan®, *hhha*! I could have renamed the book *Apoca[loose]lips*.

* * * *

I typed furiously for two hours. It might have seemed like a waste of time because I didn't replace the manuscript previously saved to my external hard drive with this updated one. But it helped release some of the anger. Pity I had no control over what then replaced the anger: guilt. That other default setting in my internal hardwiring.

Still, I might have felt guilty about making Ralph look bad, even as I justified it, but I didn't feel even a scintilla of guilt for making Sylvia look bad. I'd only written the facts. Unembroidered.

I sat back and moved my head around in a circle, trying to loosen the kinks in my neck, then I collected the used tissues strewn all over the dining room table, popped a couple of Panadol, and texted Casper and Hannah. They'd called earlier to see how I was and had left voicemail messages. I also sent a text to the newlywed. I wasn't yet in a good place for a real conversation.

> Hey, Max, fantastic surprise last night. So, so happy for you. Will call you later. xxx

She texted back.

> Thanks, hon, and so, so thrilled you were there. Hope you're okay. Speak soon. xxx

I lapsed into a mix of joy and sadness until another text alert shook me out of it. The sender's name on the screen said 'Shit-for-brains'.

Oh, joy.

My brother's wife, Tammy. I rolled my rheumy eyes. Tammy and Myron—a self-entitled pair. I'd had no contact with this disapproving duo since before my wedding.

I opened up the message.

> Myrons in hospital he had a heart
> attack

CHAPTER THIRTY-ONE

A Bad Spell

My first reaction: shock. Second reaction: indifference. First thought: Huh. Who knew he had a heart? Second thought: *Jesus H. Christ! Punctuation! Put a bloody apostrophe between n and s; put a bloody semi-colon after hospital; put a bloody full stop after attack.*

I summoned up a feeling, one that didn't convey annoyance over syntax, and texted back.

> Oh no; is he okay?

I went into the kitchen, took the Nutella out of the pantry and ate a spoonful of it straight from the jar while waiting for Einstein to string together another sentence.

> Yes it wasnt a majer one

Jesus H. Christ! Punctuation AND spelling!
I exercised restraint in my response.

Glad to hear.

Ten minutes passed before another text came through.

You could of called me

Jesus H. Christ! Grammar!

I had to make allowances for Tammy. She was majorly stupid and majorly self-absorbed. She was also majorly manipulative. I never made allowances for that.

And YOU could HAVE called me
instead of texting!

I pressed 'send' then conveyed a telepathic SMS:

Fuck off.

I assumed she would <u>have</u> been open to this. As a major airhead, she would <u>have</u> had no trouble receiving radio waves. But she didn't respond. Tammy knew better than to mess with me. Our last exchange had not ended well. For her.

I thought about Myron again, and sadness, not joy, reared up. Mostly, it saddened me that I felt so detached. It used to be very different.

Before my brother had reinvented himself as an arsehole, he'd been a bit of a nebbish. And throughout our childhood and teenage years, our parents expected me to 'be gentle' with him. Until they passed away, they kept making excuses for Myron's egomaniacal behaviour.

I nearly dropped my mobile when it rang. If it was Tammy, I wasn't going to answer it. It was Maxi.

'I know you said you'd call me, but I'm worried about you, hon. And geez, you don't sound so good.'

'I've got a rotten cold.' I told her about Myron.

'Seriously? The bitch told you this in a bloody *text*?'

I laughed at Maxi's misplaced priority. And loved her all the more for it.

She refocused. 'Anyway, is he okay?'

'Apparently it wasn't a maj*er* one.' I told her about Tammy's spelling.

'Jesus fucking Christ! Enable spellcheck if you're an idiot!' In her line of work, and like me, Maxi was pedantic. And also like me, she didn't think much of Myron. But he was still my brother.

I groaned. 'Oh God, Max, what'll I dooooo? Should I call him; should I go see him? What do you think?'

'I can't tell you what to do.'

'I know. What would you do?'

'I'd go and see him.'

This made me feel bad. Maxi seemed to have more forgiveness in her heart than I had in mine.

'Yep. If it were me, I'd go see him,' she reiterated, 'but I'd jump into his room and yell "BOO!"'

Still equal in the forgiveness stakes. We both laughed.

We talked about the wedding: her dress, her ring, the food, the music, Nemo, Nestor's speech, his romantic proposal and their fabulous apartment. I pointed out that Hector was now her brother-in-law. She pointed out that his absence was the best present she got last night.

'I told Nestor I wanted to make it a permanent thing and that I'd rather suck off the Teenage Mutant Ninja Turtles than have Hector in my home. Ever.'

I laughed and quailed at the image of Maxi giving head to Michelangelo, Donatello, Raphael and Leonardo. 'What'd he say?'

'Somehow, it turned him on.'

I sighed with envy. 'He really is like Ralph, isn't he?'

Maxi sensed the sadness in my words and told me Ralph had left not long after me. I told her about his texts. It annoyed her.

'It's like he's playing mind-games.' She applauded my parting shot. Then I told her all about Anthea.

'Oh. My. God. What an insane family tree!' she said.

'I know. It's like a rubber tree, you know, with too many invasive roots—'

'Ha, yeah. But more like an I-should've-worn-a-rubber tree!'

I laughed.

'And *her*. What a skank! Wouldn't it be funny if Ralph and his sister *had*—'

'No, Maxi. No! It wouldn't be funny.'

'Oh, hon. I'm sorry. That was a really dumb thing to say.'

And she couldn't unsay it. Last night's vengeful wish that 'Ralph and his sister had' gave way to the pain of those earlier suspicions, which now started to take root again. Like a rubber tree.

'Ruthie, listen. No way did anything happen. He might have spent years screwing his way through the fembot rank and file, but it was never more than one at a time. Ever. You know Ralph. And now, he's made a commitment an—'

'A commitment? Taking off when the going gets tough is no commitment! And I *knew* Ralph. I don't know who he is anymore.'

'Mmm.' Maxi didn't argue the point. She couldn't.

We talked a bit more. Again, I apologised for not getting a present, but I would. She didn't care, she was just glad I'd been there, and so was I. She promised to organise another breakfast or lunch with the girls.

After hanging up, I didn't want to give a second thought to the possibility of Ralph's infidelity, but I thought about Myron again. *What kind of a sister am I?*

I abandoned my poison-penning and crawled into bed.

* * * *

A scream rent the air. The gull had tapped into my memories.

'Really? *Now* you're tuned into me? Pity you weren't when you were in human form.'

She stood with her wings spread wide and flapped them once.

'Keep flapping. Go migrate somewhere.'

Sylvia-seagull threw back her head and screeched. If she'd had arms, she would have beaten her breast in woe-is-me despair. Myron, her squeaky-clean, golden child. I remembered how her ghost had tried bedevilling me with a cliché for the rest of that day.

* * * *

'Blood is thicker than water,' said Sylvia's spectre.

Whatever. Blah, blah, blah.

Sylvia's slew of clichés had lost their impetus early on. And when I was little, if she couldn't get to me with them, she'd bring out the big guns: 'Just wait till your father gets home!'

It seemed not much had changed in the afterlife. I heard the ghost of Joe: 'Friends come and go. Family is always there.'

I pulled the doona over my head and beat myself up for hours over that chant and its burden of obligation. Over and over and over.

I got calls from Vette, Iris and Rhea, but let them go to voicemail. Self-flagellation was energy-consuming. There was none left for interacting with anyone.

By day's end, I'd hit rock bottom and couldn't get up. As I lay there feeling beaten into submission, I realised that being as low as I could go meant 'up' was the only direction I could go. So I got up and took a hot, cleansing shower.

I blessed this cold that had left me feeling too crappy to act on the judgy voices in my head. And with that, the fog cleared and I saw some light.

I saw that Joe's mantra about our family came with a rider: Family is always there *like a dead weight.*

And as I dried off, I had the answer to the question that had launched my guilt ritual: *What kind of a sister am I?*

A: Bzzt. Wrong question. Right one: What kind of a brother is Myron?

Myron's need to please Sylvia had turned into a lifestyle. But yes-sir-no-sir people were dangerous. How often did you hear from the neighbours of a crazed gunman, 'Oh, but he was so quiet and polite'?

My brother the dentist wouldn't wield a gun. But for someone whose vocation was looking all day into people's mouths, he could shoot his own off in a cold, contemptuous manner. I was having none of it, which was what had caused our rift. That Myron had had a heart attack didn't surprise me. He had the feeling reality of a cyborg.

Unlike him, I felt deeply. I didn't want to become like him, so I decided to text him, not out of guilt or obligation, though. My mythical thinking had kicked in—the all-embracing approach that was more in line with my sensibilities than the either-all-or-nothing way. And like it or not, he was still my brother. That he had become a text sibling was a precedent he'd set, and one that, as it turned out, was better for my soul.

I hope you get well soon.

Not a question, it didn't invite an answer. I didn't want one. And I didn't expect one, Myron would be pissed off. Those with an inflated sense of self-importance give little but demand much.

I hit 'send' and felt stronger for it. Right timing, right reason, correct spelling, grammar, and punctuation, full stop. The doorbell ringing a nanosecond later seemed to say, *Amen to that*

But then my heart started beating hard and my breathing quickened. Was it my husband? Could be. Had he come to his senses? Although, if it was him, wouldn't he use his key? As things stood, maybe not.

CHAPTER THIRTY-TWO

Souped Up

Andy stood on the other side, a tub of soup in his hand. Like the soup, he smelled good and he looked hot. That Acqua Di Giò scent, a pale grey chambray shirt, black chinos, dark grey blazer with a herringbone pattern, salon tan.

Just as well I hadn't got into pyjamas like I was tempted to. I'd put on a clean tracksuit, no bra. My spirit was no longer sagging, but my jubblies, which had drooped in sympathy with the mood of the day, hadn't yet picked up. I crossed my arms under them to give them a bit of a lift, in the same way that Superman and club bouncers self-hug to accentuate their biceps.

'Jewish penicillin,' he said, holding up the tub.

It made me smile and his considerateness warmed me. He was looking more like a solution than a problem.

'I thought it'd be safe to deliver it seeing as the catwalk model's away.' He still couldn't say the catwalk model's name. It was fine, I was having trouble with it myself.

I thanked him and said, 'You're looking dapper.'

'I have a date.'

Oh. My spirit sagged again. The idea of Andy having a date bothered me. And it bothered me that it bothered me. Jesus! I thought I was past this. Maybe, as Maxi had said a few weeks back, I needed to cut ties. Maybe sometimes, all-or-nothing was the only way.

'I'm taking my mother to dinner. It's her birthday.'

My spirit lifted. My rack still had a way to go.

'But I've got about half an hour before I have to go pick her up. Want some company?'

'Sure.' Andy didn't know it was a catwalk model-free zone and I didn't want to tell him yet, if at all. But I could do with an infusion of testosterone. Right now, I was hardly that ballsy woman he'd perceived me to be.

We moved into the kitchen and he put the chicken soup tub on the counter. I offered him a pre-dinner cocktail. Coffee. He insisted on being bartender, told me to sit as he made a cup of honey lemon tea for me and got the dripolator going for himself.

He sat opposite me at the breakfast bar and I told him about Myron. He already knew the kind of relationship I had with my brother, he'd read it in my manuscript. I told him about the text I'd sent, but I didn't feel the need to justify my action. It was a sure sign that my decision was the right one. I didn't feel the need for Andy's endorsement, but he gave it anyway.

He'd also read about Maxi and Nestor's relationship, but I didn't say anything about last night's surprise wedding. It might raise too many questions. I told him I hadn't heard his bike since the last time I saw him. He said it was in for repairs. He was giving his car collection a workout.

When he left, he hugged me. In that moment, something shifted, and it wasn't in our nether regions.

Ralph's desertion must have cured me of Andy-lust. Now, it was just genuine affection for a friend. Doubtless, Andy sensed this. He was respectful. There wasn't anything inappropriate in his embrace. His libidinous impulses had nothing to attach themselves to.

I closed the door and looked at myself in the console mirror. I had a chapped red nose. *Respectful? Ya think? Maybe it's just that you look like crap.* Either way, Andy Ellis-Nile no longer had a mesmerising effect on me.

A bittersweet moment, it was a relief not to have to tangle with my own libidinous impulses, but I felt undesirable. Unwanted, again.

I wallowed in boohooness for a while, then called my girlfriends back one by one.

Vette, Iris and Rhea all had good relationships with their brothers, but each one supported my non-action action with Myron. Virtuous Vette's seal of approval meant the most. Betty Boop flashing her lady balls.

My bosom buddies and I discussed Maxi's wedding, and then I told them about Anthea. They reacted like Maxi, but each responded in their own inimitable way.

After hanging up, I called the kids to let them know about Myron. They were concerned about me but didn't give two shits about their uncaring uncle. I also called Norma, and her and my mother's brother, Uncle Isaac. As expected, Tammy had been too thoughtless to let them know. I cut short the conversation with Norma when she said she hadn't heard from Ralph.

And it hit me. Ralph was the one person who hadn't heard from me about Myron. I sank into unbearable loneliness.

CHAPTER THIRTY-THREE

Carrying a Torch (Batteries Not Included)

Some sludgy days followed, but I wasn't feeling quite so bad the day I had an unplanned visit from Rhea and a fruit flan.

I still hadn't told her why Ralph left and she didn't press me. She didn't know about Andy, either.

We hugged and she asked if I was feeling better.

'Yes, the cold's a bit better, and no, the heart's got a long way to go.'

I shed a few tears, she hugged me again.

'Do you want to talk about it?'

'Not really. Not right now, anyway.' I'd been so consumed with my tribulations during my isolation, not talking about it would be a much-needed hiatus.

We adjourned to the kitchen where I got the coffee going and sliced a couple of pieces of flan for us.

'Looks like whoever bought Portnoy's place has some money,' she said. 'There's a red Porsche parked in the drive.'

'Yeah. He's also got a Harley. And a Jag. Andrew Ellis-Nile is loaded.'

Rhea peered at me questioningly. 'Not *the* Andrew Ellis-Nile, the author?'

'Yep. Him.'

'Oh my God!' Her hands flew up to her cheeks. 'I'm a *huge* fan. I've read all of his books. And those last ones, the horror stories, I *love* them!'

Of course you do. You're married to Hector. Your life is a horror story.

'Have you met him yet?' she asked.

'Uh-huh.'

'Ooh, what's he like? I'd love to meet him!'

'Uh, well, why don't I call him and invite him to join us for coffee?'

'You have his *number?*'

'Yep. Actually, he's been helping me with my writing.' *He's a cunning linguist.* 'He's given me really good advice.'

No sooner had I said this than the doorbell sounded.

Andy stood there like da Vinci's Vitruvian man, that illustrated nudie inscribed in a circle in two superimposed positions with his arms and legs apart, knackers dangling. Only, Andy was fleshed out and inscribed in the doorframe, his arms out, resting on either side of it, and his legs spread apart, somewhere in between the two positions. His knackers may have been dangling (if he was wont to go commando), but I didn't know because he had clothes on. And I didn't want to know. Sort of. I sort of didn't want to know. I guess I hadn't become totally immune to his allure. Was this a good sign, feeling something, indicating some life force had returned? Or was it a bad sign, feeling something, indicating I was still under his spell? Neither and both. Not black or white.

'Well, you're looking much better than you did a few days ago,' my mentor said.

'Thanks. I was just talking about you. I have a friend here who wants to meet you.' I dropped my voice to a whisper. 'She's a big fan.'

Andy looked past me at Rhea, gave her a seductive smile, and waved. She made a be-still-my-heart motion with her hand. His chest puffed out. I made an I-wanna-vomit motion with my finger.

He tugged on my ponytail, walked past me and headed for the kitchen. He introduced himself. She gawped at him with sparkly eyes.

Are you imagining having sex with Hector while fantasising about having sex with Andy?

'Do share,' Andy said.

'Huh?'

The two of them were staring at me. 'You were laughing,' he said, his eyebrow dancing. 'Out loud.'

'Oh.' Shit. 'It's nothing. Nothing.' I poured him a cup and plated a man-sized wedge of the flan.

Rhea gushed about his books; he played at being modest. We ate, drank, and were merry. It was like watching a rerun of the first time he'd had coffee here. The man had an inexhaustible wellspring of bullshit.

He favoured Rhea with a captivating smile. 'So. Rhea. Spelled Ar, aitch, ee, ay, like the ancient Greek goddess of comfort and ease?'

Like Rhea, the ancient Greek goddess married to Cronus, the degenerate who cut off his father's balls, most likely in an I-don't-got-'em-you-can't-have-'em move. Sounds about right.

'Yes.' Rhea blushed.

'Rhea.' Andy rolled the name around in his mouth. 'A regal and romantic name, if ever I heard one.'

Oh, man.

'Thank you.' Starstruck, she broke away from his penetrating gaze and looked down at her coffee.

I shook my head at the smooth-tongued operator.

'What?' he mouthed.

'Wanker,' I mouthed back.

He flashed me a randy-Andy smile, sipped his coffee, downed a mouthful of flan, then he turned back to Rhea and re-launched his charm offensive.

'I have to tell you, I've loved that name since I first heard it, ooh, probably going on thirty years ago. I woulda been about eleven or twelve and I overheard my parents talking to my aunt and uncle. Being curious and sensing the whiff of a scandal, I hid in the kitchen and listened in. Their son, my cousin, was in love with a Greek girl called Rhea. He was a good ten years older, and she was only about eighteen. Well, he got her pregnant and her parents interfered. I heard my aunt whisper that they made her terminate. At that age, I didn't know what terminate meant, but I know it all ended badly.'

Rhea stared, her face turning a deathly shade of white.

Oh shit.

She opened her mouth to say something, but couldn't form the words. I did it for her.

'What's your cousin's name?'

'Russell. Russell Plowman. Why?'

The penny dropped for Andy just as Rhea fell off the chair. Literally. She fainted.

Andy moved quickly, caught her before she hit the floor. He scooped her up and carried her to the lounge while I fetched a clean tea towel from the cupboard under the kitchen sink, and moistened it. He gently lowered her onto the sofa and raised her legs, propping them up with a couple of scatter cushions.

'It's her, isn't it?' he asked as I sat on the edge of the sofa and dabbed her face.

'I didn't know Russell's last name, but I'd say so.' I was loath to say more. Rhea had entrusted me with her story. It was similar to Beth's, only worse. Complications from her abortion led to infertility, and like Beth's parents drove David away, Rhea's drove Russell away. Their actions drove her away from them, and right into Hector's open arms. He had two young sons who needed a mother.

'Mmm. Oh,' Rhea moaned as she came to, several seconds later. 'What happened?'

'You passed out,' I said.

'Do you have any chest pains?' Andy asked.

'N-no.'

'D'you wanna grab some water?' he said to me, then turned to Rhea. 'You feeling dizzy?'

'No.'

I brought a glass over and Andy held her head as she took a sip.

'Oh God,' she said as he lowered her head back down. She covered her eyes, then dragged her hand down her face and looked at Andy. 'You're Russell's cousin.'

'Yeah. And this is a good sign. You haven't lost your memory.'

Rhea rolled her eyes back. 'Sometimes, I wish I had.'

Andy nodded.

She shook her head and said, 'What are the chances?'

'For what it's worth, I don't believe in coincidence.'

Synchronicity in action again.

'I don't really, either,' she said.

'And seems to me you're not over him. This might be your opportunity for some closure?'

I agreed with Andy. When Rhea had told me her story, I asked why she hadn't looked for Russell. It came down to fear. But she'd also said the 'if only' feeling had never left her.

'I think you might be right.' She sighed. 'So, I guess I start by asking what happened to him?'

'Well, because of the age difference, I never had much to do with him when I was growing up. And I haven't seen him for years; probably wouldn't even recognise him. I know he got married a while ago, but I heard it was short-lived and there were no kids. But now?' Andy shrugged. 'As far I know he doesn't see his family much. I can ask my mother, though. She hasn't seen him either, but she can find out. Russell's a cousin on my late father's side.'

Rhea looked at me. I nodded.

Andy asked her if she was sure she was okay, then left with a promise to keep us informed. Ten minutes later, he called me. 'Write this down.' It was Russell's mobile number.

'I need to do this. I need to call him, to see him!' Rhea said as I handed her the piece of paper. 'I think that "if only" feeling is just going to eat away at me if I don't lay the ghost of the past to rest. And the opportunity's pretty much landed in my lap, hasn't it? It's providence.'

I nodded, but didn't dare say anything, remembering all too well what happened the last time I interfered with someone's idea of providence.

At a loose end after Rhea left, I sat on the couch staring into space for the next hour until she called.

'I spoke to him!'

'Oh my God. And?'

'And I'm seeing him tomorrow morning at West Lakes for coffee.'

'Wow! That was quick.'

'I know. But I think once I made the decision, I didn't want to wait any longer. And I feel good about that.' Rhea promised to call after they met.

The next morning, she didn't call as promised. Instead, she came by mid-afternoon.

She was barely through the door when I said, 'So, do tell!'

'Well, I've come to a decision,' Rhea said, looking more at peace, I thought, than she had in a while. 'I, uh ... Oh God, I need a drink!' Maybe not so much at peace.

'Uh, sure. What would y—'

'Just a tea. I'd love a tea, thanks.'

I made us both a cuppa and we sat opposite each other at the breakfast bar.

Rhea inhaled a deep breath and let it out a little at a time before speaking. 'I'm leaving Hector.'

CHAPTER THIRTY-FOUR

No Useful Purpose

M y mouth fell open. 'What? For *Russell*?'

'No. No. *God* no! But seeing him was a wake-up call. He's a shell of a man, Ruthie. He couldn't get it together after my parents drove him away.' She shook her head sadly. 'We talked for an hour, but it was mostly about him. No. It was all about him. He's been in and out of work and he hasn't had any meaningful relationships since me. Can you believe he didn't even consider his relationship with his wife meaningful, even before they tied the knot?'

'Geez, that's kinda tragic, isn't it?'

'Uh-huh. Anyway, my head was spinning when I left. I went and sat in a little park nearby for a couple of hours and mulled over, well, everything.' She looked down at her hands and started fiddling with her wedding ring. 'And yeah, maybe I did settle when I married Hector ...' She trailed off.

God, give me the courage to leave that one alone.

'... but, I didn't give up on life like Russell did. It just seemed like he'd attached his reason for being to me, and it made me ask myself if I'd done the same sort of thing, you know, with the idea of having an instant family in Hector and his two boys. Then I remembered when you and I talked about all this after Alex and Hannah's wedding and you made the comment that Alex and Paris were grown men now. I guess I wasn't ready to see it then, but sitting in that park, it hit me that mothering them had given me my sense of purpose. Oh, I know I'm still their mum—the only mum they've really known, but I'm no longer mothering them. And realising all that left me feeling so incredibly empty. Well, I just cried and cried.'

I reached over, put a sympathetic hand on her arm and was about to offer some comforting words, but the sudden thought that much of my life had revolved around my relationship with Ralph knocked me for a loop.

'Ruthie? Are you okay?'

'Huh? Oh. Uh, what you said, it just made me wonder how much I've attached my sense of purpose to Ralph.'

'I'm sorry. You're going through so much, I shouldn't have burdened you with my problems.'

'No. Look, it's not a burden. It's ...' I wasn't sure what 'it' was.

Rhea said, 'You know I'm here to listen to you if you need to unburden yourself.'

But it wasn't about unburdening myself. Rhea needed to hear the truth. So I told her about Ralph and Alex. Halfway through, I grabbed her hand. 'You're not about to faint again, are you?'

Her face had frozen into what looked like a silent scream, but no words came out of her mouth. She just shook her head.

I started to second-guess my decision to tell all, especially after her shock discovery and also, after having shushed Ralph for so long. But the timing had felt right.

'That explains why Alex has been so standoffish,' she said with a faraway look in her eyes.

Rhea was smart enough to know it'd be unwise to bring it up with Alex. Or to tell Hector. But we both had a stake in it. And knowing we could talk to each other about it benefited the two of us. The honesty brought us closer.

The next days blurred into one another. Rhea leaving Hector was probably the only highlight. Was it a matter of comfort in numbers? Or misery loving company? Was I at the mercy of these clichés, both hallmarks of the tribal hell I'd grown up in? In part, maybe. But mainly, no. Hector was a weenie; Rhea deserved a whole lot better.

My friends regularly checked in, Rhea and I shared feelings, and Hannah shared her feelings. Alex's parents' separation was another blow for him and he'd become moody again.

I told Andy the persistent cold had turned into flu and he'd best stay away. It was a lie. I wanted to wallow alone, and so I did. On all fronts.

Baubo the dirty bitch didn't come a-calling. It left me uninspired. Again, it was just as well I had a couple of spare articles to submit to the magazine. But as its inspirational humour writer who couldn't get it together, I felt like I was scamming my readers. Uninspired *and* humourless. There wasn't much to laugh about.

The fuck-fest next door had stopped a week ago, or had just become voiceless. Probably because I'd yelled out 'SHUT UP!' The dead air was only temporary. Bitty's baying resumed three days later, but it had lost its *je ne sais quoi*. She sounded like she'd been debarked. Two days after that, she was back to yelping at full throttle. The former lullaby was now like nauseating elevator music. Bitty's noises had become muzak to my ears.

And with still no word from Ralph, my emotions roller-coastered.

My cold may not have turned into flu, but it hung around for a few weeks and, unusually, dampened my appetite. It eased up on a Friday morning. I woke up starving and hightailed it to the kitchen, poked around in the pantry until I located the jar of Nutella, fished it out and uncapped it. It was half-empty.

No, it's not. It's half-full.

Whoa! Seeing it like this, this un-Sylvia way, made me feel better. I celebrated with a spoon until the jar was neither half-empty nor half-full.

That night, the celebrations continued with reheated leftover pizza as I watched *The Shawshank Redemption*. I was tired of crying through happily-ever-afters when mine wasn't. But man, was it masochistic to choose a movie that terrorised me and reminded me yet again that, like the protagonist Andy Dufresne, I'd often been unjustly accused?

I went to bed late and had a horrible Shawshank dream. I'd been flushed down the toilet, bounced off the walls of the private sewerage pipe and ended up in the sewerage main. I drowned in its wastewater. Never made it to the ocean, never even made it to treatment plant before the ocean.

I woke the next morning with an icky taste in my mouth, a leaden feeling in my heart, and once again, a sense that I could not go on any more.

CHAPTER THIRTY-FIVE

Fruit-Cakes

Food was the antidote. Food would assuage the hopelessness. I took my brekkie into the lounge, turned on the TV and was about to wolf a heaped dessertspoon of hokey-pokey ice cream, when I had an aha! moment.

It wasn't that I couldn't go on anymore. I couldn't go on *like this*. Couldn't keep feeding the beast.

The choice to watch *The Shawshank Redemption* last night had been an inspired one, and my dark dream was an illuminating one. Andy Dufresne was surrounded by some serious nasties in the slammer. He could have died there, but he didn't. He maintained his innocence and, in the end, he made it to freedom because he didn't let the shit stick. He pushed through it, literally, until he was out of it.

So, off went the TV and back into the freezer went the hokey-pokey. I made a poached egg with grain toast, juiced three oranges, and ate at the breakfast bar. I popped a multivitamin, showered, washed and dried my hair, then sat down to write. And write and write. The words that flowed were no longer bitter.

That night I slept like a log, didn't hear the cock rock from next door, and woke refreshed and ready to meet the day. It was Sunday and Hannah had asked me to be at her place at twelve to help her out. It was Luca's second birthday party.

Alex seemed to have suspended his sullenness. He'd just finished blowing up balloons when I got there and was now hanging streamers. The guests—little and big—would be arriving around twelve-thirty. I sat on the floor and distracted Luca while Hannah organised the food. For the purists: sushi; vegetarian sausage rolls; cheese, carrot and broccoli puffs; gluten-free, dairy-free, sugar-free muffins; fruit kebabs with yoghurt dip. For the realists: mini pizzas; real sausage rolls; chocolate crackles; fairy bread; chips; ice-cream cake.

At about twelve-fifteen, Alex stuck a note on the front door:

PLEASE FOLLOW THE ARROWS —> —>

GO TO THE BACK GATE (WITH THE BALLOONS ON IT).

DON'T FORGET TO CLOSE THE GATE BEHIND YOU.

Right on schedule, the realists started arriving: Casper; Reuben and Ida (Reuben's partner, who had moved in with him recently, just after Casper moved out to board at St Mark's, a university residential college where I'd attended many a drunken party in my youth); Leah and Ari; Greta and Rudy (Reuben's dad); Maxi and Nestor; Vette and Henry; Iris and Joel (only ten minutes late); Beth; Rhea; Paris; and friends Hannah had met through playgroup, with their husbands and little ones in tow. Norma would be coming later and, as always, partnerless. She was still married to Albie, but because no one liked the prick, invitations were never extended to him.

A half-hour passed before the mini-purists started trickling in with their parents in tow (those who were hostage to their children's timetables and tantrums).

And about fifteen minutes after that, the exhibitionist made an entrance.

I was standing near the rear sliding door with Hannah. She was jiggling Luca on her hip, kissing him and making *sh, sh* noises. He'd fallen over and was crying.

'Fuck,' she said under her breath as the gate opened and Hector walked in.

'Fuck,' Luca echoed.

Fuck. I quickly covered his eyes. Between what he heard and what he saw, the lesser of two evils was a no-brainer.

As usual, Hector stood out like a shag on a rock. This time, he was decked out in a loud tutti-frutti print shirt with images of limes, lemons and strawberries—which would have made the purists happy—and positive–negative harem pants. The trousers he'd worn to our night out almost a year earlier had reproduced: they were covered in hands. The white leg had black handprint images, the black leg had white handprint images.

Crap! Hector spotted Luca.

He made his way towards us as unanimous utterances of astonishment united the two camps. Drawing near, he held out his gift. A Buzz Lightyear doll in a clear plastic PVC toy box. Luca took one look at Hector, dropped his bottom lip and started howling.

'Aww, little man,' he said as he stroked Luca's cheek. Luca shrank away from his touch and cried even louder.

'The doll must have fwightened him,' he said to Hannah.

Kids love dolls, you idiot. You, on the other hand, would scare the shit out of Chucky.

Hannah soothed Luca and turned to talk to one of her friends, snubbing Hector. He looked around, then directed his gaze to me and switched on the sarcasm. 'So, Wuth, whewis your husband?'

You mean your son's real *father?* Tempting. Also tempting to ask him the same question about his estranged wife, even though her whereabouts were obvious. But ...

Did he know Ralph had moved out? *God, I hope not.* But who would have told him, anyway? Not Rhea, for sure. And I knew Alex wouldn't say anything that might lead to Hector finding out the paternal truth.

'Sowwy, didn't catch the weply.' He cupped his hand to his ear and raised his insolent chin.

I didn't thwow it, dipshit.

Plain to see the man was spoiling for a fight. It wasn't the first time he'd been catty with me. He'd made a caustic remark when Hannah was in labour. Ralph had jumped to my defence then, but he wasn't here now, and this blowhard had crossed a line.

I glared at him. 'He's out there trying to locate your missing circus. Catch on to that?'

Apparently, he did. Bozo's face lit up neon red, bulbous nose included, and he slithered away.

I hoped he'd stay away, but wondered, where *was* Ralph? My gut had been knotting intermittently in anticipation of his arrival. He was never late. I said as much to Hannah.

As Luca wriggled out of her arms and went back to play with his friends, she said, 'He wasn't invited.'

'What? Why? Uh, I get that Alex is—'

'It wasn't Alex. He didn't care one way or the other. I didn't want him here.'

I shook my head. 'Hannah. This is not right. Ralph shouldn't't've shot his mouth off, but—'

'But I hate what he's done to you, Mum!'

I pinched my nose. 'Look, I appreciate you being protective of me. But it's my business and my problem. I know it's been hard for you to accept, but'—I dropped my voice to a whisper—'Luca is his grandson. And Ralph's still part of this family.'

She gave an exasperated sigh, but then relented. 'Fine. I'll send him a text.' She pulled her mobile out of her pocket and quickly typed away. 'Done,' she said. She showed me the text and his reply, which came through within seconds.

> Luca's bday party here now.
> 12.30—2.30 if u wanna drop in.
> Hannah.

> Thank you, I'd love to. See you
> soon.

I checked the time. It was one-thirty. 'You trying to rub it in that he's an afterthought?'

'Hey, I compromised.' She gave me a smug smile and was about to go off to mingle with her peers when adult conversation ground to a halt. First silence, then tittering. Hannah and I followed the direction of the heads turned towards the source of amusement.

I gasped.

One of the purists stood amongst the children. A baby suckled on her right 'tittering', while her left pendulous one was flopped over the top of her half-open, flowy, hippie blouse.

'Shit,' I said to Hannah in an undertone. 'Looks like she forgot to put that one away.'

Hannah stared at the woman and shook her head. 'Nope.' She turned to me and said, 'Keep watching.'

The woman sat down on the grass and beckoned to a little boy with long, blond hair. He wore a bandana, tie-dyed cotton shorts, and a colourful T-shirt with 'Happy Earth Day' printed on the front. He ran over to his mother, latched on to her left jug and quaffed the milky contents.

'Seriously?' I said under my breath. I looked at Hannah and whispered, 'How are you friends with someone like this?'

She shrugged. 'Luca loves basil.'

'Huh?' I knew Luca had an unusually eclectic taste in food for a two-year-old, but I wondered if hanging around with space cadets was affecting Hannah's ability to focus. 'What the hell has that got to do with anything? I mean, I like it too, especially in a salad. But—'

'No. Basil is Absinthe's son.'

'Absinthe?'

'Her.'

'Oh.' *Oh!* 'Her name's Absinthe? She has a kid called Basil?'

'Uh-huh. And the baby is Sage.'

'Again, how are you friends with this person?'

Hannah looked at me. 'I met her at playgroup, but we're not friends. Luca and Basil are. Just like you and Maxi are even though her parents are total flakes.'

I nodded. We both gawked as Basil got sozzled on Absinthe, unlatched himself and resumed playing with the other children. I started to say something to Hannah, but she'd disappeared. She was now at the end of the garden engaged in an earnest conversation with Norma, who'd just arrived.

I turned and grabbed a paper plate from the food table next to me. As I filled it, Casper snuck up behind me.

'How come we only got Pin the Glove on Michael Jackson and Pass the Parcel at our birthday parties? Why couldn't we have had this kind of entertainment?' He nodded in Absinthe's direction and then Hector's.

I smiled at him. 'Hannah was scared of clowns, and call me old-fashioned, but I still believe strippers should be reserved for bucks' nights, not kids' parties.'

'Well, just 'cause you had a sheltered upbringing, don't you think it was a little unfair to put that deprivation on us?' he said in a mock-disapproving tone.

'Would you have preferred it if I'd let it all hang out in public till you were say, oh, five, which is how old he'll probably be before she weans him?'

He blenched at the thought, and staring at the flasher he said, 'Isn't her kid already a bit too old to be having moo juice?'

'I reckon he is. But it's laced with Absinthe.'

He gave me a puzzled look. 'What? She's drinking alcohol while she's breastfeeding? Isn't that a no-no?'

'She's not drinking it. She is the alcohol.' I named names.

'*Jesus!* How does Hannah attract these freaks?' he muttered as he walked off. I'd often wondered the same thing about myself.

Iris was heading towards me with an empty plate. She stopped and whispered, 'I don't care that Gaia's parading the dairy section. But she's cultivated a fucking bush in each armpit, and it's creeping me out!'

I laughed at her, and when Maxi came over and said, 'This is the only time I can say with absolute sincerity I wish your mother was still alive,' I laughed again. Judge Sylvia had cooked up a homemade AVO against Maxi after her senses were assaulted by Maxi's topless centrefold pose for a footy magazine. We were seventeen at the time. The AVO was still in place when Sylvia died two and a half years ago.

As both girls moved on to load up with some carbs, I looked across the yard and saw Norma making a beeline for me, a look of dismay on her face. Hannah, who was still at the other end of the garden, mouthed, *'Sorry.'*

Uh-oh. Seemingly, the cat, or part of it, was out of the bag—
I knew Hannah would've been selective about how much she'd
told Norma. Still, I felt relieved. Lately, I'd been questioning the
wisdom in keeping secrets. Some of them, anyway.

I watched my now-informed, beloved, dumpy and matronly
auntie as she approached. Norma had been dumpy and matronly
for as long as I could remember. And beloved. Always the
peacemaker, there had been many times she'd defended me to
Sylvia. She shouldn't've had to, but she always did.

I put my empty plate on the table and Norma hugged me.
Her lips were set in a grim line when she drew back. '*Chérie*. Is
this why Ralph never calls me back? He sends me text messages
to say he's too busy to talk, but he didn't say he'd left. Why
didn't *you* tell me?'

'Uh, I-I—'

'I can't believe he left. *Pourquoi?*' Why?

Luca's party wasn't the time or place to go into it. I didn't
want to excuse Ralph's choice, but right now, it was the better
option. 'Um, he just needs space to get his head around things.'

She frowned. 'And he needs to leave you for that? *Moi, je
ne comprends pas ça.*' I don't understand that. 'I thought he was
happy to find Beth. *C'est vraiment fou!*' It's really crazy!

It wasn't surprising that Norma knew nothing of our living
arrangements—Ralph's living re-arrangements. If he wasn't
speaking to Beth, he sure wasn't going to say anything to
Norma. And like much of her generation, she was prone to
sometimes dismissing situations in simplistic terms. You
discover you're adopted. You're sad. You discover your
biological mother. You're glad. I wasn't quite sure she'd see the
paternity issue simplistically.

She dropped her voice to a whisper. 'Does anybody else
know?'

'No.' Other than Alex, Casper, Beth, Maxi, Vette, Iris, Rhea, Reuben, Ida, Nestor, Henry, Joel, Leah, Ari, and my hairdresser.

Not wanting to cry, I changed the subject. As we chatted about this and that, I kept sneaking looks at the gate.

In spite of myself, my heart raced when it opened ten minutes later and he stepped in looking picture-perfect. He wore his navy knee-length cargo shorts, a loose white polo shirt, and light blue Tommy Hilfiger boat shoes.

His eyes searched the group of children playing in the garden. He and Luca spotted each other at the same time.

'Waph, Waph, Waph!' Luca squealed with delight.

Like Hector, Luca didn't speak 'r'. When I first met Hector, I worried that his speech impediment might be genetic and that our grandchild could inherit it. But Hector wasn't Luca's biological grandpa. And rhotacism might be cute on kids, but if Luca didn't outgrow it, Hannah would take him to speech therapy. Nobody wanted Hector saying Luca shared his 'twait', 'attwibute', 'chawactewistic' or any other synonym with or without an 'r'. *Nobody.*

Luca threw himself at Ralph, who hoisted him up, hugged him tight and kissed him. Luca and Ralph loved each other. Their bond was established pretty much from day one, before Ralph even suspected he might be Alex's father and, by extension, Luca's grandfather. Watching them together was heart-warming. And heartbreaking. I missed Ralph's arms around me, and I missed his kisses.

Ralph stroked Luca's head as he eyed him adoringly and spoke to him. Luca nodded, said something back in Luca-speak, then squirmed free of Ralph's arms. He had other fish to fry. Ralph watched him as he scampered off, then scanned the crowd. His eyes came to rest on me. He headed over and wasn't far away when a grating voice to his left waylaid him.

'Ohhhh, Waaalph?' Spoken from the sidelines in the bitchy intonation of a pubescent schoolgirl, the matching look on Hector's face said *Hell hath no fury like a man scorned* (he'd observed, with rancour, Luca and Ralph's warm interaction).

The look on Ralph's face—he who never swore—said *Shit*.

He turned to face Hector. His head snapped back in shock as he took in the little man's appearance. Ralph looked down at the ground and shook his head. A small smile played on his lips.

Hector opened his mouth to say something, but Ralph foiled him with the all-too familiar stop sign hand gesture. It brought back painful memories for me, but in this case, it was a calculated move:

'Stop. This hectoring of yours is a waste of my time. You've overplayed your hand, now back off!'

He glared at Hector. Bozo's face (and nose) changed colour again and he slunk away. Ralph watched him leave, then looked back at me. We exchanged a smile. He closed the distance between us, kissed Norma, then greeted me, his voice husky. 'Hey.'

'Hey.'

'So, I guess Hannah hadn't invited me earlier because of you—'

'Oh, enough! *Ça suffit!* That's enough, Ralph!' Norma's outburst shocked us both.

Ralph stammered, 'I-I d-didn't mean it as an accusa—'

'I don't care!' Norma was good and mad. She'd paid a price for keeping her mouth shut over the years. Now, nothing was going to stop her, even though she'd misread Ralph's intention. I knew he was referring to Hannah's loyalty.

Norma lowered her voice so as not to embarrass him further in front of the other guests. 'You hardly spoke to me for three years, and now you're treating your wife the same way. I can understand you being mad at me. I *should* have told you about your adoption when you were a little boy. But your father—Albie—he said not to. And I should have protected you from him all those times he hit you. I was wrong. *J'ai honte.* I'm ashamed.' She tapped her chest for emphasis. 'But what terrible thing has Ruthie done?' She glared at him. 'You fix this!' She jabbed her finger in his direction. 'Go and see someone together if you have to. But you fix this, Ralph.'

Ralph was left reeling. Looking vulnerable and properly chastised, he could only nod.

I didn't know whether to hit Norma or kiss her. It was what Ralph needed to hear, but it was ill-timed. And the fact that he'd come over to talk to me in the first place was a step in the right direction.

He gave me a disappointed look and moved over to the other side of the yard. My shoulders slumped in defeat.

Norma took my hand and squeezed it encouragingly. *'Ne t'en fais pas, chérie.'* Don't worry, sweetheart.

I didn't want to spoil it for her. I didn't have the heart to tell her it looked like what she'd done had set us back. The singing-a-different-tune peacemaker was high on her first burst of assertiveness. It was a big thing, particularly where Ralph was concerned. He might have been the adopted one, but he was the apple of her eye. The others were rotten to the core.

Alex called everyone to sing happy birthday to Luca. After the last hurrah, Ralph headed for the gate. It felt like the last hurrah for our relationship.

CHAPTER THIRTY-SIX

On the Rocks

Everyone started leaving. Beth, who'd witnessed the encounter from a distance, hugged me and said, 'I'm here if you need to talk.' I thanked her, but didn't say anything more. Hannah asked what had happened. 'Nothing,' I told her. I stayed back to help her and Alex clean up, some of which necessitated eating the leftovers. Before Ralph, I'd been nibbling on purist food. Now, after Ralph, I was hoovering the realist grub. By the time I got home I was queasy from a mix of gluttony and fear, and I barfed the lot.

Had my relationship with Ralph become so fragile that it couldn't withstand Norma's attack? Did he actually believe I'd be behind something like that? I needed to set the record straight. I sent him a text that night.

> I didn't tell Norma about us. What she did shocked me as much as it shocked you.

He texted back ten minutes later.

> Okay.

Okay? That's it?

That was it for the rest of the week. Ralph's response, or lack of it, left me feeling angry and hurt. Again. Still. All those weeks clawing my way out of an abyss that he'd pushed me into, just like Sylvia used to. Only, *he* hadn't extended a helping hand. And now, he was pushing me again and I was pissed off! Well, I'd got myself out before and I'd do it again. Differently, though.

When I spoke to my friends, I didn't say anything about what'd happened with Norma and Ralph. It was a step in the right direction—movement out of the bellyaching that was threatening to become a way of life.

And from morning till late afternoon, I hammered away at the keyboard. But it was the wrong kind of movement. It was escapism. A move away from the real world into a fantasy one. It would no longer do—when I stopped for the day, the gods and monsters gained on me and profound grief started to swallow me up again. But this time when it spat me out, I remembered Andy Dufresne's way out. Taking assertive action. Enough with the navel-gazing!

I sent Ralph a text on Sunday morning. I was done with Beth's advice to leave him alone to figure things out.

> It's been a week since Luca's party. Still no word from you??

His response:

> Were you expecting one?

Are you kidding? I was also done with tiptoeing around him!

REALLY?! What Norma did was
unfair & her timing sucked. And
like I said, I HAD NOTHING TO DO
WITH IT. But she had a point.
What ur doing is cruel, freezing
me out, punishing me, and for
what?! If u want out, then fucking
file for divorce!!!!!!!!

> What?! I do not want a divorce.
> I'm just trying to figure things
> out.

Married couples do that together,
work things out together. It's like
u want the best of both worlds--to
say ur married but live like a
bachelor.

> I'm not living like a bachelor.
> Having a terrible time.

So am I!! You're stringing me
along!

> Not intentional.

What bullshit! *Not intentional* was such a cop out. It spelled
n-o-t a-c-c-o-u-n-t-a-b-l-e.

> What a copout!

Five minutes passed with no response. Then the
psychologist in him answered:

> As I said, trying to work things
> out.

Yeah, and as I *said, married couples do that together! I'm not saying it again.*

Married to a stranger. Or estranged from a stranger. In a fit of pique, I threw my phone across the room, buried my head in my pillow and sobbed pitifully. When I was all cried out, I rolled on my back and stared unseeing at the ceiling. Numb.

My phone pinged. I could barely muster the energy or motivation to get it, but I had to pee. The phone lay on the floor near the bathroom door. I read the text.

> Do you want us to go and see
> someone together, like Norma
> suggested?

I didn't. It upset me that he felt we couldn't achieve anything without some kind of mediation, especially seeing as he was a therapist, and he hadn't even tried. But as Norma had said, *'Ça suffit.'* It was enough.

> Yes.

> OK. I'll ask my colleagues for a
> recommendation.

It took another week and a half before he got back to me. Tired from lack of sleep, I was climbing the walls by then.

> Appointment with Dr Jackson
> Lillicrap next Thursday at 12.00.
> Can you make it?

What? Lillicrap? You're shittin' me? Or, should that be, you're crappin' me? Oh God, I was glad Ralph couldn't see me!

> Yes.

He texted me the address, and followed it with another one:

See you then.

I didn't respond. And I wasn't going to tell anyone about the appointment. I had one week and two days to desensitise myself to this man's name. But for now, it injected a note of levity into a lillicrappy week, *ha ha ha*! It was what I needed.

As the day drew nearer, though, I feared I'd start laughing when Lillicrap introduced himself. I also feared there'd be no resolution to our situation. My stomach was in knots.

On the morning of the appointment, I was at sixes and sevens. I evacuated as many times as a ferret—Ralph had told me these animals shat often—but I still hadn't contained myself. I needed to cut the sillicrap, *ha ha ha*! I wondered if Ralph was having fun with it too. Wait ... Ralph?

Boom! Anger eclipsed the humour.

Ralph knew how I'd react. And no doubt, if he'd had two or ten names to choose from, he'd have zeroed in on this one. And if he'd had two or ten appointment times to choose from, he'd have opted for this one. Lunchtime.

Well, you can get stuffed, Ralph! I ate lunch at eleven. The need to have lunch at lunchtime would not be my undoing. The urge to laugh at the wrong time might. It meant Ralph would hold all the cards.

Maybe it was my karma. I'd taken perverse pleasure when he'd outplayed Hector, but I was hopping mad that he'd try this one on me. Still, it was a blessing. By the time I'd arrived at the good doctor's office, I no longer found his name funny. I'd become anaesthetised to it.

* * * *

CHAPTER THIRTY-SEVEN

Where's Jonathan When You Need Him?

Six hours had passed since I'd bolted from Lillicrap's office, and I was thinking more lucidly. Maybe the only appointment Ralph could secure had been the lunchtime one. But his having drawn attention to Lillicrap's name by leaving the Everett out of it made it seem like he'd been mocking me. The thought of that still chafed, but I was no longer fit to be tied.

A commotion to my right distracted me. Sylvia's posse was cawing and squabbling over morsels that a young couple was throwing. Tearing pieces of bread from a sliced loaf in a Tip Top bag, they were having fun changing the direction of their toss, then laughing as the birdbrained birds flitted and flapped willy-nilly to pounce on the scraps. I noticed it was white bread. Good, less fibre.

It made me think of my white-bread brother, who also lacked fibre. Small pangs of guilt stirred up, but they drifted away on the breeze. Coming here had been a wise choice, the ocean energy was restorative. And the experience in the doc's office started to take on a spoof-like quality.

The sun was getting low. I took in a deep breath of sea air and smiled. I always loved sitting on the beach in the evening, watching the sun disappear on the horizon as if it were sinking into the ocean. But that was a while off and my stomach was rumbling a bit. I was in no hurry to go home, though. There was no reason to rush, no one to go home to. And for the first time in two months, it felt okay.

I gazed up at the now cloudless blue. One lone seagull high up was soaring and dipping. Ah, yes. *Jonathan Livingston Seagull.*

That's me!

It was a timely reminder I didn't quite fit in with the flock and that it was a good thing. Even better, it helped me see with a bird's-eye view—a nice change from being in the abysmal village of the damned, belly-up and looking through the worm's-eye view of my primitive brain.

Now, it was big-picture stuff that I saw. A collage of images came together and fell into place like pieces of a jigsaw puzzle. Still lots of gaps that'd get filled before I carked it, but there was enough there to get the picture.

My story. Too uncultured and ridiculous to have a Shakespearean foie gras, truffle or saffronesque flavour. No. Mine was more Monty Pythonesque, the flavour of spam, canned lunch meat. It made me think of what Maxi had said almost a year ago when Vette suggested I write a book. My life was an eternal black comedy. No wonder I wrote satire. My Book of Life was a frickin' underground comic book!

The memory flashes of crazy, crass and scatological events, which had once seemed random and unconnected, were starting to interlock. But the grandstanding gull disrupted my stream of consciousness.

'*Hu-oh, hu-oh, hu-oh.*' She was puking.

Aargh. I thought I was going to lose my lunch. *Breeeathe. Breeeathe.*

I deep-breathed, she was done, we eyeballed each other.

'Swallow a bad bit of plankton?' I said. *Or maybe a bitter pill? Stupid bird.* 'Now, where the hell was I?'

I couldn't remember; looked like she couldn't either. But I was taken back to the beginning, the moment she'd crapped on me. Huh ... the power of one turd raining down on someone to trigger an avalanche of memories.

And just like that, there it was.

The rest of the answer to the question I'd asked—the one that had me wondering why the trauma of the afternoon Ralph had shattered the family with his big mouth continued to weigh heavily four months on.

A jigsaw puzzle begins with that first piece you put down. The first piece of the puzzlement that shaped my life started when I was only about the size of a pinhead and Sylvia realised she was pregnant. The original dump of fear, guilt and shame. Hers: *No, it's too soon; I don't want this child; I feel bad for not wanting this child; I hope I miscarry; I'll die from another labour* ... probably all screeched in French and bombarding and permeating embryonic me. And the noise would not have let up during that nine-month stretch. Each one of Sylvia's negative emotions cast off because she was afraid of her own shadow, but that I had to swallow. *Jesus, no wonder I shot out in ten minutes.* Still, I'd turned the nine-month experience into a life sentence.

Hypervigilance from feeling cornered had become a pattern. And feeling cornered had translated to being cornered: the common cold that should have passed after a few days, not dragged on; remaining in toxic relationships way beyond their expiry date; feeling traumatised by an event long after it had passed because auto-absorbing other people's garbage weighed me down, and often took too much strength and endurance to jettison.

I needed to overlay this predominant pattern with an autocorrect option; to move from Sylvia's *what's mine is yours, what's yours is mine* to a healthy alternative: *what's yours is yours, what's mine is mine.*

I felt lighter. And grateful.

'Hey, thanks for the memories, harpy,' I said. 'And yeah, maybe thanks for shitting on me all those years.'

The gull bobbed her head in what looked like a don't-mention-it gesture. Hmm. Unusually humble for Sylvia. Was she showing signs of benevolence? Still ...

'Let's not get carried away—it was bad parenting. *Bad, bad, bad!*' But at least it had fertilised my lizard brain, home of primitive survival instincts and the habitat of my dirty goddess. I added, 'Well, as of now you can keep your shit!'

And Ralph could keep his.

My mind drifted back to just after our wedding reception wound up. I'd been worried he might be knocked six ways to Sunday if the paternity test was positive, and also, if he found his biological father. I figured my role would to support his fall. Not break it.

But I had tried to. I'd been driven by that *what's-yours-is-mine* thinking, which meant if he fell, I'd have to fall too. And I was sick to death of falling. So yeah, it wasn't so much about protecting Hannah, as Ralph had accused. It'd been in the interest of self-preservation that I tried to break it by nagging and gagging him. And gagging myself.

Sylvia-gull launched into a shrill trill that seemed to say *Ha ha, telle mère, telle fille.* Like mother, like daughter.

CHAPTER THIRTY-EIGHT

Flying the Coup

'**B**ullshit!' I yelled at my *not* benevolent mother. I was no chip, flake or even splinter off the old block. 'I might have the harpy within me, Sylvia,' I snarled, 'but unlike you, I own my harpyness, it doesn't own me!'

The couple throwing bread bits looked at me like I'd come unhinged. I recognised that expression, I'd worn it myself. But I didn't care what they thought of me.

They scooted off. She, sing-songing the word 'Kerrrazy!' But I didn't care what they thought of me. Their scrounging fan club followed the scent of the half-full Tip Top bag, but Sylvia-gull looked like she was settling to roost here. Sylvia, who clearly still had much to learn in the next world; Sylvia, who'd assumed many disguises that concealed her own spirit—harpy, vulture, albatross around my neck—stood transfixed and stared. I leaned forward and outstared her.

'All those years, you demanded your pound of flesh, but I don't owe you. I'd say we're done here. Time to cut your losses.'

And we had lift-off!

I watched the low-flying gull disappear, then stood up and stretched, taking one last look at the ocean. I felt a sense of acceptance for what was. I felt like a yeeros.

After shaking the sandy blanket and folding it, I gathered up the food wrappers, water bottle and tissue box, made my way to the loos on the esplanade, then headed back to the main drag and bought myself a yeeros charcoal lamb pack with chips, a Greek salad, a slice of scrummy baklava, and another bottle of water. Back in the car, I polished off the whole meal. As I dusted the crumbs and some residual sand from my lap, a bit of grit flew up into my eye. Damn!

I squirted some water into my palm and blinked into it several times. It worked. I switched on the interior light, flipped down the sun visor and leaned in close to the vanity mirror, pulling out upper and lower eyelids for added insurance. All good. No. Better than good. Something had changed.

There was grit there of a different kind, a determination that had deserted me for too long.

I'd lived through Sylvia's constant reminders—through her words, actions and non-actions—that I was an interloper. And now, I was surviving Ralph's kiss-off.

By losing myself in my writing during these difficult weeks, I'd found a place where I could completely be and express all of me. I was writing my spirit back to life. And like Rhea had had her epiphany—the revelation after the apocalypse—I now had mine. Ralph was not my raison d'être ... I was.

Through the windscreen, I saw a lone seagull circling above. It couldn't be Jonathan this time. No. JLS had purpose and direction and wasn't afraid to fly high. I wound down the side window, stuck my head out and yelled out to the recycling bird, 'And by the way, I forgot to add, I don't owe Myron anything, either.' Then I said, as much to myself as to her, 'And maybe

Ralph won't put up with me. But that's not because I'm unlovable. Fuck you, you with your endless trash-talk in my head! Well, I'm now putting you on notice. You can keep trying to run circles around me, and I'll just keep kicking your sorry arse back to where it belongs.' I jabbed my finger at her. '*You are not wanted! How's that make you feel?*'

I didn't care how she felt. As for me, well, I knew there'd be more grief in store if Ralph, the great love of my life, didn't want me. He used to tell me if I had to struggle for something, it wasn't worth it, it wasn't meant to be. It made me sad to think about how these last several months with him had felt like a struggle. The seeds of doubt Andy had planted about Ralph and me being Twin Flames were now full-blown weeds. But I knew that no matter what, my spirit would sustain me like no one or nothing could.

It felt like the end of another odyssey. I was Odysseus, the brave warrior who'd fought, got lost, felt hopeless, then persevered, rediscovered his mettle, and was on the way home.

The breeze picked up a little and sent some invigorating sea air my way. *Peace.* Wanting more of both, I knew what I had to do once I got home.

I started the car and turned on the radio. Gloria Gaynor's 'I Will Survive' was playing.

'Yeah, yeah, yeah! Synch-ro-ni-cityyyy!' I whooped, and then belted out my version of the lyrics as I drove.

I pulled into the garage, killed the headlights and amped up the volume for the grand finale.

'Mmm, mmm, I'm gunna surviiive ...' I froze midway, my hands in a death grip on the steering wheel.

Oh shit.

CHAPTER THIRTY-NINE

Home Sweet ('n' Sour) Home

Gloria would survive with heaps of love to give, but I might have little time to live!

The door leading into the laundry had swung open and an ominous, backlit, shadowy figure loomed large in the doorway.

Ah-ha-ah-ha-ah-ha. Get a grip, woman, no time to wuss out.

I threw the car into reverse and was about to back out like a stunt driver at breakneck speed, as in *The Fast and the Furious*, when the garage light went on.

Oh.

Him.

My pounding heart stilled, but it didn't become all aflutter like it would have a week earlier. Or several hours earlier.

I shoulda changed the bloody lock.

I stared at the catwalk model through the windscreen. Nobody would hire him in the state he was in, he looked a right mess. His shirt was hanging out, his hair was mussed and his face wore a pinched expression. It reminded me of that morning four years earlier when he'd come back to apologise for recklessly declaring his love for me the night before.

Man, I'm beginning to hate anniversaries.

'I've been calling you for hours,' he said as I stepped out of the car. His voice was ragged.

The panic returned. 'Is something wrong? Has something happened? Are the kids okay? Luca?'

'No. Yes. They're fine. I was worried about you! Where have you been?' It came across as a subtle reproach.

I stood stock-still, thunderstruck. At first. Then I walked towards him and looked up into his bloodshot eyes. 'Under the circumstances, you don't have the right to ask me that.'

The great love of my life no longer looked so great, and my inner Yoda and inner peace just went down the toilet.

Without giving him a chance to respond, I pushed past him and walked through the door leading into the lounge. I headed for the bedroom, grabbed my nightie from under the pillow and took it into the bathroom, locking the door behind me. I ran the shower hot and shampooed twice, sloughing off any remnants of bird shit, and taking natural oils with it. Then I ran the water cold. I felt salty from my time at the beach, and peppery because of Ralph's sudden about-face. It took me back to another time and another face. My first boyfriend, sixty-day Zach.

> Zach Cohen had used and re-used chicks, but he couldn't sustain a relationship for more than sixty days. He probably couldn't have sustained an erection for more than sixty seconds, only getting off on the thrill of the chase. Once he'd nabbed his quarry, he lost interest. It'd peak again when she moved on, then he'd chase her for another sixty-day go-round. He eventually found a wife. He eventually left his wife and found a husband. Only then did I stop asking myself what I'd done for him to leave me. And then leave me again.

I wasn't worried that Ralph might secretly bat for the other team. I was annoyed about his fickle-mindedness. By the time I dried off, I'd cooled off.

I padded barefoot into the kitchen. Again, I got a shock when I saw him. It wasn't like I'd expected him to leave; I'd just become used to his absence and I wouldn't have cared if he had taken off. A defensive stance, but it suited me fine to feel nothing. It had to be that way. I'd felt too much in the last couple of months.

With slumped posture, he was leaning against the bench looking downcast and down at his feet. He straightened when he saw me.

'Can we please talk?' His voice was strained.

I responded with an apathetic shrug.

He sat on one of the stools. I remained standing and folded my arms. The analyst in him took this in. His body drooped, then he squared his shoulders and faced his hostile audience.

'I swear, I didn't know about him.'

Him? I gave him a confused look.

'The therapist.'

Oh yes. How could I forget? Humpty. Fat Bastard. *Oh no*. I wanted to laugh, but I couldn't afford to. As a writer, my imagination could take me into all manner of feeling. I drew on that gift now, thought of horrible things. Road carnage, terminal illness, paralysis, flared trousers as a fashion statement. It worked.

Ralph continued. 'I called you a few times but your phone kept going to voicemail.'

Oh. I'd forgotten to turn my phone back on when I left the dumpling's office. But I didn't tell Ralph that. I didn't answer. It wasn't a question.

'I got real panicky a couple of hours ago and started calling hospitals—' His voice broke. I could tell he was remembering the night of my accident.

'—that was after I called Hannah and Casper and Maxi and Vette.' He gave an embarrassed half-smile. 'And Beth.'

Jesus! 'Well, I need to let them know I'm home.'

'I already did. While you were in the shower. And if it makes you feel any better, I got an earful from all of them. Even Vette.'

Yep. Makes me feel a whole lot better.

'And I deserved it. I've done the wrong thing. Opening my mouth when I shouldn't have. I've messed up big time.' He looked down at his hands, then looked up at me again. 'Especially with you.'

If you're waiting for a there, there, *you needn't hold your breath.*

'It's just that you were so—'

'Oh, no-no-no. No you don't! Whatever I did or didn't do, you made the decision all on your own to move out. Don't even *think* about putting that on me.' I glared at him. 'You can go home right now if that's your intention.' I pointed towards the door to enforce my point.

'No, it's not.' He put his hand over his heart. 'I take full responsibility.' His eyes welled with tears and he quickly wiped them away. 'But, I thought ... I thought I was home. Aren't I?' he said, his voice cracking.

It was hard to keep the annoyance out of mine. 'Well, hell, I dunno. Are you?'

Sadness clouded his features. 'I wanna move back in. I wanna work this out with you. Please?'

'Moving back because you were afraid something might've happened to me is not a good enough reason.'

He shook his head. 'No, that's not why.'

I stared at him, narrowed my eyes and made him wait. And wait. And wait. Then I spoke. 'I can't stop you from moving back in any more than I could stop you from moving out. But you're not sleeping in my bed.'

My bed. Not *our* bed. I could tell that one cut deep.

He nodded. 'I'll stay in Casper's room.'

I hated it when Hannah or Casper responded with *whatever*. It was rude and dismissive. 'Whatever,' I said. 'I'm tired. I'm going to bed.' With that, I walked away.

'Ruthie?'

Now what? I half-turned.

'Please don't let this overshadow what we had for all those years before.'

I looked at him for a long time before answering. 'You did.'

His shoulders sagged. I turned back and made my way down the hall towards the bedroom and closed the door behind me. I hit the power button on my mobile. There were thirty missed calls and worried messages from Ralph, Hannah, Ralph, Maxi, Ralph, Vette, Ralph, Beth, Ralph, Casper, and even Reuben. I felt bad for what I'd unintentionally put my family and friends through. Then again, it was what Ralph had put them through. And his idea of calling a 'few times' amounted to eighteen. I didn't care what I'd put him through.

I texted Reuben to say I was okay, and called the others. It didn't matter that Ralph had let them know. They needed to hear it from me. I didn't go into detail, but promised to speak with them the next morning. There were another couple of calls I had to make.

The first one was to the Sheraton Noosa. Did they have any rooms available for five nights from tomorrow? Yes, they'd just had a cancellation! I didn't have to struggle, it was meant to be. The next call was to the airline. Did they have any flights to the Sunshine Coast, outbound tomorrow, homebound Wednesday?

Yes, they did, early afternoon there, mid-afternoon back, and at a discounted rate! I didn't have to struggle, it was meant to be.

I climbed into bed with a satisfied smile, and turned off the lamp.

A good five minutes passed, when there was a soft knock on the door.

Go away.

The door opened a crack and a sliver of light from the hallway filtered through.

'Ruthie,' Ralph whispered, 'okay if I come in and get some pyjamas?'

I simulated the even breathing pattern of sleep, throwing in a soft snore for good measure.

After a beat, I heard the rustle of his trousers, then the *piaaaak* sound of the wardrobe's plastic rollers on its metal track. I pricked up my ears. The sounds were heightened. It was like having the auditory system of a bunny on the alert (thank God I didn't have the large upright ears). And with Ralph standing only a few feet away and me being in a supine position, I felt open and vulnerable.

He wouldn't be here long, though. Where my drawers were shambolic, Ralph's were shipshape. Everything was neatly folded and coded. Light on top, gradations of colour in between, dark on the bottom. I opened one eye and saw him dig deep into the drawer. *Jesus, you're only sleeping in them! The light ones'll do.* Then again, he probably wanted to match his state of mind.

He finally settled on a pair of boxers and a T-shirt. But seeing the way his broad shoulders and tight buns moved brought back memories of all the action that had taken place in this room, excluding solo performances. It also brought back that familiar kindling down-under. *Shit.*

As if he sensed it, he turned to look at me in the semi-dark. I slammed shut the eye, but felt him staring.

Hey, remember how you left without a word two months ago? Do that again now. He must have heard the thoughts. My bunny ears heard the fade-out rustle of his trousers and the door closing, swallowing up the sliver of light.

Trying to release the stirrings was not as easy. And it got harder when I heard the *swoosh* of water rushing through the pipes. He was having a shower. It meant he was naked, soaping those tight buns, his washboard belly, broad shoulders, toned pecs—

Stop it! What if he picks up on these *thoughts, and returns? I'll be screwed. Every which way. Think mass destruction, think inferno, think torture and drowning.* Good. I was no longer thinking dirty, but my beaver wasn't working in concert with my mind. Not so good.

Oh God, I needed protection. I needed a team of cheerleaders.

Give me an A

Give me an N

Give me a G

Give me an E

Give me an R

What do we get? We get ANGER!

What did I get? Nothing.

'Nothing' was good. Or was it?

That state of nothingness was like revisiting my lost years. Back then, Ralph had helped me come back to me. Now, he'd come back home to me, but I was leaving me again. Worse, I was entering that droid universe Joe once occupied, and Myron still inhabited. By comparison, Sylvia's Anger Central was looking infinitely better than this barren place, where you were neither dead nor alive. Tomorrow and Noosa couldn't come soon enough.

With nothing on my mind and nothing in my heart, I dropped off, only to wake a few hours later with heartburn. Back in Sylvia's angry world, but my stomach had picked up the slack and was speaking on my behalf.

I stumbled out of bed and made my way to the kitchen, switched on the pelmet light, blinked away its assault on the eyes, then ferreted out the bottle of Eno from the untidy—yes, cluttered, disordered, look-who-did-it-and-ran—pantry.

I dropped a heaped teaspoonful in a glass of water, waited for the bubbles to subside a bit, downed it in one go, and let rip a humungous burp that would have woken the dead. *Just, please, God, not my mother. Don't let it wake my still-uncharitable mother.*

I groaned, released a couple of aftershocks and rubbed my sternum.

'Are you okay?'

I started. In my semi-dazed and dyspeptic state, I'd forgotten Ralph was here.

'Sorry. I didn't mean to frighten you. Are you okay?' he repeated, his forehead creased in a distressed frown as if he'd read my chest-rubbing gesture as a precursor to a heart attack. 'Ruthie?' His voice had risen in pitch, like he'd sucked from a helium balloon. His over-concern was tantamount to being stalked by my over-reactive mother.

'Yes, I'm okay,' I responded with impatience. 'It's just indigestion.'

That should have been the end of it. I mean, what can you say to someone who's just told you they have indigestion?

'I love you, Ruthie.'

What? I just belched like a power saw and you're professing your love for me?

'I meant what I said earlier. I really wanna work this out with you.'

The yeeros was repeating on me. Ralph was repeating on me. I couldn't stomach either at the moment.

I gave him a cynical look. 'Uh, is that supposed to fill me with the warm and fuzzies? You, laying it on thick? From nothing, to this? Just like that?' I clicked my fingers for emphasis.

'No.' He shook his head. 'It's not like that. There's a lot more to it than meets the eye. Please let me explain things—'

'Not now. Right now, I can't take anything else in. All this is making me feel crazy. My head's full. I need to get back into my body.'

Damn. Poor choice of words. His eyes glazed over and he fixed me with a look that said, *I need to get back into your body, too.*

My body responded and I was rooted to the spot. I needed to move, and quick, or I'd be rooted *on* the spot!

Too late.

That physical reaction to Ralph immobilised me. We stood there staring at each other. And then, he closed the distance between us.

CHAPTER FORTY

Simply Irresistible

He cupped my face and kissed me. Softly, tenderly, his tongue started to probe my mouth as his hands moved down towards my waist. He wrapped his arms around me and drew me to him, holding me firmly against his growing hardness. Weak woman that I was, I slid my arms up around his neck.

Our kisses became urgent, both of us moaning with unbridled ecstasy. I was losing myself. But then ... I sensed a presence in the room. And much as I tried to ignore it, it was insistent. It spoke. In French.

Toi, tu comporte comme une pute! You're behaving like a slut!

Hello, God—did I not say 'please' before? You know, when I asked you not to wake my dead mother? God—omniscient, omnipresent, omnipotent, omnifuckingdeaf.

Then again ... I'd taken leave of my senses and she snapped me out of my foolish reality.

I've learnt that prayers are often answered in convoluted and unexpected ways. Angels, winged messengers, aren't only those adorable, fat little cherubs. They come in many forms, harpies included. And even though it was typical of Sylvia's mothering style, this time, it felt like a healing poison. God— omnismartarse.

I pulled away from Ralph, took a step back. 'No. No!' I shook my head. 'I'm not doing this with you.'

He was stunned. Forlorn, even. An erection going nowhere was cause for forlornness.

He winced. 'I'm sorry. It's too soon, I know. I just ... it was just that ...' It was just that his voice turned husky. 'It's just, well, being in close proximity to you, it's hard to resist you.'

What? His words knocked me sideways; words failed me. But not for long.

'Really? *Really?* We were in the same bed for two months before you moved out! Close proximity doesn't get much closer than that, Ralph. Yet, you had no trouble resisting me. Oh, and I was so goddamn irresistible, you managed to stay away in your own apartment for another two.' I was tasting bile now. 'And during that time, you only initiated contact once and it was through a text! After Maxi's wedding, where we were also in "close proximity", but you had no trouble keeping your distance there!'

He looked down at his feet, then looked up at me. 'I know. I was thinking we might resolve things back then. But your response was defensive, so I—'

'It was a text message. You sent me a *text* message, Ralph! You would never advise one of your clients to resolve things through text messaging. Come to think of it, you'd never advise a client to walk out on his wife with no good explanation. Make that, *no* explanation.'

'Ruthie, I didn't walk out on you. You're my wife. You never stopped being my wife.'

'No,' I said in a strained voice. 'But you stopped being my husband.'

He opened his mouth to speak. I cut him off before he could say anything. 'I'm going to bed.' I needed to get away from him, couldn't stand the sight of him. Was that what it had been like for him when he left? Didn't know, didn't care. I turned towards the bedroom, took a few steps, but then turned back to look at him.

'You know, you don't get to mess with my heart and my head again. You don't get to do that.' I strode down the hall and slammed the bedroom door behind me. *Bite me, Troyboy!*

I expected to hear a voice in the wings saying 'Cut. Print it. That's a wrap.' My words had sounded scripted. And I'd been so dramatic, the whole scene could have come straight out of a romantic movie, the parting words spoken by the tragic leading lady.

I slumped against the door and facepalmed.

Sylvia, the Mills & Boon junkie who still didn't occupy a place in my heart two and a half years after she'd shuffled off this mortal coil; Sylvia, who'd been awakened by my man-sized burp, still resided in my head, still headed up the monsters' think tank. Unmarried Chick had taken a back seat. At this very moment, my mother was the leading lady in my psyche.

Someone, shoot me.

CHAPTER FORTY-ONE

Due North ... Going South?

The next morning, I woke with my head in a fog. Or a fog in my head. It was after eight; I'd slept in. All that sleep and still weary. I yawned, then froze. What was that noise?

Someone had broken in. *Aargh.* I grabbed the inert mobile from the bedside table and powered it up, scuttled into the bathroom, locked the door, and waited with finger on standby to hit 000.

Come *on*! I could be dead before this phone came to life.

Another noise, this one a loud clattering. An amateur burglar? I moved to the door, put my ear against it. *What the ...?* The intruder was emptying the dishwasher?

Oh. I forgot the intruder had moved back in last night.

I showered and threw on some casual clothes: combat fatigues. A pair of shorts and a loose, tatty T-shirt over the oldest and unsexiest bra I owned: a sports bra. Like the original jockbra inspired by two jockstraps stitched together, it was the kind that prevented breast bounce—and boners.

The infiltrator looked up as I traipsed into the kitchen. He had just finished preparing a damn fine-smelling breakfast feast: scrambled eggs, hash browns, sourdough toast, smoked salmon, avocado, freshly squeezed orange juice, tea. I was grateful I had all the ingredients in stock. It said *Screw you, I've managed quite well on my own.*

'Good morning,' he said sheepishly.

I noticed he was dressed casual. He must have slipped into the room to get his clothes while I was in the shower. But why casuals? 'Why aren't you at work?' Was it Saturday today? Had I slept through Friday? Oh, no. Had I missed my flight? Oh n—

'I postponed my appointments for today. I'll go get my things from the apartment this morning, then I was hoping we could spend time together and, you know, talk.'

I opened my mouth to tell him I wouldn't be here, but thought better of it. He might postpone going to the apartment. All those months I'd wanted to you-know-talk, but he hadn't. Now he wanted to, but I didn't. We didn't want the same things. Was it a sign?

He spooned the eggs onto the plates, then pulled out a chair for me. Over the top, obsequious, but when food awaited, I could overlook anything.

'Would you like to go out for lunch? Or if you're busy, then maybe dinner?' he asked as I sawed a piece of egg-topped toast.

'I'm going away this afternoon.' *Big mouth.*

'Oh. Um, where are you going?'

I hesitated, then said, 'Up north.'

'Up north?'

'Yep.'

He nodded as if giving some thought to what he'd say next. 'Where?'

'Noosa.'

'Oh.' One second passed ... two, three, four, five, six, seven ... 'Who with?'

It was rude to speak with a mouth full of food. Never bothered me before, but now it was rude. It was better for the digestion to chew slowly. Never thought that way before, but now I did. I finished chewing before answering. 'Myself.'

'Can I come with you? Plea—'

'No!'

He looked crestfallen, but said nothing.

Ralph had mastered and milked the hangdog look at seventeen after it had landed him a pity-fuck. All these years later, it'd become naturalised. I had to turn away. It wouldn't do for me to feel sorry for him. He needed to remember actions have consequences. It was one of Sylvia's many clichés (which apparently didn't apply to her), but it was the best I could come up with in the interest of immunity.

I scarfed down the rest of my breakfast because I had to get away from him. What irony.

For the rest of the morning, Ralph was the perfect husband. If you wanted a Stepford husband. I didn't, but it suited me for the time being. I wasn't up for D & Ms or confrontation. He heard what I didn't say and heeded it.

He went to his apartment to retrieve his things and I made my calls. All brief, all along similar lines: Ralph had moved back in. Was I okay with that? Time would tell, but right now, I needed to get away from Adelaide.

I also rang Norma. I loved that my aunt worried enough about me to call and drive me crazy every day. But she'd beaten herself up long enough for her catastrophic decision to withhold important information from Ralph. She needed to have her mothering affirmed, so I made it a point to tell her Ralph took her suggestion on board and that we saw a therapist. It wasn't a lie. She didn't need to know he was fat and that I'd cut and run.

She was thrilled that Ralph had moved back in, but she wouldn't have been thrilled to know I was going away sans him. I didn't tell her.

The others hoorayed my getaway and I felt buoyed by Casper and girl-power. Dr Lillicrap would be a killer conversation starter for another time.

Ralph came back with his stuff and said he'd pick up some groceries after dropping me at the airport.

'I've booked a cab.' *Remember how I wanted to take you to the airport when you and the scrubber went to Canberra, but you booked a cab?*

Another slap in the face, another woebegone look. He nodded and proceeded to clean the house, top to bottom. Not that the place was dirty, but my goddess of tidiness could sometimes be a lazy bitch. Ralph's presence was annoying, so was his OCPD. I didn't complain, though. The maid was back! And he didn't complain when I splashed away and left watermarks on the chrome tapware.

By the time the cab arrived, Ralph's lips were firmly affixed to my arse.

By the time I arrived in Noosa to a balmy 27°C, it was 'Ralph who?'

I sent texts to Casper and my female cheer squad to let them know I'd arrived safely and that I was on retreat for the next five days. I checked in to the hotel, unpacked, donned Bermuda shorts, a T-shirt and espadrilles, slapped on a smattering of sunscreen, and strolled down to the beach. En route, I bought a bottle of water and an ice cream.

The sand was warm. I sat down, dug my feet into it, and savoured the double scoop of mocha almond fudge in a waffle cone, and the fresh, salty smell of the ocean air. The taste and scent of freedom. When I was done, I licked my fingers and saturated the serviette with some of the water to remove the last vestiges of stickiness, then lay down, placing my bag under my head to prop it up a little. I felt good. No. Make that great. I felt great!

With eyes closed I took in the sounds: the sand crunching underfoot as people walked past, the waves gently lapping against the shore, children's laughter, seagulls cawing ...

Plop.

CHAPTER FORTY-TWO

Same Shit, Different Day?

I sat bolt upright. *Déjà vu. Déjà poo.* It was synchronicity in action and a cosmic joke.

Hard to believe it'd only happened yesterday, but this time I laughed as the bird alighted and watched me wipe the droppings off my hairline with the wet serviette. Again.

She squawked. It sounded like she was saying *Change doesn't happen overnight.*

'No, it doesn't. And on this issue, it won't. At all. I stand by what I said yesterday.' I leaned forward and aimed a finger gun at her. 'You wanna try dumping on me? Go ahead. Make my day.' I loved Dirty Harry. He got the shit-end of the stick, but did he put up with it? No. I wasn't going to anymore, either. I fired my 'gun'. *Poomb.*

The gull flew away. 'Hasta la vista, baby,' I said. I didn't like The Terminator because he was a cyborg. Like Myron. But I loved that parting shot.

Sylvia would be back at some point in one guise or another. But she didn't need to hang around now and she didn't need to appear as often. I wasn't feeding her. Freedom had just increased from the taste and scent of it to a keen sense of it.

I went back to the hotel and showered. As I was drying my hair, my phone pinged. A text from Ralph.

> Are you okay?

> Yes.

> Is there anything you need me to do?

Yeah. I need you to get lost.

> No. Text only if there's an emergency.

> Okay xx

xx? Ralph rarely xx-ed in texts. His transmission carried both disappointment and a bit of desperation. It wasn't my problem. He was in Adelaide; I was a thousand miles away. Literally. I wanted it to be that way metaphorically. Then why choose to come here of all places?

It was in Noosa about five years ago during a weekend away with Ralph, Maxi and Vette that things between Ralph and me had started to change. My marriage was coming undone and, feeling stale, I took myself off to Hastings Street for a makeover: new hairstyle and colour, provocative little dress. Back at the hotel, Ralph didn't recognise the new me, and he tried to hit on me!

I laughed at the memory, but then I felt sad. And sadness wouldn't do. I was here to float for a while, not dive. So, I escaped into Utopia. Beach walks, dips in the pool, sunbaking, delicious meals, reading, and retail therapy. Contentment. The rest of the holiday flew by and so did the birds.

It was a warm day when I got back to Adelaide. But the lightness and liberty I'd felt up north had gone south the minute the cab pulled up in front of my home. Being greeted by Bin's fat arse didn't help. He was on all fours, pulling weeds. I wondered if I could sneak past unnoticed. I wondered if he and Bitty did it doggie style. It was probably the best mating position for a pair of upright and inverted triangles.

I slipped out of the cab, quietly closing the door. The driver took my case out of the boot, then slammed the door. No, no, no!

Oh, great! Just great.

Bin swivelled his head. He sat back on his heels and smiled. 'Will, looks like someone's bun on holidays!'

Yis, end I hed five blussful nights of not hevving to lusten to the shut thet goes on un your fucking beardroom! I lifted my hand in response and almost tripped over the suitcase in my hurry to get away from him.

Inside, I collapsed against the front door and looked around.

I so don't wanna be here. And so, I wasn't. A darkness enveloped me. It was that same awful non-feeling of disassociation I'd experienced at Maxi's housewarming-cum-wedding. Here, but not here.

A hot shower did little to wash it away, but there was always food.

And what food! The freezer was filled with a collection of Tupperware containers of cooked meals, as well as two new tubs of ice cream. The fridge was stocked with trays of cold cuts and assorted cheeses, and a big box of gateaux, all of which were my faves. Everything had been stacked by the book: lower shelves, the warmest part of the fridge, for raw ingredients; middle shelves for jars of tapenade and whatnot; higher shelves, the coldest part, for dairy. The 'maid' had also cleaned out the crisper. Tired old veggies had been tossed. The nightshade family that had sprouted long before my holiday had probably walked out by itself. A younger bunch of spuds had moved in.

'Jesus, how long can someone be stuck in the anal stage?' I muttered as I tried to decide what to eat.

I was gorging on a slice of mille-feuille when I heard his key in the door. Early. *Shit*. My gut spasmed.

CHAPTER FORTY-THREE

Same Day, Different Shit?

'Welcome back,' the stranger said with forced cheeriness.

'Thanks.'

'You look well. Nice and suntanned.'

'Thanks.'

'Beautiful.' His voice was low and rough and it hit the spot.

Don't even go there. I turned away from him.

He cleared his throat and returned to neutral. 'Did you have a nice time?'

'Yes, thanks.' *Did you have a nice time with your slutty sister?*

Ohhhh, I wanna go back to Noosa where I can walk around without masks and armour, and where bitchy is off-limits. God forgive my bitchy thought. I didn't mean it. I meant slutty half-sister.

'That's good.' A nervous clearing of the throat. 'So, uh, would you like to go out for dinner tonight?'

'No. I'm tired.' *Energised from five days of doing nothing, drained from five minutes of deflecting you.*

He didn't question it. He was tiptoeing around me in much the same way I'd skirted around him in the months leading up to his departure.

I went off to unpack while he thawed out a container of beef bourguignon. He made mashed potato and a green salad to go with it.

We exchanged civilities as we ate, but he had to do all the work.

'So, what did you do up there?'

'Read, went for walks, shopped a bit, sat by the pool, swam, sat on the beach'—*talked to my mother the seagull, told her to piss off*—'stuff like that.'

'Mmm. Mmm. Sounds idyllic. Sounds idyllic.'

'It was.' *It was.*

We ate in silence after that. Well, I did. He *mmm, nom nom nommed.* I rolled my inner eye.

'I've noticed a ute parked in the neighbours' driveway. Have Phoebe and Zac moved out?'

'Yep. Around the same time you did.'

Oops. Impetuous. He gulped and followed it with a down-in-the-mouth look again. I thought he might cry. I started to waver until I heard the unwelcome voice: *N'oublions pas ce qu'il t'a fait.* Let's not forget what he did to you. Sylvia. Back again in a familiar form: the elephant in the room. *Welcome. Come join the herd that's taking up residence.*

Ralph rallied on Thursday morning and tried again. And no thanks, I didn't want to go out for dinner. Again, he didn't question it.

That night, he thawed out a chicken curry and served it with fluffy white rice, mango chutney and some greens.

When he tried to broach the hot topic, I gave him a taste of his own medicine. I was now the 'talk-to-the-hand' traffic cop. The pot was in no position to call the kettle black. And on Friday morning, the pot had to eat on his own. I was meeting Maxi and Vette for breakfast.

I was about to walk out the door when he said, 'How about tonight? Would you like to go out for dinner tonight?'

'I already have plans.'

'Oh. Um, with the girls?'

'No. Casper and I are going to Hannah and Alex's.'

This time, the tears started pooling in his eyes before he looked away. It aroused guilt and pity, which vaporised when Wednesday's message repeated itself: *N'oublions pas ce qu'il t'a fait.*

No. I couldn't afford to forget what he'd done.

As I pulled up outside Stella's, I remembered our meeting here a year earlier, same time, eight-forty. Again, it was two days after getting back from my time away. Again, the restaurant was quiet, and the same table was available. Synchronicity or sameness?

It didn't matter which. After the topsy-turvying of the weeks and months before, no change was a refreshing change.

Again, Maxi and Vette both turned up at the same time, five minutes after me, and we three hugged. We ordered the same breakfasts and had the same waiter. But it was a sliding doors moment.

My honeymoon with myself had been relaxing, and it was the first time in a year when getting together with my besties wasn't tinged with discontent or fraught with pain. I didn't want to talk about Ralph, not because I was avoiding reality, but because he'd consumed way too much of my time, thoughts, words and energy.

But I did tell them about Lillicrap and they laughed. And when I told them about Sylvia-gull, they laughed with me, not at me.

I asked Maxi how married life was.

She sighed with pleasure and went all moony. 'I still can't get enough of Nessie.'

Nessie?

I loved monikers. They were terms of endearment. Being called Ruthie made me feel lovable and important, and that mattered a lot because my parents never called me Ruthie. To them, I was just single-syllable *Ruth* or single-syllable *pest*. It was odd that this pair, who worshipped quantity over quality, didn't extend my name, and often addressed the many-syllabled Myron Stephen Lawrence Roth as *My*. Then again, it was an appropriate moniker for someone like Myron.

Anyway, I'd have thought that Nestor would be *Nes*, pronounced Nez. *Nez* had a manly vibe. A human one. 'Your nickname for Nestor is Nessie? Like the Loch Ness Monster?'

'Oh, no.' Maxi gave me a lewd smile. 'That's not my nickname for *him*.'

The same, no holds barred, dirty girl talk that had coloured our interactions for years never got tired. Vette and I laughed at her and the three of us nattered and giggled about other things. It was this intimacy that nourished the soul.

Networking with my friends and, later, with the kids was uplifting. But then coming home that night was like wading through pea soup. And over the weekend, the pea soup felt like it was congealing.

On Saturday morning over breakfast, Ralph asked, 'What are you doing today?'

'Working.' *Be good if you did the same. At the office.*

After showering, I settled myself in front of the computer in the dining room. I'd donned an old, rumpled, brown shift dress that had escaped the last couple of wardrobe cleanouts. Ralph had once told me brown was not my colour.

I worked on my book all day, he worked at domestic stuff.

Sunday was a repeat of Saturday, and Monday couldn't come soon enough. By the time he left for work, I was over the ingratiating maid service and was hoping he'd move back out.

CHAPTER FORTY-FOUR

The Big Freeze

'What's the point of you being here if you can't be you and I can't be me?' I said to Ralph a week later. He wasn't here, though. He was at work. It was a practice conversation and one that needed to be had. See-sawing between irritation and iciness, I was becoming a bitchcicle—a Sylvia–Joe compound.

It was spilling over into other areas, like my writing. And Andy, who'd been on a book tour the last few weeks but was now back, must have sensed the freeze because he hadn't dropped in as promised.

I was spinning my wheels at the computer on Friday morning in a cycle of writing biting crap, paraphrasing it, refining it, then deleting said crap, when the phone rang.

Beth.

'Hello, darling. How about I take you out for lunch today? Are you free?'

For Beth, I'd make time. And it wasn't like I was on a writing roll. We arranged for her to pick me up at twelve. We'd spoken a couple of times since my return, but the conversations had been brief because she was away camping again, and mobile service was scanty.

We went to Glenelg; her idea. She found a parking spot in a small side street off Jetty Road.

'Will we grab something and sit near the beach, or do you want to eat in a café?'

'Let's sit near the beach.' Sylvia-gull might show up to make my day. I was ready for her and I had reinforcement this time—Beth knew all about the kind of relationship I'd had with my mother. It angered her and made her all the more protective of me.

She bought a falafel roll for each of us, hot chips for me, and two bottles of water. We found a semi-shaded spot on the grassed area near the jetty. I sat cross-legged like a pre-schooler at story time, stooped forward with elbows on knees. She sat upright and as if she was riding side-saddle. She nibbled, I tucked in and waited for the onslaught.

Beth was both amused and outraged as I recounted my head-to-heads with the seagull. But talking about her was like summoning her and her cohorts. And there they were, a dozen or so blow-ins. Gate-crashing garbage guts assembling in front of us.

Beth glared at them. 'Which one is she? I'll give her what for!'

'The one that's squawking the loudest. That one, I think.' I pointed to the cackler towards the middle and on the outskirts of the flock. She was no longer in a position of leadership. I'd demoted her.

'Get lost!' Beth said, and threw a piece of her falafel at the bird.

They all attacked it violently, like a bunch of desperadoes swooping on a department store's bargain bin during a Boxing Day sale.

I gawked at this learned woman who had a swag of letters after her name. 'Really?'

Her cheeks pinked and she burst out laughing. 'Clearly, I'm not thinking straight.' Beth then put her roll down on its wrapper and turned serious. 'And I also wasn't thinking too straight after I got Ralph's call that day you went missing. He was in quite a state.'

I didn't say anything. We both became pensive for a beat, then Beth said, more to herself than me, 'Almost as bad as he was on the weekend.'

'The weekend?'

'Saturday. You know, when he dropped in to see me?'

'Oh. No. I didn't know.'

'Hmm.' She nodded and seemed to be weighing up whether she should say more. I waited her out. I wasn't big on patience, but this was her process, just like it was Ralph's.

'He's pretty devastated, Ruthie. He thinks he's lost you. It's the first time he's cried in front of me. Sobbed, actually.'

I looked away. Hearing this a couple of weeks earlier, knowing that he feared losing me would have been music to my ears. Now, hearing that he was suffering made me want to dance to the music. Bitchcicle.

'I know it sounds harsh and heartless,' I said as I turned back to face her, 'but I don't much care, Beth. For the past two months, there've been many times when I just didn't wanna be here anymore.' My voice had become thin and thready as my own words weakened my façade.

'Oh, sweetie.' Warm-hearted Beth's eyes welled. 'Why didn't you tell me?'

Beth and I had spoken regularly over the last few months, and more so after Ralph moved out. She knew it had been hard for me, but she didn't know the extent of it. I'd never let on.

She tenderly brushed a strand of hair off my face. This intimate gesture made me want to cry, but I fought back the tears.

I shrugged. 'I dunno. I guess I just didn't want to be a poor-me like my mother.'

'Ruthie. Being honest about your pain is not being a poor-me. Exploiting it is. And you most certainly don't do that!'

If you only knew the mileage I've been getting out of this. I felt ashamed, but said, 'Thank you.'

As if sensing I had more to say, Beth remained silent.

'I also didn't want to put you in an awkward spot, you know, with Ralph being your son an' all.'

'Darling. Yes, he is my son, but I haven't known him. These past couple of years I've been getting to know him. And you. And I love him dearly, but I love you just as much.'

And I loved Beth even more now for not trying to defend Ralph. It brought on the thaw and my own meagre defences collapsed. I put my lunch down and started to cry.

Beth took my hand and waited till I wiped away the tears. 'Look. I'm not about to dispense advice to you. And I didn't with Ralph. It's not my place to. It's nobody's place to. All I can say is I hope you two can work things out. You're meant to be together. I know what it cost David and me not having fought for each other and I'd hate to see that happen to either of you.'

I nodded. And though I felt conflicted, I also knew I needed to look after myself and my own well-being. 'I don't want it to happen to us either, but he strung me along for weeks, Beth. Months. And this is not about avenging him. I don't trust him.'

It made me sad to have finally put my overarching feeling into words. And Beth looked saddened by this disclosure, but I sensed she knew where I was coming from. Still, she remained true to her word. She didn't defend Ralph, and she didn't collude with me.

'So,' I continued, 'at the moment, forgiveness it not really on the horizon.'

'And that's okay. These things take time.'

We ate in silence for a bit. She ate like a bird—more like a baby sparrow than these rapacious seagulls—and had hardly made a dent in her lunch. I'd almost finished mine when I had a thought.

'Did Ralph ask you to speak to me?'

Beth shook her head. 'No. Well, not in so many words. He kind of hinted in an off-hand way. You know, saying that maybe I could put in a good word for him when I spoke to you.' She took a sip of her water. 'Look, having lunch with you today was about you, not about him. I needed to see that you're doing okay, and I appreciate that you were honest with me. But please, *please*, promise me you'll keep being honest with me?'

I did, we hugged and I said, 'Did Ralph tell you about the couples' therapist?'

'Um, on that day, he mentioned something about you two seeing a therapist and that it didn't happen, but he was so frazzled, he didn't elaborate. And he hasn't said any more about it. But, uh, you have that wicked look in your eyes. Why do I get the feeling I'm about to start laughing?'

That wicked look in my eyes found its way to my wicked lips. 'Well, for starters his name is Jackson Byron Everett-Lillicrap.' I drew out the first L and emphasised that last syllable.

Beth laughed at me. 'Oh, I can just imagine what you did with that one!'

As I gave her some of the details, she screeched and hooted. When her convulsive laughter had dwindled to hiccups, she shook her head and stroked my cheek. 'Sweet girl. Your mischievousness is one of your most delightful qualities. And I love that you make it safe for me to express my inner earthiness.'

I favoured her with a broad smile, which then turned wry. 'I wish I could say you make it safe for me to bring out my inner lady, but I don't think I have one.'

'Oh, you do!' She waved it away. 'And believe me, gentility is'—she looked around to make sure no one was within earshot—'fucking overrated!'

I *woo-hooed* and grabbed and squeezed her hand.

We sat chatting about this and that for another two hours: her camping adventure, my book, her projects, her kids, my kids, Luca. Not Ralph, though. Beth was wise enough to know that a newly planted seed shouldn't be overwatered. My gorgeous mother-in-law was like a tonic. Yet, I didn't feel better after I got home. I felt worse.

I couldn't even write crap, like I had before getting together with Beth.

Throwing my arms up in frustration, I yelled, 'What the hell am I gonna do?'

My thoughts were as woolly as Bitty's hair. But then ... a sweet, incisive moment of clarity. The simplicity of the solution released a flood of endorphins and I couldn't wait for Ralph to get home.

The conversation at dinner that night was strained and excessively polite on his part, once again. Maybe even more so than usual, or what had become usual.

He took the garbage out while I cleared up. He lined the bin with a new bag, but then just stood there. I sensed his eyes on me.

'Ruthie?' he said, his voice tight.

I stopped loading the dishwasher and turned to look at him.

'I, um, I'm trying. I'm doing my best here, but it feels like we're going nowhere. What is it that you want from me?'

I gathered up my courage and bit the bullet. 'A divorce.'

CHAPTER FORTY-FIVE

Locking Horns: Olé and Touché

Ralph's jaw dropped, his face turned ashen. 'What?' he cheeped.

'Let's be honest here. You and I were at our best when the dust settled after we became an item, when we weren't married, when we weren't under the same roof—'

'Look, I know it's been a terrible year,' he said as he raked his fingers through his hair. 'And the first year of marriage is supposed to be the hardest—'

'Yeah, and you're supposed to ride it out. To work through stuff together. But you bailed out!'

These words hit home. It was hard to look at his stricken expression, so I averted my gaze.

'No!'

His gruff-voiced command made me jump. I jerked my head back around.

'No?'

'Yeah. No! We're gonna work this out. Now! I've given you enough latitude.' His eyes stayed heavy on mine.

'You've *what*? You've given me enough "latitude"? Wow. You have got some nerve!' I sneered at him. 'As I recall, I gave you *considerable* latitude after you made the executive decision to move out. I had no say!'

'I admit, I should have involved y—'

'*Involved* me? Are you kidding?' My tone was bordering on the piercing falsetto of a Bee Gees song.

'Okay, okay. Then, have your say.' He was trying to placate me with a calm-down hand gesture. It further incensed me. *Grrr!*

'Have your say,' he repeated. 'Give it to me. Just spit it out because I can't take the indifference and unfeelingness anymore.'

I felt my face flush with anger. 'How dare you! Don't you talk to me about indifference or unfeelingness after *you* shut me out for months before you even moved out.' I was yelling at him. 'And I did nothing *but* feel!'

'And you think *I* didn't feel?' He raised his voice. 'My whole life was falling apar—'

'That was your own bloody fault. But you made it mine.'

'I did not make it yours!'

'No. You just took steps to make damn sure I'd go to hell with you!'

'Oh, you did that all on your own.' He started pacing. 'You were so caught up in your stupid worries about upsetting this one or that one, you couldn't see beyond it to what I was going through.' He snorted. 'Typical.' And with that, he got my Achilles Heel.

He hadn't said the word 'selfish', but the implication was there. It was enough to trip me into a shame spiral. And when I was saturated with shame, I couldn't think straight. Ralph knew it. It angered me that he'd try and shoot me down this way. But then, if I was aware of all this it meant I *was* thinking straight. I fired back using his form of ammo.

'Ah yes, a classic example of projection. As I recall, I tried to be there for you when you were at your worst, when your father died. But did you let me? No. I kept getting'—I made angry air quotes—'"I need to be alone right now" or "I can't talk about this at the moment" or "Not now, I'm going to work".' That I remembered these words verbatim kind of scared me. It was the Sylvia-esque way.

He glowered at me, I glowered back. We had a stand-off, but it didn't last long. Mr I-take-full-responsibility from a couple of weeks ago now tried to relinquish it.

'Well, it was too little, too late,' he muttered. 'I discovered long before that that I had a son and I'd missed twenty-five years of his life and you stopped me from having tha—'

'I "stopped" you? What rubbish! I'm not your bloody mother!'

'No? You sure acted like it.'

'Well, maybe it's because you were behaving like a child! And anyway, you already had a relationship with Alex. It's not like I stopped you from seeing him, for God's sake.'

'But you tried to stop it from going further.'

'Bullshit! You did that by opening your big mouth. Don't you dare blame me for your fuck-up. Just like Andy Dufresne, you—'

'What? What the hell does the neighbour have to do with this?'

'Not Andy Ellis-Nile. Andy Dufresne from *The Shawshank Redemption*.'

He looked at me, his mouth agape with incredulity.

'Well he got falsely accused and imprisoned and then he got out of his shitty situation into freedom and like him, I want out!'

'*What?* You're comparing a fictional character's situation to ours?' His lips curling in contempt, he said, 'I don't even know how to respond to that. But hey, a couple of minutes ago you were accusing *me* of being a child, of bailing out. And now, you're the one wanting to bail. So, who's the child?' He shook his head. 'Amazing how you can be a child and Sylvia at the same time. Oh wait, same thing.'

Another shot in the heel. I gnashed my teeth and clenched my fists. Then I screamed with all the lung power I could muster.

Ralph inhaled a sharp breath and took a step back. 'Have you gone *completely* mad?'

'I *am* mad and I HATE YOU!' I shrieked.

He returned fire. 'I HATE YOU BACK!'

Two children.

We continued like a pair of enraged bulls, goring each other with words until the doorbell sounded.

That bloody doorbell had become a red rag, and my response was like Pavlov's rabid dog. I snarled, stormed to the door and ripped it open.

I scowled at the familiar face and barked, '*You* again!'

CHAPTER FORTY-SIX

Law of the Jungle

Because of the checked pattern on their peaked hats, Joe had nicknamed the police 'chequerboard cuntstables'. A pair of them stood there. The surly burly one, who was momentarily taken aback, fit the bill. And he was no happier to see me than I was to see him. 'Yes. Me again.'

He had fronted up on my doorstep just over two years earlier when Luca had his foreskin removed. A ritual circumcision is a cause for celebration in the Jewish religion, and it was—for everyone except Luca. We celebrated the snip at eight o'clock in the morning with food and drink and loudness. Portnoy had complained to the authorities about noise pollution. This testy officer they'd sent out wore the uniform like a second skin, one he'd have done well to have removed.

The complaint this time around was about a more specific form of noise pollution: domestic violence.

My jaw dropped. 'Are you fucking kidding?'

He glared at me. 'You might want to watch your language, Ma'am.'

Seriously? 'Uh, why? You gonna arrest me for saying fuck?' I glared back at him and then, with a boldness that surprised even me, I added, 'Fuck, fuck, fuck, fuck, ffffuck.' *Lock me up, see if I care.* All those months in Sylvia's uterus and all those years under her roof, I already had the framework for prison life. And just like Andy D, I had the balls to get out. *So yeah, go ahead, make my day.*

Or not.

Alarming thoughts filled the space between my ears. I wasn't Dirty Harry ... and where the hell was Ralph? Assuming no responsibility. Again. It was a soundless transmission, but the anti-hero must have heard it. I felt his presence next to me and about bloody time.

The cuntstable eyed me with open disdain that was barely contained by his tone. 'I think you need to calm down, Ma'am.'

I shot him daggers. 'Please don't patronise me.'

He shot back, 'I'm not trying to.'

'What? It comes naturally?'

The cuntstable's face and neck reddened. He seemed hypertensive. If he had a heart attack right then and there, I was determined not to resuscitate him.

Ralph intervened. He knew I was playing with fire. 'So, you just want some facts, right?'

I spun my head around and scowled at him. *Really? You're making nice? You gonna kiss his arse like you have mine for the last few weeks?*

I sensed the bully cop's eyes boring into me as he answered Ralph, 'That's why we're here, sir.'

'Well. My wife and—

'Who reported us?'

'Sorry, Ma'am, we can't reveal our sources.'

Jesus. Looks like I'm not the only one who watches too many cop shows. 'Was it the people in the adjoining duplex?' If it was, I'd report them for fucking too loud and keeping me awake.

The cuntstable looked and spoke robotic. 'Again, we can't reveal our sources. Suffice to say, you could be heard all the way down the street.' He dismissed me and turned to Ralph. 'Go on, sir; you were saying?'

'I was saying my wife and I were just having an argument. Don't you have arguments with your wife?' Ralph cocked his brow. 'Or, husband?' And there it was. Ralph's special brand of sticking it to someone. He'd just redeemed himself.

Cuntstable snapped, 'Wife!'

'Whatever. The point is, do you see any upended furniture?' Ralph turned and made a sweeping gesture with his arm, taking in the room behind us. He turned back. 'Do you see any black eyes?'

He glared at both of us for a long moment. 'Maybe just try and keep it down.'

'Hmm. It's a little hard.' Ralph gave him a wry smile. 'These kinds of fights lead to some great forms of making up.'

Cuntstable's sidekick, who'd remained closemouthed throughout, started to laugh, just like he had two years earlier when Casper had wielded his smart mouth. Officer Cheerful was no longer a rookie, but he still hadn't toughened up. Keeping South Australia Safe? My arse.

Cuntstable stiffened but said nothing. I hoped he was quicker on the trigger in genuinely dangerous situations.

They left and I slammed the door behind them, took in a long, slow breath, and exhaled. I turned to Ralph, who favoured me with one of his irresistible, lopsided, schoolboy grins. 'I can't believe you said all that to a cop,' he said.

My breath caught in my throat. And then, I died.

CHAPTER FORTY-SEVEN

Bang on!

I didn't really die. Not in the physical sense. It was more akin to the phenomenon reported by those who'd had near-death experiences, where they'd seen their life flash before their eyes.

In an instant, a whole lot of images from my past presented. *Bang-bang-bang-bang.*

Bang 1: As kids, Ralph and I may not have fought often, but when we did, we screamed at each other, uninhibited.

Bang 2: As we advanced into adolescence and adulthood, we'd chosen not to scream at each other. Instead, we kept our distance for a bit when we were miffed.

Bang 3: Reuben and I rarely fought. He was non-confrontational, so he gave me the silent treatment if I raised my voice. I got that marriage was easier that way. But pussyfooting around each other had bred resentment that irreparably damaged what we'd had at the outset.

Bang 4: Since Ralph and I had become an item, I didn't yell like Sylvia had, except in texts. Instead, I sniped, like Joe had.

I flashed back to a much earlier time.

I saw my father putting up the newspaper to screen out my mother's rants. Even earlier, I saw myself covering my ears to shut out her tirades; myself at age four failing a hearing test and being taken to hospital to have my adenoids removed as a means of warding off permanent deafness. I saw Sylvia systematically shaming me when I expressed anger. And I saw Ralph's pain at Norma's repeated directive not to fight back and further incense his abusive father. I saw this becoming Ralph's pattern.

Yet, here we were, again having faced authority figures because of our blatant expressions of anger. Only, this time, we'd defended our right to vent, and thumbed our noses at those who would challenge that right. I thought about what I'd told Andy, about how suppressing our natural emotions could lead to disease. I got how Ralph and I censoring ourselves and each other had started to cripple our relationship. And I got why Ralph, who'd held back for too long, had suddenly exploded that day and spilled the beans after months of me trying to muzzle him.

'Ruthie?'

'Huh?' Ralph's voice brought me back to life. 'What?'

'I said, d'you want to pick up where we left off?' There was that lopsided smile again. 'Whose turn is it to yell?'

I opened my mouth to say something, but then started to laugh. So did Ralph. We cracked up. We doubled over shrieking and howling. It lasted almost as long as our earlier screaming session. And when the laughter petered out, when our sides ached, Ralph looked at me and I looked at him, and we went at each other again. Only this time, not with words. And not like a pair of incandescent bulls locking horns. But like sex-starved, horny teenagers.

We clung to each other and kissed with an unparalleled passion. Deep, urgent kisses. He moved back a step, removed the ugly brown shift dress, which was not my colour, balled it up, and threw it across the room. Then he deftly unhooked my bra and removed that. He grazed his hands over my breasts and we both released a throaty moan. I grabbed at his T-shirt and pushed it up. He threw it off and reached for me, crushing me against his chest. I threaded my fingers through his hair, he slid his down, clasped my butt cheeks and tilted my hips against his, pressing his hardness into me. With lots of groping and within minutes, his shorts and our briefs were discarded. And somehow, we'd moved from the entrance hall to the bedroom and ended up rolling around on the bed. All the earlier yelling followed by the laughter had constituted foreplay, and neither of us could wait. Sex with Ralph had always been intense, but this was stratospheric! Release was quick and explosive, both of us crying out in ecstasy at the same time.

Panting and sweating, we remained connected as he rolled onto his side, taking me with him.

He stroked my face with the tips of his fingers. 'God, I love you so much.'

These words caught me unawares. They hurt. I tried to mask the pain by closing my eyes.

'Oh, Ruthie ...' He held me closer and tighter.

He pulled back and looked at me. 'Do you still love me?' he asked hesitantly.

I nodded. 'But I don't trust you.'

Ralph rolled onto his back and covered his face with his hands.

'Can you blame me?'

He shook his head slowly and muffled, 'No.' Then said to himself, 'What have I done, what have I done, what have I done?' He was sorry. So very, very sorry.

'Sorry doesn't erase anything, Ralph.'

He rolled back onto his side, a profound sadness showing in his eyes. 'I know. And I know you find it hard to believe, but what I did, I'll never do that to you again. I promise.'

I looked at him impassively.

'Can we please talk about it? I just want to explain why I did what I did.'

'Not right now. I'm wiped out. Honestly, I just wanna go to sleep.'

'Okay.'

I turned away from him, onto my left side.

'I'm tired too.' He started moving in to spoon me, but I stopped him.

'Not in here.' I turned back to look at him. 'I'm not ready to share the bed with you.'

I was ready to share my body, but somehow, having him in the bed for the night felt too intimate. And I wasn't ready to share the insights from the 'near-death' experience. That also felt too intimate.

He nodded, knowing better than to question it.

I still wasn't ready two weeks on, but Ralph didn't push. It probably helped that we were having regular sex. He referred to it as lovemaking, I saw it more as a series of booty calls. Mine. With my ballsiness back, my testosterone levels had surged. But with frostbitten emotions, I didn't yet crave the connection that women typically do. I just needed to get laid! He was accessible and had the goods. Shallow, maybe, but at the moment, carnal depth was all I could handle.

Again, the poltergeist reminded me that I was behaving like *une pute*. I didn't argue the point. I wasn't au fait with role-playing the ho. But it was curiously appealing, so the label didn't offend me. I guess Sylvia and I were in sync. For once.

And Ralph and I were more in sync. Even so, the lingering resentment lingered. It would surface late afternoon when the sun started going down and the shadows grew long. Seemed I was also in sync with nature.

On the Friday night, I went to bed early. I couldn't sleep. I lay on my back and stared into the dark, silent void, the space between my ears infested with a collision of thoughts. Through the cacophony, I heard the soft clunk of the pipes as Ralph turned off the shower.

About five minutes later, as I tossed and turned, ending up side-on facing the window, he opened the bedroom door. I assumed he'd come in to get something from the closet. I waited for the sound of the sliding door. Nothing. But then the doona was drawn back.

CHAPTER FORTY-EIGHT

Well-Laid

I rolled over and looked at him. The dim nightlight in the hall meant we could discern each other's face.

'What're you doing?'

'I'm coming to bed.' He climbed in and lay on his side facing me.

I sighed. 'Ralph, I'm still not ready for—'

'Ruthie. I know. But the longer we leave this, the bigger the breach. And I don't wanna make the same mistake. I should never have left it as long as I did—'

'You should never have left, period!' I said in a tight voice.

He winced. 'You're right. And I can see what it's cost me.'

'*What?* What it's cost *you*?'

'I meant, what it's cost us. Look, I didn't handle things well. I should have talked to you about my feelings. And moving out was a bad choice. I know that now and I don't blame you for being angry about it. I get it, really, I do get—'

'You don't get anything!' I glowered at him in the semi-darkness. 'I can't believe that you can't see past the obvious. Or won't. That all you can see is I'm angry because of your stupid choices!'

Tellement stupide! Et il s'appelle un bon psychologue? So stupid! And he calls himself a good psychologist? Oh yes. My other-worldly mother's worldly-wise take. In her embodied form, she herself had been *tellement stupide*. She couldn't see the obvious in any situation. In her embodied form, it hadn't taken much for me to piss her off. She often responded by hanging up on me, or storming off. *Feel free to do the same now, Sylvia.*

I ignored the internal yammering and continued. 'The breach between us, it's mostly because of that breach of trust!'

Judas Iscariot, pth, pth, pth! Sylvia's inescapable load of bitchy? Hardly. *Pth, pth, pth* was her style (the spitting sound to scare off the evil one), but the name Judas Iscariot would have meant bupkis to her. He wasn't a Harlequin Romance or Mills & Boon character. Still, the voice spurred me on.

'You were my everything. Since forever, you were my best friend, my confidant, my lifeline, my protector. And then, my lover and husband. And you took it all away from me, just like that!' My voice quavered. 'You know, if Reuben had cheated on me when we were married, it would've been terrible, but because of what you and I have had, what you did felt like the worst kind of betrayal.'

Ralph's face crumpled in pain and tears shimmered in his eyes. Articulating this for the first time shattered my defences and I started to cry. Ralph pulled me towards him and held me. 'I'm so sorry,' he whispered, his voice tremulous. The two of us clung to each other and wept. He calmed, then silently held me while I continued, my whole body shaking as I cried out the residual trauma and despair. And when I was done, he took my face in his hands.

'You're wrong, what you said. I didn't take away what we had—what we *have*. I lapsed. Badly. And I'm hundred per cent accountable for that. But you and I, we have an unbreakable bond. And I believe it can survive anything. You just have to believe it too.'

I disentangled myself from him, rolled onto my back and stared up at the ceiling. He was right. *Un bon psychologue.* I thought back to a time many years earlier when I'd been offered a job in Sydney. It'd been tempting and meant getting away from my mother. But I'd knocked it back because I didn't want to be away from my best friend. Now, I knew, as certain as I was that I'd never get away from Sylvia, I would always find my way back to Ralph. Without a doubt, he was my Twin Flame.

We made love, and then lay entwined, both lost in our own thoughts. We still hadn't had that talk; there was a lot of ground to cover and I was ready. As if he sensed it, he took the initiative.

'No excuses, but I do need you to know where I was coming from.'

I looked at him and nodded.

'I know it seems like I was only thinking of myself, but I wasn't. I wasn't trying to hurt anyone. And I know you're protective of Hannah. Your mum wrapped you in cotton wool and—and please don't take this the wrong way—it's like you were doing the same with Hannah. But there was never going to be a right time. I thought about how much pain I went through when I found out I was adopted, and how a lot of it could have been spared, or not been so all-consuming. It was hard enough dealing with that sense of betrayal over being adopted out. But if I'd been told earlier, I wouldn't have also been burdened by Norma's betrayal.'

'I hear you, Ralph. But I've had my challenges too. A divorce, the flak I copped for being with you— the worst being from my children and Maxi not speaking to me—both parents dying, Hannah getting pregnant at eighteen, me becoming a grandmother, and the list goes on. But I didn't run away from you—'

'I know. I know. But I wasn't running away from you.' He blew out. 'I was running away from me. I was stupid. I should have taken a leave of absence from work, like you did when you went through your stuff. Trying to absorb everything in my sensitive state and working with people who had major issues while I was in that space, well, it wasn't a wise move. I wasn't coping. At all. I just wanted to hide from everyone and everything. I had to take time off in the end—it was just after I moved out—because I thought I was having a breakdown. I turned to Dawn for some counselling, but mostly I was angry at women.'

It was like Beth had said.

'I was angry at Beth for giving me away, and at Larissa for not telling me she was pregnant, and at Norma for not telling me I was adopted. And for letting her husband beat me, then begging me not to fight back because, heaven forbid, I might incite him more.' He shook his head. This one still stuck in his craw. 'And when you kept telling me to keep quiet about Alex being my son, all I heard was Norma's voice in my head telling me to back off. Well, it stirred up all those feelings I'd shut down because I'd shut up to keep her happy. Then, when you and Hannah turned on me for opening my mouth, even though I deserved it, it did my head in. And the Anthea and David thing, well, it tipped me over the edge.' His expression revealed the pain of what he'd been through.

I took his hand. 'If you'd shared all that with me and told me it was why you needed to move out, I'd have accepted it, even though I wouldn't've been happy about you leaving. And I understand you got lost, but the way you went about it all had me believing it was my fault, that you were moving out because of me.'

'No, Ruthie. I'd dug a hole for myself and kind of buried the best part of me in the process.'

We both became pensive, then Ralph said, 'But ... I did let you know.'

'Huh?'

'After Maxi's party. Her wedding. I texted you.'

'Yeah. I remember the text. But giving me a clichéd "it's not you, it's me" isn't an explanation. It's an insult—'

'Yes. Which is why I didn't just leave it at that. It's why I apologised and explained.'

'What are you talking about?'

'The text I sent after that.'

'Uh, as I recall, you told me I was projecting. How do you see that as an apology?'

'No. The one before that.'

I gave him a curious look. My phone was on the bedside table. I switched on the lamp and the phone and searched my messages until I found our exchange. There was nothing in between the two texts in question. I held the screen towards him.

His brow furrowed. He got out of bed and disappeared into the kitchen to get his phone. He was scrolling through the messages as he got back into bed.

'Why can't I find it?'

He then groaned. 'It didn't send. *I* didn't send it. It went into drafts. Oh God. I remember now I'd just finished typing it when a message from Dawn came through. It was late, but she knew I was going to Maxi's party and she wanted to see how I'd held up. I answered her, and then your message came through, the one about me sounding like your mother. And it made me angry.

The way I saw it, I'd just sent you an explanation about where I was at and you attacked me. Thing is, I wouldn't have blamed you after what I'd originally said. But, here's the unsent text.'

He held the phone out to me.

> Sorry. That sounded lame. What I meant is I'm overwhelmed by everything and everyone right now and want to shut the world out. Not even going to work.

'Oh no. *No!* If I'd got this, we could've worked things out weeks ago.'

He shook his head. 'No. It was meant to unfold this way. I think we both needed to go through what we did to get to where we are now.'

And there it was. Synchronicity, again. Not always delivering what was desired, but what was necessary.

I sighed. 'You're right. But Ralph, I can't go through this again. You *have* to communicate with me. And not use providence as an excuse to do what you want, when you want.'

'I know, I know. But these were extreme circumstances—'

'Doesn't matter! There's no guarantee we won't go through crazy stuff like that again.'

'No. There's not. And I can't guarantee that I won't hurt you again any more than you can guarantee you won't hurt me. But what I can guarantee, what I can *promise* you, is that I'll fight fair. You have my word on that.'

I slowly nodded and then said, 'Same.'

He drew me into a tight embrace. I wanted to ask him if he'd cheated but wasn't sure how to word it. 'Did you cheat on me?'

He pulled back, stunned. 'What? N-no! Why would you even think that?'

'Well, the way you and Anthea—'

'Anthea? Ugh, God. Anthea's my half-sister!'

'I know. But before you both knew that, the woman was flirting with you!'

'No, she wasn't. She was just being friendly.'

Seriously? You, who whored your way through late adolescence and most of your adult life, read that as 'friendly'? Ralph was no idiot. But this? *What an idiot.*

'So, what about you?' he said.

'What? What about me?'

'The neighbour. The author.' *The author.* Mr no name, just like *The catwalk model.* The author and the catwalk model— grown men, but a pair of mean girls.

'Andy?'

'Yeah. Him. I didn't like the way he looked at you. Or the way he was touching you. I didn't like it at all.'

'Mmm. He was just being friendly.'

Ralph made a wry face, then gave me a tentative look. 'Were you, uh, attracted to him?'

Fuck, yeah! I screwed up my face in a pretend-apology. 'Sort of.'

He looked crushed.

'His attention made me feel good about myself at a time when I was feeling pretty shit, Ralph.'

He nodded. 'He didn't try anything, did he?' Good move that, putting the onus on Andy.

'No! And I wouldn't've allowed it.' *Imagining bonking him doesn't count.*

He nodded but left it there. I turned off the bedside lamp, we both got lost in our thoughts, then drifted into a peaceful slumber until his voice woke me.

'Ruthie. Ruthie.'

'Mmm?' I was groggy and disoriented. And panicky. 'Wha? Wha's wrong?'

Ralph's head was raised off the pillow. 'What's that noise? It sounds like a dog's been hit. I'm gonna go take a look.'

'No.' I grabbed his arm. 'Ish not a dog. Not in ve lit'ral shensh. Ish our new neighbour, Bitty. I mean, she looksh like a poodle.' I sounded like Sylvia used to, in the morning before she put her teeth in.

I rolled over and rubbed my mouth awake. '*Shh*, listen. She's coming.'

Bitty's tone was a tad croaky this time. I knew she had a cold. I'd heard her sneezing throughout the day, and her sneezes were like her orgasms: Ah ah AH CHOOOOO!

I conducted without a baton. I had the tempo down pat; Bitty's opus never varied. My hand moved faster as she reached a crescendo—'Uh oh ah oh uh uh uh. Oh Bin ...'—and I punched the air at the climax—'AAAAAAAH YES YES AAAAH OH GOD!'

Gesundheit.

Ralph's eyes went wide. He was speechless. I told him all about Mr Pumpkin and Mrs Bumpkin, about Mr Pumpkin's daily grind, and about their nightly, country and western bump 'n' grind.

He laughed. But when I told him about Myron, he cried.

Not for Myron. Ralph couldn't stand my brother. He cried for the fact that he would have been the first person I turned to, and yet, he was only finding this out a few months later. Even Norma hadn't said anything. It wasn't an intentional twist of the knife, but it had that effect. I felt sad for him, but I wasn't completely above feeling smug.

Still, there was a significant shift. It all came down to divine timing. For his part, it wasn't about dropping the ball, then claiming the timing was right. For my part, it wasn't about claiming the timing was wrong because it would make someone unhappy. It was about letting things happen in their own time, an act that was beyond human control and one that wouldn't please everyone. I'd wanted to let go, and the timing was now right. Earlier, it hadn't been. There was no point beating myself up for that and I had to let Ralph off the hook for the same reason.

I thought about Sylvia, who'd never let go. She hadn't wanted to and it had made for a tragic life. I didn't feel sorry for her, though. She'd made her own bed. But I didn't want her in mine.

Things were looking up. Often. We spent the whole of Saturday in bed. We made love on and off all day, and we talked. We even ate in bed and I purposely dropped crumbs on the Egyptian cotton, 1200 thread count. *I am such a bitch.* But Ralph left them there. He got his own back because I was the one with the granules clinging to my arse when we boffed again. And we boffed and talked late into the night. Then we stood by the window giggling like a pair of naughty school kids as we listened to Bin and Bitty boning.

Ralph wolf-whistled after Bitty's finale. I liked that he had this he-man talent. He'd learned it as a small boy. At the time, such a harsh, ear-piercing noise coming from him had seemed incongruous. It was hard to reconcile the man today with the short, skinny little boy he'd been. Bookish, with disproportionately huge teeth in a tiny, pale face, and sporting black-rimmed, coke-bottle glasses that magnified his eyes, he'd looked like a cartoon character.

'I would have come home sooner if I'd known about this performance!' he said.

I knew I'd come to a level of acceptance, that final stage of the grieving process, because I took his comment in stride.

And things had shifted for Ralph. The next morning, he said he wanted to go and see Hannah and Alex. He wanted to apologise.

CHAPTER FORTY-NINE

Dweeb ♥ Geek

Hannah eyed Ralph with suspicion. She'd put Luca down for his afternoon nap half an hour before we got there, and now, the four of us were sitting in their lounge. Ralph and I were on one couch, Hannah and Alex sat opposite. The coffee table between us served as a barricade, with no peace offering of coffee and cake on it.

Alex's shoulder was twitching. Normally reticent, he plunged in before Ralph had a chance to speak.

'First things first, you need to know that as far as I'm concerned, Hector is my father.'

It was oddly comforting to hear these words. Only because it meant Hannah was married to a loyal man. No other reason. None.

Alex folded his arms, set his jaw and stared at Ralph.

'And I wouldn't dream of coming between you.'

Alex relaxed his stance a little and Ralph continued. 'I want to humbly apologise to both of you. I regret what I did. I wanted you to know the truth, but I went about it the wrong way. And I guess I filtered the whole situation through my own experience. I really believed that if I'd known earlier I was adopted, it would have spared me a lot of pain and the feelings of betrayal by my birth mother and my adoptive parents. But it wasn't fair of me to assume it'd be the same for you. Our situations aren't the same. You weren't adopted, and it's pretty clear you've grown up in a loving family. I need you to know, though, if Larissa had told me she was pregnant, there's no way in the world I would not have been involved in your life.'

Alex's expression softened. He unfolded his arms, but wrapped them around himself. It was a telling move.

'Alex, I love kids and I think you know that. You know that too, Hannah.'

She nodded and looked off into the distance, no doubt remembering Ralph's regular presence and involvement in her childhood.

'Not having them has been one of my biggest regrets. And when I found out I had a son, I think I wanted to make up for lost time. But obviously, I didn't think it through. And I'm sorry for the hurt I caused you, both of you. All of you.'

Alex and Hannah exchanged a long look. Then he stood up, crossed the divide and held out his hand to Ralph. Ralph stood up and warmly shook Alex's hand. The tension in the room evaporated even more when the two of them spontaneously bridged the gap and moved into a man hug. They parted and looked at each other a little awkwardly. But it passed as they launched into an analysis on the art of hugging, from a psychological perspective.

Hannah and I rolled our eyes.

As she went into the kitchen to organise coffee, I stood observing the two men. I remembered back to when I first met Alex, and how I thought it strange that Hannah had found someone like Ralph rather than like her father. Now, and I could have been imagining it, it wasn't hard to see other similarities beyond their height, physique, intelligence, and weirdness. There were small mannerisms, their intense dispositions, and their laughs.

I joined Hannah in the kitchen, leaving dweeb and geek alone in the lounge to get their rocks off. We stayed all afternoon, had takeaway with them, and left after Ralph, at Luca's insistence, put him to bed for the night.

And very gradually, conditions started to change for the better. Alex asked Ralph to go with him to several of the Adelaide Festival of Arts events, the kind that didn't interest Hannah or me: opera, theatre, classical and contemporary music, cabaret and literature. He didn't see Ralph as his father, and might never, but Ralph knew enough to let their relationship develop at its own pace. And it did. Alex and Ralph often did things together and were establishing a solid friendship.

Life was good all round. Baubo was now playing ball again and there was a surge in my writing. There was also a surge in our social life. We triple-dated with Maxi and Nestor, and Vette and Henry. We were also seeing more of Nick and Donna. And Beth's daughter, Amelia, was overcoming her resistance to meeting Ralph. They spoke on the phone. It wasn't an instant rapport, but it was a step forward. I talked to Rhea often. She was grieving, but her health had improved since she'd left Hector. Little niggly things stopped niggling. I resisted the urge to say he made me sick too.

And Ralph got to meet Bin and Bitty. It made him happy. With Hector no longer on the scene, he'd been feeling a little bereft, he'd said. The yokels were as good a replacement as any. A superior replacement, he'd said. I got why when, one night, midway through one of our hot and heavy love sessions, he jumped out of bed to open the window. 'For some fresh air,' he said.

'Either the window stays closed or my legs do,' I said. I wasn't going to be a pawn in his pissing contest!

But my trust in him was slowly restoring itself. We talked about things we'd skirted in the past, and we sometimes fought. But as we'd promised each other, it was fair fighting. Ralph and I became a different fit. A new–old one. Our relationship was well-rounded. We played like pre-schoolers, fought like middle-graders, had make-up sex like teenagers, and resolved our arguments like mature adults. We compromised, but there were some things I wouldn't make concessions for.

Like Anthea.

After she dropped in uninvited on a Saturday morning, I said to Ralph, 'She might be your sister, but she's not welcome here.'

He was about to put up an argument, but I put up the stop sign. 'I don't care how often you see her, just not here. And I'm not budging on this one. You can cry foul all you like.'

He spat the dummy. 'Fine, but I don't want the author here either!'

I agreed. 'The author' hadn't been here, anyway, not since he'd finally moved into the spook house. He'd abandoned the pursuit, either because he'd seen Ralph's car in the driveway every night, or he sensed he was no longer getting inside my head, which meant he'd have Buckley's of getting inside my pants.

I was a little disappointed because I thought we were friends. But maybe Maxi had been right. Maybe Andy had been playing me all along, or maybe guys like that couldn't be just friends with women.

I got used to his absence over the next few months, but then came the day the catwalk model, the author, and the harlot would be under the same roof at the same time.

Synchronicity could be a bitch.

CHAPTER FIFTY

Split Ends

I held an 'alignment' party. After four shitty, turbulent years of war and death and ruptures and reconciliations, it seemed the planets were aligned. Not just for me, but for everyone close to me.

I'd slain the Goliath. Ralph and I had made it through our first year of marriage and were thriving in our second. Maxi and Nestor had defied the odds and were smooth-sailing through their first year. Vette and Henry had moved in together. Alex was more forthcoming about his feelings, so his relationship with Hannah was on an even keel. And both of them were much calmer because Luca had graduated from the terrible twos (he'd started at eighteen months. He was well ahead of his time). Hannah had gone back to uni to complete her degree (Luca was in day care three days a week; he had a large pool of babysitters to help out on the other two days). Rhea was very happily separated from Hector and had now separated from her mo and mouche (I was going to miss the mo and mouche). Reuben and

Ida were engaged, and Casper had a lovely girlfriend, Daphne. Leah and Ari had announced they were expecting, and Iris and Joel were over the moon about becoming grandparents. Beth had started dating a colleague and she was glowing. Norma was also glowing. She was no longer taking crap from her dropkick husband or the three disappointments she'd given birth to. And I'd finished my novel, which I'd retitled *Cupid F*cks Up*. I'd submitted a few chapters to a publishing house and they'd come back to me, requesting the full manuscript.

My nearest and dearest were now gathered in the lounge and dining room, chatting, laughing and eating. Everyone had arrived on time, even Iris and Joel—it was a first. Nick and Donna were there also and it pleased Beth no end to see her two sons in the same room and in a burgeoning relationship. I wasn't looking forward to having Anthea in the same room as me. I didn't care that she and Ralph were half-siblings. I didn't like her and didn't want to invite her.

'It might upset Beth,' I'd said.

'Why?'

'Hello! Because she's the daughter of the man Beth had you with.'

Beth was fine with it. And in the end, I only gave in because Anthea asked Ralph if she could bring Andy. They were dating. Who knew?

'First I've heard of it,' Ralph had said.

'Hmm. And it hasn't made the social pages. How the hell did they meet?' I'd asked, trying to hide a hint of jealousy from him and myself.

'When she left here after dropping in on that Saturday a couple of months ago, he was just getting on his bike to go out. And she went over there to speak to him. She loves bikes.'

Why wouldn't she? She's the town bike.

'Well, apparently, there was an attraction and it just went from there.'

'Huh.' Another little prick of jealousy, another attempt to ignore it.

Thinking about it now, though, I smiled to myself. Andy and Anthea, like the fairy-tale prince and princess, like Ken and Barbie, belonged together. It was just a matter of time before he got bored with her because she was available, and she'd feel torn between wanting to fix him, yet realising if she succeeded she wouldn't be getting laid. Having them at the party would be fun. Watching them both work the room would be free entertainment.

They arrived fashionably late and made a grand entrance.

'Holy shit!' I whispered as Ralph and I made for the front door to greet them.

He squeezed my hand and whispered back, 'Beeee nice.' He'd seen what I saw; he knew me well. 'Keep reminding yourself you're the hostess.'

Andy, looking dishy in skinny black jeans and a Polo Ralph Lauren V-neck sweater the same colour as his eyes, gave me a warm hug and whispered, 'I've been crazy busy trying to meet a deadline. My editor strong-armed me, otherwise I would've dropped in. I've missed you.'

It made me all gooey inside. Uh-oh.

Andy's intimate gesture wasn't making Ralph go gooey inside. I disengaged, smiled self-consciously, and turned to Anthea, politely extending my hand to her and making sure she saw my manicured, squoval-shaped nails painted in a micro-glitter lilac. My body language said, *A handshake, tolerable. But a kiss and/or hug are out of the question.*

'Nice to see you,' I lied. It took infinite restraint to not say, *NOT nice to see so much of you.* And that had nothing to do with frequency, and it had nothing to do with her low-cut, canary-yellow, alpaca sweater that barely contained her hooters. Like Andy's pants hugged his manhood, Anthea's sheath-like, silver satin pants hugged her womanhood. But hers hugged a little too tightly. She had a giant camel toe.

The men in the room who saw it were probably digging the look. The women in the room who saw it were probably screaming inside *'One giant setback for the sisterhood, you tart!'*

One thing was certain, though. Anthea would get at least two humps tonight.

Then again, if she successfully upstaged the master of centre stage, then all bets were off. It would not be good for their relationship because the sex addiction counsellor was not equipped to deal with limp-dick.

Ralph had extended his hand to Andy. As Andy shook it, he said, 'You're a very lucky man to have this amazing woman as your wife.'

Ha, fuck you, Anthea, you silicone sex toy! You, with your flawless skin and luscious locks. It's me he'd rather build a nest with. Me, with my large pores, split ends and concealed labia.

'I know,' Ralph said as his left hand slid around my waist possessively. His little green monster had come out. I knew his other monster would come out after the party.

There was no need to introduce Andy and Anthea to the other guests. Andy went off to consort and Anthea trailed him like an overzealous paparazzo. Speaking of which, where the hell was Derek?

Maxi had arranged for Derek the photographer to take some formal pictures to mark this occasion. He'd snapped Hannah and Alex's wedding, and mine and Ralph's.

Maxi called him for me. 'He's on his way, hon, shouldn't be too long. He had an accident—not a big one.' She then nodded in the direction of Andy and Anthea, who were talking to Rhea and Vette. 'So, you invited the skank and the skunk, huh?' she said under her breath.

'A last-minute thing,' I sniggered, then lowered my voice. 'Ralph wanted the skank here; I only succumbed because she wanted to bring the skunk.'

Maxi eyed me warily.

'Don't worry. Only for the entertainment value.'

Iris approached and whispered, 'Is that Ralph's sister?'

'Mmhmm. Half-sister.'

'Hmm.' She turned to stare at Anthea, then looked back at me. 'More like half-sister, half-brother. Interesting pair of suggesticles on her.'

Maxi and I laughed.

Andy and Anthea were now moving on and introducing themselves to Reuben and Ida. Rhea and Vette came over to join us.

'Andrew—Andy—asked me about Russell,' Rhea said. 'He's just as considerate as he is gorgeous. And such a romantic.'

'Yes,' Vette said. 'He's very into the Greek mythology. He credited you with that. He introduced Anthea as his Aphrodite, goddess of beauty.'

'*Pfft,*' Iris snorted. 'Should've introduced her as his *herm*aphrodite.'

Maxi and I laughed again, but Rhea and Vette gawked at Iris, perplexed.

'Don't tell me you haven't noticed? Have a good look.'

Both turned. We watched as their eyes bugged out.

'Oh no! Do you think we should say something to her, you know, let her know?'

'Geez, Boop, you can be so naïve sometimes!' Maxi said.

'You really think she's aware of it?'

Maxi gave Vette a cross-eyed *duh* look.

'Why would she intentionally go out like that?' Vette whispered to herself.

Yep. Naïve.

Iris turned to me. 'Seriously, doll-face, between you and Hannah, I swear next time I have a party, I want your guest lists.'

Before I could say anything, the waiter shoved a tray under my nose. Ralph had insisted we get the party catered so I could relax and enjoy myself. There was food set out on the sideboard, but a server was also moving amongst the guests with the hors d'oeuvres, while the caterer was doing things in the kitchen.

I looked over at Ralph, who was huddled in the corner of the dining room with Alex and Beth. They were debating information and misinformation in the information age. The three generations seemed to be going around and around in circles. The fourth generation, Luca, was next to his father, also going around and around and around and around ad nauseam in his own little circle.

I shuddered. All the spinning made me feel dizzy. It reminded me of when Hannah circled Alex seven times at their wedding—a Jewish tradition—then another three times—a Greek tradition. Luca stopped turning and was now teetering like a drunk. I shuddered again. It reminded me of when Portnoy was alive and making her way to her letterbox at night. She'd always taken the road less travelled, too shitfaced to walk the straight path.

My wobbly grandson smashed into the wall.

'Waa! Waa! Waa!'

Hannah rushed over and picked him up, making soothing noises to him, then not so soothing noises to Alex. 'You're supposed to be watching him! Can't I have five minutes to myself?'

I grabbed two madeleines from the kitchen and took them over to Luca. It did the trick.

'Lovely, just lovely. Teaching him to comfort eat, like you do!'

'Piss off, Sylvia. You weren't invited.'

Ralph grabbed me and pulled me against him, his arm encircling my waist, his cheek resting against mine. He'd always been affectionate, but since we'd reconciled, since I'd let go, he tended to hold on more tightly, like he was afraid I'd slip away. I didn't mind; I loved the sheer physicality of it all. And maybe, to a teeny extent, the feeling that I had him by the balls like Vette had predicted at my birthday breakfast. I didn't want to be that person. *Must work on it.* Not now, though. Now, I needed to eat; the kind of eating that celebrates life, not comforts its ailments.

I moved to the sideboard, filled a plate and then stepped back from the huddle. As I looked around my lounge room the words *divine design* came to mind, like they had when I first started writing my book. I remembered the thought that had accompanied the words: that divine design was a beautiful thing, if only I could see the perfection in its placement with my stupid family, and that maybe writing the book would help me. It had. It had crystallised vague feelings and thoughts and ideas. Having Sylvia as my mother was divine design. I'd read somewhere that mothers are supposed to provide spiritual guidance for their children. Mine had provided spiritual weights. Not a bad thing. I now got that it was neither in spite of her, nor because of her, that I'd come to this place in my life. I'd arrived here because of *me*, just like I'd given birth to me.

Sylvia and Joe had played their part, to be sure. Maybe I wouldn't have devoured the nonsensical myths if I'd had a normal childhood. For the first time in months, in years, everything made sense.

I was bursting with deep affection for all these people here (save Anthea).

'Off with the fairies?' Andy's voice startled me out of my loved-up reverie. He was looking down at me, an eyebrow raised and an amused glint in his eyes. Before I could respond, he leaned down and whispered in my ear, 'I meant what I said before about the catwalk model being lucky to have you. You're the one that got away, you know.'

He drew back and looked at me long and hard, with penetrating eyes that held not a hint of mockery in them this time, and eyebrows that didn't budge. I gawped at him as I struggled for words, and with them: *That's flattering Are you kidding I'm married Ooh that makes me feel good What the hell are you doing You're in my home with my husband and my kids and my friends and your girlfriend and Oh God help—*

CRASH!

Conversation stopped as everyone turned towards the hapless red-faced waiter, who'd dropped a fully-laden tray of mozzarella sticks and dipping sauce on the tiled floor next to the breakfast bar.

Synchronicity.

I took a step in his direction, but the caterer said, 'We've got this.'

I turned back to Andy's steady, intent look, and still, no words would come. Only a thought—*Heeeeelp!*

Ding-dong.

'That'll be Derek,' Maxi called.

A synchronic back-up plan. There might not be another one. I shoved my plate at Andy, made a dash for the door and opened it.

Derek stood there, a folded tripod in one hand, a camera slung around his neck and large camera bag looped over his shoulder. 'Sorry I'm late. Didn't allow for an accident.' He made a wry face.

I asked if he was okay.

'Yep, all good. Just a bit of a bingle; the other driver's fault.'

Standing next to him was an attractive woman who looked to be in her late twenties. No doubt she was his assistant; she was holding another camera bag. She looked uncomfortable, though, and started to protest even as I ushered them in.

'I just ... he asked if I could help him. He was juggling his equipment,' she said awkwardly.

'And thank you. You've been a great help,' Derek said as he put his apparatus down in front of the console table and relieved her of the camera bag. He turned to me. 'So, some candid shots and some posed?'

'Huh?'

'The pics. Did you want a mix of candid shots and posed ones—happy faces? Are you okay? You look shell-shocked.'

'Oh, uh, yeah. I'm fine. And yes, please.'

Derek nodded, bent down and started fossicking through one of the bags as I shook off the jumbled thoughts and feelings from Andy's confession.

Now, clear-headed, I added, 'Also, some full body ones, posed.' *Specifically, a full body, front-on shot of Anthea.* No need to say that out loud, Derek was a bloke.

I turned to the young woman, who hadn't moved much beyond the front door, and smiled at her.

'I-I'm not with him,' she stammered.

I narrowed my eyes quizzically. 'So, then, who are you?'

She opened her mouth to speak, but closed it again. She licked her lips nervously and stared at me.

Hello. It's not a trick question.

'I'm, uh, uh, does Ralph Brill live here?'

'Yyyeah.' *Shit. A nutjob client with transference issues? How does she know where he lives? Did she follow him home after work one day?*

I turned towards the philosophers' corner and called out, 'Ralph?'

With a plate in one hand, and wildly gesticulating like a maestro conducting a fast tempo with the other, Ralph looked like he was on a winning streak. His hand froze mid-air. He scowled at me and mouthed, *'What?'*

Geez, sorry for interrupting your esoteric rap session. I beckoned him over.

He put down his plate and sloped across the room. 'What's wrong?'

I held my hand out towards the woman.

He gave her a questioning look. 'Hi.'

She stared at him with an awed expression. *Jesus.*

'Can I help you?' he prompted, then he squinted at her. 'Do I know you?'

She shook herself out of her trancelike state. 'N-no. Um, I'm Amy Don's daughter.'

Ralph gave her a nonplussed shrug.

'She was Amy Cilla. Her maiden name was Cilla.'

He seemed to register a flicker of recognition.

She drew a deep breath, squared her shoulders, then said, 'You're my father.'

No End in Sight ...

Thanks for reading!
If you enjoyed this book, I'd be very grateful if
you'd post a short review at your favourite online retailer.
Your support really does make a difference.

Paula Houseman lives in Sydney, Australia, with her
husband. No other creatures. The kids have flown the nest
and the dogs are long gone.

Paula is the author of the Ruth Roth Series—
Odyssey in a Teacup, Cupid F*cks Up and
My T(r)oyboy is a Twat.

And—the saga continues: The next instalment is underway!

Connect with Paula at
https://paulahouseman.com
to get pre-release news of Book 4
in the Ruth Roth Series.

www.ingramcontent.com/pod-product-compliance
Lightning Source LLC
Chambersburg PA
CBHW021403110726
47901CB00008B/2033